THE FIRST CITY

THE KINDRED FEW BOOK TWO

HEATHER KINDT

Published by Midnight Tide Publishing

Cover Art by BRoseDesignZ

Edited by Megan Dailey

✿ Created with Vellum

CHAPTER ONE

Mari

THREE WEEKS

For three weeks, he hasn't returned, making me afraid I've lost two of my brothers.

I walk through the warm grass in bare feet, sitting crisscross beside the garden. Levi's flowers are in full bloom as they soak in the springtime sun. Birds chirp from the trees surrounding me as if anything is possible, but the ominous feeling in the pit of my stomach tells me otherwise.

I unfold the paper in my hand, then fold it again, a ritual I've undertaken every day since Bastian left. His words will hurt too much. They will hold a promise of hope for our future, one that no longer has any validity. He handed me the note on the way to Frostacre before we retrieved the prophecy.

Before we knew he was the second savior from the First City.

Before Levi was killed by the king of Frostacre.

But I've told myself I need to face him, even if it's only his words. Looking into Levi's garden, I speak out loud as if he can hear me. "What if he's like them?" It's a fear I've held onto. That deep down, Bastian is like the Miscretes we faced in Tenny Rocks—deceptive, manipulative, and wanting to control the other savior. "What if he's lied to us all along?"

A robin lands on the ground beside me and cocks its head to the side.

"You're right. He's Bastian." When I come outside, I feel Levi's presence around me, in the flowers, the birds, and in the whisper of the breeze. It's why I've resorted to speaking out loud to my dead brother, hoping the others aren't listening. "I know him." But my reaction to the second part of the prophecy is part of the reason he left.

And why I need to face him now.

I unfold the letter with trembling hands.

MARI,

I'm not sure how today will turn out, or any of our days. All I know is I want you in them. You have a way of challenging me unlike any person I've ever met. It's a challenge to love fiercely and with reckless abandonment, something that never motivated me in the past. I don't know if I'm drawn more by the animal, mental, or emotional pull I feel toward you.

But I digress. Whatever bewitching spell you hold over me, I can't name it anything but love.

This is why I want to leave you with my deepest secret, something I've never told anyone because it's too frightening to speak it aloud. In case I don't make it out of Frostacre, it's important for someone I trust to know about me.

When I was thirteen, I discovered a loose floorboard in our barn when my father had me sweep up the mess my friends and I made after a hay fight. Chilon, my brother, was mucking the horses in the

2

stall, not paying much attention to me. I snatched a crowbar from my father's tools and lifted the board from the flooring. Beneath it was a package wrapped in canvas. Checking to make sure my brother remained occupied, I hammered the board down and slipped the package beneath my shirt.

In the safety of the woods, I pulled at the strings tying the canvas securely around its contents. Hidden within were documents and this necklace, proof of where I'd come from. Jaresiah and Sarah Hale were not my blood parents. They were tasked with keeping me hidden because there were many out there who would want me dead if they knew of my existence.

The paperwork contained a lot of legal jargon which I didn't understand, but after scanning the entire document, I couldn't find the name of either of my parents. Jaresiah had signed it, agreeing to raise me until I was of age. He didn't make it that long.

The necklace is my only clue to my birth parents. If we both make it out of Frostacre alive, I want to find them. Not to derail our mission to find the other savior and take down the cities, but as a side mission. If I can find my parents, it will help me discover who I really am and what role I need to play in this world. If I train you along the way, maybe we can go together.

I don't want to do this without you, Mari.

You are the one person who makes this life worth living.

Love,

Bastian

HE KNEW the Hales weren't his parents. They had adopted him like they had Levi. And he wanted me to help him find his birth parents. Why didn't I read this letter weeks ago? He must be searching for them alone.

I touch the pendant around my neck—the red gem encased in intricate metal scrolling. It's a clue about his lineage, and he left it behind with me.

Evie, my sister, comes out the backdoor, skirts the garden, and sits beside me.

"I can feel him out here too," she says, inhaling and lifting her chin to the sky as she closes her eyes. "It's as if he left behind a piece of his soul in this garden."

As much as I want to talk about Levi, Bastian's letter is at the forefront of my mind. If he left for the First City, and Arazian finds out he's one of the saviors, he could be in danger. "I think I know where Bastian is."

She opens her eyes. "How?"

I hand the letter to her. "The Hales weren't his parents. They took him in as a baby. Like the prophecy says, he's from the First City. I think he went to find his parents."

Evie jumps up with the letter still in her hand. "Of all the stupid Bastian things to do." She storms to the backdoor with me on her heels.

"Gray!" she shouts, laying the letter on the table. "Get down here."

My oldest brother, Grayson, barrels down the stairs of the cabin at his girlfriend's command. "What is it?"

She points at the paper, her green eyes flashing at him. "Bastian gave this letter to Mari before we left for Frostacre. He's in the First City."

Grayson picks up the letter and tilts his head to the side. "I could've told you that. Where else would he go for three weeks? The Crestone Caverns?"

"No." Evie crosses her arms and frowns. "That's just stupid. But going to the First City without backup is insane. I know he's got a few screws loose in that brain of his, but I thought he had common sense."

"It's his family, Evie. He wants to know more." Grayson sets the letter down, leaning against the table. "What we really need to talk about is his profession of love for Mari." He looks at me and winks.

"He won't live long enough for that to matter!" Evie paces the floor beside the table. "We need to leave now. Operation Demolish the First City must commence."

"Chill out." Grayson pushes off the table and places a grounding hand on his girlfriend's shoulder. "Bastian's the most capable among us. He'll gut the First City from the inside out if need be."

Still standing in the kitchen, horrified that both Grayson and Evie read Bastian's words about his feelings for me, I twist a loose string on my shirt between my fingers. I've already made up my mind that I need to go after him, but if I bring it up to them, they'll make me stay here.

Crossing his arms, Grayson leans against the counter beside me. "We can't launch a full-on assault yet. We don't have Bastian and Mari's not ready." He reaches over and pinches my cheek. I elbow him in the ribs. He clutches his side in mock pain, his lips still holding onto his infectious smile. "We initiate a mission. Enter enemy headquarters, rescue the commander, and get the lay of the land."

"Won't we stand out among the Miscretes?" The thought of facing the Dark King's creatures again makes me want to curl up on my mattress and never come out. But the thought of not going alone comforts me.

"There are people in the First City." Evie rolls her eyes as if I'm the dumbest person she's ever met. "Arazian attracts all the crazies—fifth-in-line-to-the-throne princes, rejected vampires, former members of the Avrenian Council. He keeps his creatures locked away beneath the city until he needs them."

My heart stutters at the mention of former Council members. The Northern Duke, as my father is known in the wilderness, keeps company with Arazian. They were on the Council together years ago. Arazian was forced to leave the city and from what I know, my dad left voluntarily. "And they all agree with their leader's tyranny in the wilderness?"

"As far as we know." Grayson snatches an apple out of the fruit basket and takes a bite. He continues to chomp as he says, "It's not like either of us have dared to enter its gates."

Evie narrows her eyes at him. "We know from reliable sources that the First City contains the worst criminals and creatures in the land. It's a refuge for those rejected by Avren and the Supe strongholds."

A criminal in the eyes of Avren's Council is not always a criminal in the wilderness. "A vampire is Arazian's second-in-command," I state.

"Yes, Sterling never leaves Arazian's side." Grayson tosses the apple core into the trash basket. How did he eat it that fast? "It's rumored the old vamp feeds off his master in a warped symbiotic relationship." He wipes his hands on his pants. "But besides the Caverns, there's reps there from Frostacre, the Downs, and Rumsford."

"Rumsford?" Maybe Grayson means humans turned into Miscretes.

"It's a werewolf stronghold." He plunges his hands into the soapy water in the sink. "That's why Bastian wanted to string Levi up by his toes after he found out the two of you went to Mafekadi. You were lucky one of them didn't sniff you out the night you spent at the inn. Must not have been a full moon."

That night, Levi and I spent time eating in a room packed with people on the main floor of the Iron Horse Inn. Quinn Malum, the fae bounty hunter sent by King Cirrus to collect me, stood out as the main attraction due to his glamour. I don't remember any details of the other people in the room. Not that I'd recognize a werewolf in its human form. "And what's the Caverns?"

"The Crestone Caverns." Evie hops onto the table, pulling one leg into her chest. "It's in the Elmridden range and holds the largest nest of vampires known in the wilderness. Queen Isle brought in the refugees from Avren, both vampires and humans, intent on increasing her influence."

"With all the supernatural beings inside the First City, won't they sense my presence?" The chill of the vampire's breath in the meadow still haunts my dreams. My blood still screams *Avrenian*, so the Supes are attracted to me for some reason I don't quite understand.

"And that's why you'll wait outside for us." Evie slides from the table and opens the weapons cabinet, assessing the vast array of daggers, swords, and other equipment. "We'll visit the old Hale farmstead to look for clues and find a place close by where you can stay safe."

"We need to take this seriously, Mari." Grayson removes a curved sword from the cabinet and sheathes it on his belt. "Bastian's already at risk. Having both of you waltzing around the First City before we're ready to attack will sabotage our primary mission." He lifts a weapons strap from the door of the cabinet and places it over Evie's head, looking her in the eyes as he tightens the straps. His fingers linger on her hips and trace her neckline.

I return to the dishes, my cheeks flaming. It's uncomfortable at times, sharing the cabin with the two of them, but my best friend and my own *lover* are gone. Grayson's actions also bring me back to my time in Tenny Rocks with Bastian. Before I knew he was the other savior. Before I knew he was from the First City. After the initial shock wore off, I came to my senses. But I hurt him with my reaction. He'd never betray the Kindred Few.

"If you think my presence will put Bastian's rescue at risk, then I'll stay away." I lift a plate from the soapy water and dunk it in the clean water before placing it on the counter. "But what if the soldiers come back after we've left?" Over three weeks ago when we traveled to Frostacre, Avren's soldiers visited the cabin looking for me. When we returned, the only clue of their presence was muddy boot prints on the floor. When his friend told him they were coming, Grayson had left the cabin unlocked so they wouldn't break down the door. Anything of value or that pointed to me was locked away in a camouflaged underground strongbox in the garden.

"I'll lock the cabin this time so they don't grow suspicious. If only we had wards that protected against humans." Grayson taps his lip with his finger, staring up at the ceiling as if in deep thought. "Might have to talk to Ben about that one."

"As long as you keep him away from my bones." I dry my hands on a towel and cross the room to retrieve my boots. Ben Finch is a magician who lives a day's journey from here in a tiny village of like-minded necromancers. When I broke my ankle, he melded it back together—painfully.

"Ben means well." Evie hands me a quiver filled with arrows and then my bow. "You'd still be up in your bed mending if Bastian didn't take you to him."

Her comment has my mind playing a game of cause and effect. *If I was still in my bed, the others would have made Levi stay behind to watch me while they traveled to Frostacre, and he'd still be alive.* But is that true? Avren's soldiers visited the cabin while we were gone. If we had been there, they would have killed Levi and taken me to Avren. Bastian would have thought about this. *He'd carry me to Tenny Rocks and have Levi and I stay back while they climbed the mountain to Frostacre.* No. The Miscretes would have sniffed me out, killed Levi, and carried me off to the First City.

The games I play in my mind aren't fun because some things were written in the stars before time began.

"What do you think we'll find at the Hale farm?" I loop the quiver over my shoulder and attach the buckle across my stomach. With the warmer air, we don't need our cloaks, only a simple tunic and lighter pants. No one is wearing their fighting gear.

"Hopefully some clues that survived the fire." Grayson scans the room before opening the front door. "The Hales knew who Bastian's parents were. And something happened that upset Arazian. He claims he wanted the land, but I'd bet it had to do with the commander."

I clutch the stone of the red necklace hanging over my chest hoping it will lead me to Bastian and the truth.

CHAPTER TWO

Bastian

FOR THREE WEEKS the only thing I've felt is numb.

After my time with Mari in Tenny Rocks, I felt more alive than I had ever felt. She gave me hope for a future in a liberated wilderness.

But then Levi died, and we opened the damn prophecy, and my life changed forever.

The black rocks scrape against my skin as I scale the rugged hillside, leaving a smear of blood on my palms. I'm not sure why I'm sneaking in. If I stroll up to the massive front doors and announce myself, I'll probably be welcomed with open arms. This is where I belong. As much as I've tried to be a good person, deep down I know the demons that lurk within me. The ones I hide from the people closest to me—my family, my brothers and sisters, Mari.

Leaving her was the hardest thing I ever had to do.

I need to know the truth about who I really am. But finding out might lock me within the walls of this city forever. Looking up, the tall spires of the onyx structure reach into the darkened sky above, carving an ominous hole in my heart.

My hand clasps another jagged outcropping before I move my foot to another hold. The only thing that would add to this ill-fated atmosphere is a rainstorm with bolts of lightning threatening to strike. But it is a clear night with the stars winking at me from high above on their ethereal perch. My heart settles slightly at the thought of Mari looking up at the same sky through the window of our room in the cabin.

Not staying behind to work out a plan with the others is selfish. I need Mari to stay within the safety of the cabin. I've willed it so many times, hoping somehow she could feel my wishes through our connection.

The two saviors.

How in the world am I a savior? Sure, I'm built for battle, but inside, I'm broken. The time I spent with Mari healed a tiny part of me, but watching one of my brothers die and hearing the other, damaged me. My pursuit of Arazian is not only to free the wilderness from the tyranny of his Miscretes; it's to make him pay for what he did to my family.

I look up as I near the end of my climb. A man stands on the top of the ridge, backlit in the moon's glow like a dark angel. Long brown hair catches on the breeze, whipping around his shoulders. He's slender compared to me, but I know he could snap my neck in an instant. Instinctively, I wrap my fingers around the shaft of the wooden stake at my hip.

"Welcome, Bastian Hale." The vampire glances over his shoulder. "Leave it to you to take the difficult road. Arazian waits for you in his dining quarters. You must be famished after such a strenuous climb."

Sterling. The leader's second-in-command.

If I reveal my true intentions, will the bloodsucker drain me? "I didn't come here to dine with Arazian." Despite my better judgment, I heave my leg over the top of the ledge, then pull the rest of my body up. I'm lying at the feet of a vampire, completely exposed.

"No, of course not." Sterling's eyes flash, his steel-toed boot inches from my hand. "But when he heard you were coming, he reserved you a seat, not realizing what an insolent young prick you are."

Sterling doesn't want me here.

Shifting to stand, I brush the dirt away with one hand, keeping my second firmly on the stake. The vampire wears a silver studded burgundy suit coat that extends down to his knees. Gaudy ruffles from his dress shirt poke out below his neck.

"I don't intend to kill you, Bastian, so you can relax with the stake." He walks along a pathway leading to the front doors of the city. Blood -red roses grow on either side of the gravel trail.

I remain quiet, intent on taking in my surroundings for my future escape. At the wave of Sterling's hand, the heavy iron doors open to his command. It isn't magical. Two men stand on either side of the doors when we enter.

The roof of the city extends the length of the structure, creating a massive space. But it isn't full of stone passageways, dungeons, bats, and screaming prisoners. No image I ever conjured in my mind compares to what stands before me. People mill about, living their lives. A woman carries a basket of vegetables, two boys kick a ball around a grassy area, and three girls huddle together and giggle. Homes line the cobblestone streets much like the cottages in the Grove. This isn't how I pictured the First City. This is how I picture Avren.

As Sterling strides along the cobblestones, people stop and stare, their attention drifting from him to me. Could my parents be among them? My clothes are torn and dirty from my climb, and the vampire still hasn't confiscated my weapons. He marches me along as if in a parade, sure in its intent to humiliate me. But I learned long ago to let other's thoughts of me roll off my shoulders.

A large white building stands at the end of the road. It's two stories high and lined with windows looking out over the city. On the second-floor balcony, a man with gray hair and a beard looks out, his eyes following us. He wears a white robe and spectacles. Like the city, the leader's appearance doesn't match my expectations. A man as great and evil as Arazian would stand at least a foot taller, wear a black cape, and hold a specter as he analyzed the city with his penetrating eyes.

Sterling leads me through the front door of the building and up a grand marble staircase to the second floor. I wrap my fingers around the hilt of a dagger, my heart beating against my chest. In a strange way, this makes me more nervous than if the city were full of skeletons and bats.

"Do you like caviar and wine?" The corner of Sterling's lip lifts. He's making fun of my upbringing, the opposite of the extravagance he's always been privileged to.

"Like I said, my intent is not to share a glass with Arazian," I grumble. The creepy old man is sure to poison or drug me with the drink. "My parents live in the First City, and I want Arazian to help me find them."

Sterling stops before reaching the top stair and taps his chin with a pointed red fingernail. "Your parents. Hmm... I'll store that one for later."

He leads me along the upstairs corridor to a pair of golden doors that swing open with the same grandiose flourish of Sterling's hand. "Master, I've brought the savior. Time to pop the cork."

Great. They know about the prophecy. This wasn't how I wanted things to go down. My goal was to ask around quietly about my parents and get them the hell out of this place.

Arazian already sits at a round table set for three. A four-pronged candelabra decorates the center of the table. Besides that and the plates, the only thing on the table is a bottle of wine. "Come and have a seat, Bastian Hale." He holds out a hand toward the chair to his right. "You're much larger than I had imagined."

My hand hasn't left my dagger since we entered Arazian's home. The thought of this guy knowing my name freaks me out. "I get that a lot."

Arazian purses his lips before breaking into awkward laughter. "Did you hear that, Sterling? He's also funny." He leans his elbows on the table, pitching forward. "I never thought I'd have an actual savior standing in my parlor." He reclines in his chair, crossing one leg over the other. "It's a bit unsettling. You, destined to destroy this wonderful place I've erected, and I, determined to stop you."

"Then why invite me to your table? It's like the cat asking the mouse to join him for a meal." I remain standing as the vampire pulls a chair out to the left of Arazian. I'm outnumbered, but I need information if I want to find my parents.

"Our relationship can be mutually beneficial, Commander." Arazian lifts his glass, tilting it slightly in my direction. "It doesn't have to be a case of the psychotic former leader of Avren versus the hero of the wilderness. There's more to a situation than meets the eye."

"And how can you benefit me?" This is the same guy who sent Miscretes after Mari, and his creatures killed Lyden.

"By helping you find your parents, of course." Arazian takes a long sip from his glass before placing it on the table. "And in return, you'll command my army in our rise up against Avren."

"What of the prophecy?" I don't trust this man any more than the Council in Avren. Revenge and hatred have hardened his heart. "According to the fae, I'm to be your downfall."

The so-called Dark King smiles, and from this distance I can see where the red drink has stained his gray whiskers. "Ancient words won't hold me back, young Hale. They are often misconstrued or changed over the centuries. Rumor has it that you are the best in the land, and I want you in my arsenal."

"And if I refuse?" Mari and the conversation we never really had about me being the second savior make me long to return to her. "Surely, you must have a vampire, or even a werewolf, crazy enough to step into the position."

"People don't refuse the Dark King." Sterling moves with stealth speed, standing over me in an act of intimidation. "If they do, they never again see the light of day."

Arazian rests his arms on his chair. "Sterling, don't harass our guest." His attention shifts to me. "Stay in my best room as a guest until I can change your mind. I'm afraid our lovely city has gained a nasty reputation, and I want to rectify that."

Another vampire appears at the door wearing a similar velvet suit coat to Sterling's. "Your guest has arrived, my lord."

"Invite him in." Arazian stands and crosses the room to welcome them.

The large, red-headed man stands a foot taller than Arazian. He's dressed like the rebels of the wilderness in his tunic and woolen pants. He wears a ragged coat with a long sword hanging from his belt.

The two embrace.

"Do you have news from the northern realm?" Arazian nods to Sterling who pulls out the third seat for the stranger.

The man reclines in the chair, crosses one leg over the other, and pulls a pipe from his pocket. He lifts a snuff pouch, emptying the black powder into the end of the pipe before striking a match on the leg of the table. He appraises me before speaking. "All is in place. Our informants from within tell me the groundwork is almost laid. A month, maybe two."

"And the Council suspects nothing?" Arazian folds his hands on the table.

"They know of the girl and that the second part of the prophecy has been confiscated from the fae." He takes a drag on his pipe letting the smoke hang over the table warping his image from my viewpoint.

"We must protect the girl at all costs." With a flick of Arazian's wrist, Sterling leaves the room. "She, along with the boy, are our best weapons."

"I thought you didn't believe in the prophecy," I grumble, not liking how they're reducing Mari and me to weapons.

"I said I believe that one could misinterpret the prophecy." He glares at me as if he'd forgotten I was there. "Bastian Hale. I'd like to introduce you to the Northern Duke, one of my greatest allies."

I cross my arms and give him a curt nod. Any friend of Arazian is no friend of mine. Though I'm curious about having the First City's full arsenal at our disposal when facing Avren.

"Looks like your friend thinks he's too good for the likes of us, Arazian." The Northern Duke slams his pipe onto the table causing a puff of smoke to billow above it. He leans closer to me, his lip curling. "You'll learn soon enough who you can trust."

"I trust my family." I don't intend to give them any more information about the Kindred Few. "That's it."

Arazian claps twice, and Sterling appears at the door, his hands behind his back. "Take Bastian on a tour of the city. Be on the lookout for his parents. Dax and I have things to discuss."

Sterling raises a well-manicured eyebrow. "Very well, sir."

Given little choice, I scrape back my chair and follow the bloodsucker out of the room. I don't trust anyone here. There's no way the Dark King has my best interest in mind. He wants to use me for my *savior* status to take down the city that kicked him out. But why was he given the boot in the first place?

I walk behind the vampire, lost in my own thoughts as we follow the cobblestone streets through the residential area. "Do you know where to look?"

Sterling sighs, the weight of the world heavy in his exhale.

"Pick any of them you'd like. I'm done with his fruitless missions."

"I'm not going to just pick out random First City residents to be my parents." I glance at the people milling about the streets, hoping to catch a resemblance. "What do you know?"

Sterling shrugs and sits on the edge of a wall, his lithe legs impossibly long. "Your parents are dead, Bastian Hale. Arazian had them turned into Miscretes two decades ago. He wanted you out of the room so he could talk strategy with the Northern Duke."

My blood boils so hot beneath my skin I think it might catch on fire. I storm through the streets, intent on ripping the Dark King's throat out. But I suddenly run into a rock-hard body blocking my way.

"I can't have you disturbing them." Sterling glares at me with ancient hazel eyes. "My instructions are to keep you away for at least a half hour."

It's no use. I could kill the bastard with the wooden stake beneath my cloak, but I don't want to deal with the ramifications.

I sit on a wall, tossing pebbles into a nearby pool to pass the time. The tiny ripples remind me of the impact of the decisions we make.

Why did my parents give me up? Maybe to save me from their fate.

Why did I let Mari and Levi go alone to face the fae king? And why am I so intent on learning about my lineage that I left her vulnerable to Avren's guards? Not that I don't trust Gray and Evie to protect her; it's just that I feel a gaping hole in my heart when she's not near me. And maybe it's the connection we have through the stupid prophecy, but I don't care. My feelings for Mari have morphed into something more than a piece of parchment containing ancient words. They've wrapped themselves tightly around my entire being, giving me hope for the first time since my family died in the fire.

When we again climb the stairs to the upper room of Arazian's home, I've made up my mind that I'm ready to return to the cabin. I'll say *no thanks* to the Dark King's proposition and be on my way. With my parents off the table, there's nothing else he can offer to convince me to remain as his commander.

The Northern Duke is gone when we enter the room. Arazian sits by a fireplace in a high-backed chair.

"Come and join me, Bastian." He motions to the chair beside his.

Sterling leaves, closing the door behind him.

I stand for a moment beside the chair, resting my hand on the embroidered material. Never in my life have I seen such opulence. My anger has morphed into smoldering ashes, ready to be stoked when it is time to kill this man. But now is not that time. Now is the time to negotiate my release. I sit in the chair, unsure of what to do with my hands. I finally rest them on the arms.

"Any luck finding your parents?" He keeps his gaze on the flames in the hearth, knowing full well the answer to his question.

"You can't hold up your end of the deal, so I'm ready to leave." I move to the edge of the chair. "My parents are long gone, and I want nothing to do with this place."

"You're wrong about that." He looks at me through his spectacles, reflecting his crystal-blue eyes. "I'm your father, Bastian."

CHAPTER THREE

Mari

THE FORMER LOCATION of the Hale farm is northeast of the Grove, closer to the First City then I've been before. This both thrills and terrifies me. Since our night in Tenny Rocks, I've longed for Bastian's touch. Images and feelings from our time beside the pond haunt me, searing into my dreams at night. Sleeping in his bed, among his things, makes everything so much more vivid. But I'm also worried about his safety, because the First City also holds the Miscretes—the creatures who occupy my nightmares.

Come, come, Maribel. Imagine taking the throne as princess in the First City. We have a horse waiting for you outside to whisk you away from this place.

The creature's voice, disguised as Levi's, fills every tortured dream. If we go to the First City to find Bastian, will I ever return to the only freedom I've known in my life?

Evie, who has taken the lead on this trip because she knows the area well, turns back to us. "The remnants are on the eastern edge of Moss Ford. We should stick to the woods instead of waltzing through town where we might be recognized. The Supe element is high here."

I stare at the various weapons strapped to Evie's back and attached to her belt. Coming here was a risk.

Grayson drapes his arm over my shoulder. "No need to worry. Word has gotten out that you're the savior and kick-ass fae-slayer. They won't lay a hand on you."

"But what about the other Supe leaders? Don't they want me to gain control over the wilderness?" This makes me more nervous about Evie and Grayson's safety as my companions. If I'm such a valuable commodity, what Supe wouldn't want to impress their leader by dragging me back to their lair?

"Sure, but right now, we have a singular focus; getting Bastian back. Spending time in the First City must be terrible on his complexion." Grayson squeezes my shoulder and releases me.

Smoke from the nearby village drifts through the forest as my feet crunch through the leaves. I have my arrow nocked, ready for action. Evie told me all types of Supes congregate around Moss Ford, so I chose a regular arrow in hopes it would distract long enough to grab the right weapon. My companions hold daggers in their hands but appear more relaxed than I feel. I'm not sure if I'll ever grow used to this—killing other creatures in the name of our freedom.

We travel far enough from the village that I haven't seen a single building, but the smells and sounds indicate it's a lively place. Under different circumstances, I might enjoy Moss Ford.

"The tavern where I work on occasion is here." It's as if Evie can read my thoughts. "There, I'm known as Everleigh Rose, the bartender who can pour you a whiskey bourbon almost as quickly as she can slit your throat."

"That's not a shocker." I skirt a hole in the ground that appears to be a grave. "You're as good, if not better than Bastian and Gray." Since Bastian left, Evie and Grayson have taken turns training me and her dagger holds deadly accuracy.

"I grew up in Moss Ford." She keeps her eyes straight ahead, wiping quickly at a tear running down her cheek. "It wasn't always this way."

"What happened to your family?" I don't want to upset her more, but it's something we've never talked about.

More and more holes appear, dotting the forested landscape, which I find strange. But other than walking around the edges, I ignore them.

Evie buries her fingers in her red locks as Grayson turns back to us, the corner of his lip upturned in a half smile of encouragement.

"My parents owned the tavern and the adjoining inn. As I grew up, it was a thriving business. Moss Ford is close to the sea, so people traveled here on holiday. That is, until the First City was fully constructed." She strings a lock of her hair behind her ear, her freckles vibrant in the muted sunlight. "I had a twin sister—Ferrish. Unlike me, she was outgoing and had all the boys in town wrapped around her pinkie finger. One boy was aggressive in his pursuit of Ferrish's hand in marriage—Samuel Roy. On the night of the annual town dance, he insisted on taking her." Evie stares into a far-off place before continuing. "She looked so beautiful in her pale green dress with her red hair tied up in ribbons."

"If she looked anything like you, darling, she was a knockout," Grayson pipes in, not really attuned to the gravity of the story.

I glare at him.

"She was so beautiful. Samuel came to pick her up from the inn and take her to the barn on the outskirts of town. The entire village seemed to be there that night because the tavern was empty. I stayed back to clean and organize and insisted my parents go and have a good time." A slight sniffle from Evie tells me this is not going to end well. "It was the first night the Miscretes came to town. They hit the barn first, carrying off those they didn't kill. When they swept through the village, I hid beneath the floor in a trapdoor my father had installed."

"About three-fourths of Moss Ford was killed or taken that night." Grayson's voice is somber, as if he's finally sensing his girlfriend's pain.

"And what happened to your family?" I hate to ask, but I know whatever it is must be worse than holding my mother's hand as she succumbed to the sickness. Hearing Bastian and Levi's stories has shown me this.

"The next morning, I traveled to the barn with a few of the other survivors. Hundreds of dead bodies lay strewn across the grassy field. I found my parents lying beside each other, eyes open. Kneeling, my heart full of grief and rage, I clutched them in my arms and sobbed, telling them I loved them for the first time in my entire life." She chews on her lip and glances at me. "If you haven't noticed, I'm not exactly an emotional person."

"You hold it inside." I understand this. In Avren, emotions were a sign of weakness, but it was difficult to suppress them without the daily vitamins. Here, in the wilderness, without the assistance of drugs, I'm an emotional wreck. Fear and terror are at the top of the list.

"I never found Ferrish's body." She lets that statement hang in the air because we all know what it means. The Miscretes probably dragged her back to the First City to become one of them.

The very thought of this makes me want to hurl. Somewhere, there's a mutated Evie intent on killing humans.

"A few months later, the Supes moved in. They saw Arazian's attempts to spread his influence, pushing his boundaries into the wilderness. The Miscretes won't bother with the Supes." Evie removes an apple from her pack and takes a bite. She's done talking about it.

"And what are all these holes?" I ask, directing the question to Grayson. They're so numerous now, it's becoming difficult to avoid them. I put my arrow away and string my bow over my shoulder to keep my balance.

"The Supes in Moss Ford are renegades, at first sent by their leaders to block Arazian's advancements but then enjoying their freedoms from the establishments of their respective allegiances." Grayson points to the holes closer to the village. "They've made it their mission to kill as many Miscretes as they can get their hands on, dump their bodies in holes, and burn them."

Now I really want to hurl.

"But why? Don't the Miscretes mostly kill humans?" I walk around the perimeter of a hole, noticing a burnt-up corpse inside for the first time. Turning to the side, I hold my hand over my mouth as I blanch.

"And who do the Supes rely on for their food supply? If the Miscretes diminish the human population, that effects all of them. And then there's the fear that the First City aims to be another Avren, bringing its heavy hand down on the people and creatures of the wilderness." Grayson opens the back of Evie's pack and removes two more apples, tossing one to me, though I'm not sure I can eat it. "The renegades in Moss Ford don't believe the leaders of the Supes are doing enough. They sit back and for the most part, let the two great powers take over."

"Do you still own the tavern?" I ask Evie.

"Nope, sold it a while back to a werewolf named Max. When I work there, the vamps really enjoy having a human bartender." She slides her hair to the side to reveal two pinpricks in her neck.

Shocked, I hold my fingertips to my neck, knowing I'd never willingly let a vampire drink my blood.

"Don't knock it until you try it, Avrenian." She smiles and

nudges my shoulder. "Just kidding. I'd never wish that on my little sister."

Two men and a woman race through the forest in a blur, stopping a couple hundred yards in front of us. They each carry a mutated corpse on their back, which they toss into holes. In a burst of light, fire fills the holes, sending ashes and sparks into the sky above.

Evie and Grayson freeze beside me, so I do the same, not even reaching for an arrow. I feel like the deer I see in the early morning in the meadow. As Bastian and I approach, they freeze as if we won't see them if they remain perfectly still.

In an instant, the three vampires stand five feet in front of us, assessing their prey from head to toe.

"Everleigh Rose, what have you brought us today?" The tallest of the three has dark skin and a smooth, hypnotic timbre to his voice, making me wonder if I should let him take a sip.

"We're only passing through, Gabriel. We have an errand in the First City." She holds her head high in her defiant stance—a look I can only aspire to. "Let us pass, and I'll give each of you a draw the next time I'm working."

The female vampire laughs and tilts her head to the side, her eyes locked on Grayson. "But you've brought us Avrenian blood. And this one's your mate." She saunters closer to him, her wavy brown locks catch on the slight breeze. A blood-red fingernail trails down Grayson's chest to his waistline. "Tell me, is he any good?"

"Don't touch him." The anguish on Evie's face is apparent. It's difficult for her to hold back.

The third vampire, slightly shorter than the other male, circles me. Feelings from my first morning in the meadow with Bastian come rushing back. That morning, a vamp had his eyes set on me, drawn by my Avrenian blood. Before Bastian killed the vampire, the creature's breath on my neck chilled me to the core.

"Oh, come now, Everleigh Rose." The female is dangerously close to Grayson, reaching behind him to grab his ass. She turns to the male vamps. "I don't know about you humans, but the three of us are ready for a full-out orgy."

My heart is in my stomach, knowing that any one of the vampires could snap all three of our necks in an instant and still take their fill of blood. I straighten my back as the blond vampire's fingers slide along my lower back, around my hip, and to my stomach, which tightens with the chill. "I'm one of the saviors destined to bring down the two cities. These humans are my guards, entrusted to bring me safely to the First City."

The ice-cold fingers leave my stomach.

"The savior?" Gabriel assesses me, his narrowing eyes telling me he's not very impressed. "Did you sense it, Alfred?"

The blond vampire moves beside me, his creep-factor at an all-time high. "She is one of the two."

"You must let us pass. Arazian holds the other savior captive, and we don't have time to lose on any type of distracting activity." I touch my neck, hoping they accept our story. "I've been told that the Supes who live in Moss Ford want to fight back against Arazian and the Miscretes. According to the fae prophecy, you need us to take them down completely."

"Then I will lead you safely to the boundaries of the First City," Gabriel states. "There are plenty who would take advantage of three humans traveling alone."

Including you.

"We need to visit the Hale farm before going to the city." I look to Evie for help, but she only gives me a slight nod. "After that, we can travel the rest of the way on our own."

Gabriel's blood-red eyes widen. "You seek out a gravesite? Whatever could it hold of importance to you?"

"A friend of mine grew up there, and it might hold a key to his past." Too many details will make this entire situation muddier than it already is.

25

"I see," he says. "After leaving the farm, you'll more than likely be torn apart in the Canyon of Whispering Souls, but I can only do so much to warn you."

"And we appreciate it." I lift my quiver to my shoulder as the other two vampires disappear into the forest. Thankfully, now we only have one to deal with. "We'll need to take our chances from here on out, or I have no right to claim the name *savior* of the wilderness."

CHAPTER FOUR

Bastian

MY INSIDES CRUMBLE the way I always imagined the walls of the First City falling when the Redeemed attacked. I can't seem to organize a coherent thought.

Arazian? My father? Impossible.

My fingers curl around the arms of the chair, turning my knuckles white.

"When I lived in Avren, I was a powerful man. Almost as powerful as I am here. I was the second-highest sitting Council member, and I wielded my rank with a carefully crafted reck-lessness." He lifts a pipe from the glass side table beside his chair and holds it to his lips.

I want nothing more than to march out of the room and never return. He's lying. He must be.

"I was the one who came up with the idea to oust the Unde-sirables. All Supes had to go first. They were a danger to our perfect city. Although some were upstanding citizens, they all had to go to prove my point." He taps his finger on the table, sending my nerves even further down the road to wreckage. "I think Carl brought up the idea to dismiss the ones with defects, or maybe it was Noki... either way, we had a plan set in motion to develop the most perfect civilized city in the world. And it was all under our control."

"And you fucking messed up people's entire lives." I can't take this anymore. What does he expect? That I'll fall at his feet because he sired me? "You ousted people and then expected them to serve you."

Arazian holds up a hand. "And I didn't agree with that. I also didn't agree with the pregnancy law. Raven believed if we controlled the process before birth, we'd have fewer defects and wouldn't have to banish people."

"Then I guess you get a shining star." I push up from the chair and pace the floor in front of the hearth. "A majority of Avrenians released into the wilderness are killed the first night by Supes. You threw innocent people out to be slaughtered. Don't you understand that?" My fingers grip the hilt of my dagger. I'm tempted to run him through. "And now? You start a new city that supposedly does things better, but you've become a pillar of terror to everyone. *You killed my parents and brothers.*"

"I didn't lay a hand on your adoptive caregivers. They played their role well, raising you and making sure you grew up strong. I gave them clear instructions to follow." He takes a puff from his pipe.

I lay an arm on the wooden mantle above the hearth, resting my head on it. This is all too much. "And you were kicked out because you disagreed with the rest of the Council?"

He clears his throat, so I lift my head and turn back to him. "It was a farce. You are not a test tube child, son. Your mother Raven and I had you the natural way. If my relationship with Raven had come out, it would have been scandalous. The rest of the Council would have banished us. She hid her pregnancy, feigning illness when her condition could no longer be hidden."

He wrings his hands, not looking at me as he speaks. "Before you were born, we had a falling out about how to raise you, whether to make our relationship public, and about the dealings of the Council."

I hear his words, but they're not processing. It's like he's dropped me into a nightmare and there's no coming back from it. "Lady Raven is my mother?"

"Yes! Are you listening to me at all?" He sits forward in his seat and tents his hands. "Her plan was to give you over to another Citizen family to raise and have you join the guard when you were old enough. I couldn't let her get her claws into you. She had plenty of time to show me who she truly was, and it wasn't what I wanted for myself or my son. One night I left with you hidden beneath my cloak, and we never returned."

"Everyone always talks about the grand ceremony where you and your followers were forced to leave Avren. Your story doesn't match up." This guy will never give me a reason to trust him, blood or not.

"No one saw my face because they put a mask and a red cloak over my poor stand-in." He twists his lip into a slight frown. "I think it was a fire-breather who got him." Shifting in his seat, he stares into the glowing hearth. "Spend the night, Bastian. I've had a room waiting for you for twenty years. It's a lot to process, and I'm sure you'll have questions for me in the morning."

My tired head battles with my ravaged heart. Never once did Jaresiah or Sarah provide any clues to this hard truth. They treated me the same way they treated my two brothers. And I'd never fault them for trying to give me a normal life. "Where's my room?"

A sliver of a smile crosses Arazian's lips, and he claps twice.

Sterling appears at the door.

"I'll have Sterling show you. I can only imagine how tired you are of my face at this moment."

That's an understatement.

I follow the vampire down the hall to a set of double doors as impressive as the ones leading into Arazian's room. He opens one of the doors and ushers me inside.

The first thing I notice is that the room mirrors the other exactly, except this one is blue where the other was white. Double glass doors open to an enormous balcony overlooking the city. The far wall beside the hearth contains floor-to-ceiling bookshelves filled to the brim with an unthinkable amount of tomes. An enormous four-poster bed, complete with a deep-blue satin comforter stands against the far wall with an impressive view out the window.

"The bathing room is in here." Sterling opens a door beyond the bed. "If you wish to dine with us this evening, we'll see you downstairs in an hour. If you do not, he says he understands."

When did the two of them have a chance to discuss this?

"You can tell *Arazian* to feed my dinner to the dogs and go to hell." All I want to do is wash up, curl up in bed, and dream of having Mari here with me—under much different circumstances.

"As you wish, Master Hale." Sterling gives a slight bow of his head and exits, leaving me alone in the massive room.

I unbuckle my weapons belt and drop it on the chair beside the bed. It's definitely a "dagger beneath the pillow" kind of night. My head spins, making me long for my family. If only I could have an archery competition with Evie, or a game of cards with Gray, or hold onto Mari so tight that I knew I'd never leave her again.

I open a glass door to the balcony and walk out, disappointed. The air out here is as artificial as it is in my bedroom. One must walk outside the city to experience my world—the one I came here to fight for before my parents got wrapped up in it.

Instead of making a spectacle of myself on the balcony, I

start a bath and hope the hot water will clear my head. Sinking beneath the suds, I close my eyes, pushing out the negative energy of my conversation with the Dark King and pulling in thoughts of Mari. Our time by the pond in Tenny Rocks seems like a distant memory soiled by the reading of the prophecy. What will she think when she finds out Lady Raven is my mother? That Arazian is my father?

I break through the surface and shake my head. Having the two of them as the birth parents of a savior destined to destroy them provides a warped sense of irony. I rub the soap bar between my hands and work the lather into my hair, dipping below the surface again to wash it out.

As the commander of the rebellion, who better to play the spy and find out what Arazian really wants? Revenge is a strange word, filled with so many hidden motives. The Dark King seems to lack the unhinged emotional passion that getting back at an ex usually holds. There's more than anger at being ousted. And as much as I want to get out of here and return home, there might be information I can gather.

Stepping out of the tub, I yank my tunic over my head and pull on my trousers. A looking glass sits on the ornate dresser in my bedroom, so I rake my fingers through my hair and check for circles beneath my eyes.

Arazian's living quarters is a straight shot down the hall from my room, but I turn down the stairs instead. The house is so empty, I can hear the echo of my feet in the grand entryway. Anyone in earshot will know I'm here.

Sterling is there to greet me with his creepy grin and arm held out like it's meant to have a napkin draped over it. "Arazian waits for you in the dining room."

I follow the vampire into the room where a long table is laid out with a black cloth. It doesn't seem to fit the white décor in the rest of the mansion. Two elaborate candelabras sit about a third of the way in on either end of the table. And there's a feast ready for thirty rather than three. Birds, hogs, fruits, breads, desserts, and multiple bottles of wine.

My stomach growls, although I'm unsure if I should trust my host's offerings.

"Come, Bastian my boy. My cook outdid himself tonight, knowing that my wayward son has returned to me." He nods to a man dressed in a black suit, who pulls a chair out for me.

After sitting, I watch as the same man pours me a tall glass of wine. "Uh… I don't think I can be wayward if I had no idea you existed."

Arazian holds up his glass as Sterling sits across the table from me. "A toast. To my clueless wayward son. May the First City bring light to his eyes and clarity to his heart."

The Dark King clinks glasses with Sterling before turning to me.

I stare back at him, tempted to leave but understanding that I have a bigger mission. Without any flourish, I lift my glass and tap it against his. "And to my father. The one who abandoned me as a baby."

"I never abandoned you." The man's temper doesn't manifest. He's continually lukewarm, making him seem even more dangerous to me. It's as if he lacks emotion. "Merely had good friends raise you. I never was one for children."

"And you had your *good friends* killed. My parents and brothers were mutilated and burned to death." The core memory fills me with so much rage, I'm surprised I have the restraint to not strangle Arazian to death.

"I did no such thing." He stabs a piece of meat with his fork, examining it in the candlelight before plopping it in his mouth, chewing as he speaks. "I asked the Miscretes to retrieve you. My error was not being more specific about the method. They get a tad bit overzealous at times."

"If Jaresiah and Sarah were friends of yours, which I highly doubt, couldn't you have just asked them to bring me to you?"

None of this makes sense to me. Growing up, I was taught to fear the First City and Avren. And Evie, Levi, and I have stories of how Arazian made us orphans. No matter who this guy says he is, he's a lying bag of shit.

Arazian lifts his wine glass, swirls the red liquid inside, then takes a sip. "People lose their faith in the wilderness, Bastian. When we left Avren, I had a core group who were loyal to me. They understood the urgency of stopping the Council and creating a place where freedom outweighed progress." He sets his glass down and splays his white fingers on the black cloth. "If you haven't noticed, son, everyone is welcome in this city. Test tube babies are outlawed. The Avrenians need to know there's a better way to live."

"There has to be a reason the Hales stopped following you." I recline in my chair and cross my arms. "As I see it, you're as manipulative as the Council. It wouldn't surprise me to know you have your own diabolical plan to take down Avren and the wilderness in its wake."

A flash flickers through Sterling's eyes. Why does a vampire leave his queen to come serve with this crazy son of a bitch? Arazian and I may share blood, but from what I've seen, we're miles away in core values.

Lifting his napkin, Arazian wipes his mouth. "I had hoped we'd come to an agreement. Sterling always accuses me of holding too much optimism. Ever since you were born, I had hoped we'd stand side by side in the First City's fight against the Council and Avren's soldiers. But you have too much of your mother in you—cynical, calculated, unwilling to listen to other points of view." He pushes back in his chair, and it scrapes against the stone floor. He nods at Sterling, then walks toward the door. "I can't have a savior stopping my plans."

I reach for my stake.

Sterling slowly rounds the table, his hands behind his back as if he's out for a stroll. To drive the weapon into his heart, I need to get close enough, but there's no way I can catch him off guard. The smile on his pallid lips is really creeping me out. If Arazian's orders were to kill me, he's enjoying every second of this cat-and-mouse game.

"Do you enjoy being my father's second? I'd think a vampire would hate working for a human."

"Who do you think is really in control here?" He lifts a chair with one hand and throws it at me as easily as if it were a rock.

I duck before it smashes into the wall, breaking to pieces.

"The Dark King gets the title. In return, he gives me an unlimited blood supply. Living in the Caverns, I had to hunt. How *pedestrian*. And the old bastard relies on me. The Northern Duke is the only ally he has left." Sterling knows better than to get too close with my fingers wrapped tightly around the stake. "And he has this obsession with you—a hero to give us the edge in our war with Avren. All I see is a scared little boy with mommy and daddy issues."

"I was fine until I came here," I growl, ready to stop this vampire's self-indulgent speech. It's not like I haven't killed several dozen vamps in my life. "The man and woman I consider my real father and mother were good parents."

The same maniacal smile crosses his lips again. "It's too bad I had to rip your mother's throat out as she screamed."

Emotions I've tried to suppress since entering the First City boil over. With all the anger and hatred in my heart, I rush at Sterling, ready to end his miserable existence. But he's too fast. Before I know it, I'm flying through the air in his arms, then my back comes down hard in the center of the dining table. It cracks, and I crash to the floor, covered in mashed potatoes and red sauce. Sterling is on top of me, his ice-cold fingers around my throat.

"You were the one wildcard," he hisses. "I should drink you dry, but I want to remain in your father's good graces."

The stake flew from my hand as Sterling drove me into the

table, leaving me vulnerable. I squirm beneath him, but it's no use. He's holding me like an iron cage.

"A warning." He lowers his lips to my neck, tugging gently at the skin before piercing me with his fangs.

Pain courses through my veins as he draws on my most precious resource. Lightheadedness overtakes me, and my thoughts drift to Mari. She's in the garden by the cabin dressed in a white shift. It's sheer and I can see the shape of her body beneath. Her beautiful brown hair hangs loose, catching on the light breeze. She lifts a hand and beckons me with a finger to come to her.

As can only happen in a dream, I'm instantly there, lifting her shift over her head. I remove my shirt as she stands naked before me, the most wondrous sight I have ever laid eyes on. She unbuckles my belt, letting it drop to the ground before slipping the buttons of my pants through the eyelets and shimmying them to the ground. She kneels before me and gives me a coy smile, setting my blood on fire. The moment she's about to take me into her mouth, I'm startled awake.

Sterling draws back, his lips dripping with blood. "Mmm... I think I've just found my new source. I enjoy where your mind wanders." He settles back on his hands, crossing his feet at the ankles. "I'd have let you take it further, but I already drew a little too much."

My heart stutters as I feel any remaining blood drain from my face. He must be able to read my thoughts when he's drinking from me.

"Your father wants me to lock you in your room." Sterling glances at the mess he made. "I'll tell him you were naughty and fought back." He lifts a shoulder. "It's understandable. You're used to your freedom." In a fluid motion, he rises to his feet. "And Bastian, I look forward to meeting this woman of yours."

CHAPTER FIVE

Mari

THE REMAINS of the Hale homestead are about a ten-minute walk from the village. Tall grasses grow over charred wooden beams. A corral still stands in a meadow, its occupants long gone. Pink and white flowers dot the landscape as chipmunks and tiny birds skitter and hop around the wood. New life exists everywhere, reminding me of Levi's gravesite.

"I didn't know Bastian growing up, but the Hales were good people. They left Avren with the Great Exodus." Evie crouches beside a beam to pluck a single pink flower pushing its way up through a crevice, stands, and sticks it behind her ear. "Life always finds a way, even when it seems all hope is lost."

"I'll leave you here." Ezekiel looks back to the village. "Miscretes came back last night, so we have a fresh pile to bury. I don't think they realize most humans have left."

"According to our sources, Arazian has ramped up his efforts to expand his army. He's also actively searching for the saviors. He sent his creatures after Mari in Tenny Rocks a few weeks back." Grayson walks the perimeter of what was probably once the Hale home. "If he can get at least one savior on his side, they can convince the rebellion to attack Avren and keep the focus away from the First City."

His words catch me by surprise. "Do you think that's what he'll do with Bastian? Convince him to change his mind about making the city our first target? He's the commander, so he holds a lot of sway."

"There's nothing I'd put past Arazian," Ezekiel says. "Watch yourself with that one. There's a reason the Council in Avren exiled him. Good luck on your quest." And before I can blink my eyes, he's gone, leaving us alone at the Hale gravesite, thankful to be alive.

It seems overwhelming to start digging around in Bastian's world. We stand for a moment, absorbing the enormity of it all.

"Good thinking back in the forest." Evie joins Grayson in assessing the remnants. "They don't give me too hard of a time in the tavern, but apparently three humans waltzing through the forest, mostly out of sight, are too tempting to resist."

"But you could have killed them, right?" For weeks, I've felt safe in the forest when one of my brothers or my sister was with me. They have the skills and weapons needed.

Grayson scratches his neck and shoots a look at Evie. "Maybe one, possibly two, but they're too fast and strong. If you hadn't spoken up, we would have experienced our first vampire sex, been drained of our blood and dumped in one of the graves."

"Speak for yourself." Evie crouches to lift a wooden beam and toss it to the side. She drops to her knees, lights a match, and stares into the hole. "There are stairs here into the basement."

Grayson helps her move more of the charred wood. "Well, I think their intentions were pretty obvious. If Mari hadn't told them about..."

"No, no." She grunts and heaves a large log to the side. "No, I agree with that. It just wouldn't be my first vampire sex."

"Oh." Grayson stands still. His face is white. "But I…"

Evie steps onto the first stone stair leading to the basement, lighting a torch from her pack with a match. "Get over yourself, Gray. No, you weren't my first time. I had a life before I met you, but I don't want to discuss this in present company." She looks at me and rolls her eyes. "Let's get down here and see what we can find."

I follow Evie down the stairs to give Grayson his space. He and I had both grown up in Avren, a place with strict rules about sex. It didn't happen until you were married and even then, it was minimal. Evie may have been his first lover. And although Bastian was my first, I knew he had been with others. It was something I had to accept. But he also told me I was the only woman he'd ever loved.

The temperature drops as we descend into the dirt-lined basement. Parts of the upper floor have collapsed into the vast hole, but there are still areas that are accessible. Shelves line the walls with tools Mr. Hale probably used on his farm. Spiderwebs crisscross from shelf to shelf and among the hammers, wrenches, and other iron gadgets.

"What exactly do you think we're looking for?" Grayson stands near the top of the stairs, the blue sky so bright above him, it is difficult to see his face. Is it still white?

Evie rummages through metal boxes. "Whatever it is, it won't be right out in the open. They would've hidden it from Bastian and his brothers." She slams a box shut before holding her torch to the dirt walls, stopping when she reaches a small metal door in the wall. Etched across the front are the words: *Danger. Keep Out.* "I wonder…"

Grayson is now at the bottom of the stairs, moving beside a workbench. "That's just the fuse box. And you should heed those words. Old homes like these don't have the safest wiring."

I ignore Grayson's warning and join Evie, curious about what's behind the metal door.

She struggles with the latch, which squeaks and moans as she jiggles it. It's rusted shut. Reaching into her pocket, Evie removes a dagger and runs it along the seams of the door.

"And *that's* real safe. Why don't you stick your knife into an electrical socket? Your imminent death will happen a whole lot faster."

Grayson's little pity party is getting on my nerves.I whip around, ready for him to drop whatever grudge he's holding toward Evie. "I'm sure whatever electricity this house had stopped working many years ago."

The hinges squeal open as I'm facing Grayson.

"It's not a fuse box." Evie reaches into the hole behind the door and pulls out stacks of credits.

The Hales were rich.

Evie piles the money into my arms before pulling out a stack of papers. She shoves the torch at Grayson. "Here, hold this." She tilts the top paper toward the torchlight. "It's a birth certificate from Avren." Her finger trails down the paper. "For Bastian Aiden Valeria."

"The Hales adopted Bastian?" Grayson lowers his head to get a better look. He points to the parent section. "And Arazian Valeria is his father? I don't see a mother listed. Didn't know a male could have an immaculate conception."

"He was a test tube baby." I shift the credits to one arm and take the paper from Evie. "How else could Arazian have a child with no mother? This must be the reason he was exiled from Avren. But why work so hard to have a child and then have other people raise them?"

"You think nothing happens behind closed doors in Avren?" Evie reaches back through the doorway. "Leave it to you to assume everyone has a purity badge in the city."

I ignore her, no longer bothered by her degrading wit. When

Bastian gets this information, it will break him. His family, although dead, grounded him. They gave him a reason to press on in the rebellion. The leader of the city he planned to destroy is his birth father.

"Look at this." Evie holds a second piece of paper to the torchlight. "It appears to be a declaration of some sort. 'We, the former leaders of Avren, reject the direction the Council is taking the city. By exiling us to the wilderness, their intent was to isolate us, but it has made us stronger. In the end, we swear to come together to defeat the powers of oppression and exclusivity that walk the halls of the place we once called home. With the rise of the two saviors, we will once again walk in the light of day to fight alongside them. Arazian Valeria, Daxon Barellis, Lucy Song, Cirrus Meadowlark, Isle Calista, Jaresiah Hale, Sarah Hale, and Cage Hilder.'"

Although I recognize two of the other names, my body and mind go numb when Evie reads my father's name. He wants the same things the Kindred Few wants—the defeat of Avren's Council, peace in the wilderness—but he's siding with people and creatures of questionable character. Arazian uses imperfect test tube babies to build his army. Isle rules over a nest of vampires wreaking havoc and fear on newly exiled Avrenians. Cirrus killed Levi.

Cirrus killed Levi. That alone is too much for me to take.

"Well, that's a load of crap." Grayson points at the names. "You'll never get vampires, werewolves, and fae to cooperate. And the Northern Duke? The guy has a few screws loose. I once heard he forced his troops to sludge through the Murky Swamps because it was faster than going around."

"No way!" Evie looks up at him. "What happened?"

"Lost about half his regiment."

"Serves him right." Evie places the paper on the bottom of the stack and continues to read through the documents.

"What's wrong with the Murky Swamps?" I have some sense

of direction in the wilderness, but the only things I know that are north of the Grove are Tenny Rocks and Frostacre.

"They're haunted by the spirts of the Miscretes who died there. Their bodies sink below the surface, but if you dare to enter the water, it is said their boney hands reach up and grab you, pulling you under." Grayson's eyes light up in the flickering torch as if he enjoys telling ghost stories.

I shiver at the thought.

The man the others are describing to me is nothing like the father I knew growing up. He'd tell me bedtime stories, kiss me on the forehead, and bring me presents like the music box. This man seems to lead his people with an iron fist, his goals the only thing on his mind.

"I once thought I wanted to work for the Northern Duke." Grayson leans against a barrel and crosses his arms. "You hear the stories growing up in Avren, never thinking you'll experience them. My parents worked for the resistance within the city walls. It was extremely dangerous. When you meet in secret planning an overthrow of the government, you eventually get caught." In the torchlight, Grayson's eyes grow watery. "One night, my parents didn't return to our apartment. Soldiers ambushed their meeting and shot them. When the Council ruled in favor of my exile, I didn't have anyone to lead me to a warm cabin."

I close my eyes and take a deep breath. Every one of us has a tragic story. I didn't push Grayson for his because I knew the pain ran deep. Instead of trying to find an awkward condolence, I place my hand on his arm and squeeze. The men and women in that group died for my freedom—to help those who are blind to the oppression they live under in the city.

"Alone in the wilderness, I longed for the familiar. This meant finding other exiles from Avren who understood what I was going through." He hangs his head as a tear trails down his cheek. "I traveled north in search of the Duke, stopping in the first human village I could find." He tilts his head to the side so his sandy bangs sweep over his forehead. "I know it's difficult to believe, but at almost eighteen, I was a strong, good-looking kid."

Evie looks up from the documents to roll her eyes at me again. "With little to no ego."

"Exactly." He's joking, but in the glow of the fire, I can see the pain etched across his face—no dimple, worry lines creasing his forehead, the slight downturn of his lips. "When I entered the village, I was approached by a woman at least ten years older than me." He holds out a hand in my direction. "As you know, I wasn't allowed to look twice at a woman in Avren. And this one, with her blonde curls and low-cut dress, made me want to break that rule. She led me like a puppy dog to her home. Turned out it was a brothel, and losing my virginity saved my life that night."

"Because it made you realize what you were missing out on?" I glance at Evie to see if she looks upset over Grayson's story. She's still engrossed in the papers.

"No. The next morning, the madame of the house told me that three vampires had tracked me and waited for me to leave all night. The whole *'fresh Avrenian blood'* thing." He scratches the back of his neck. "I did find myself in trouble because I couldn't pay for the night before with Holly. So I stayed and worked in the brothel until I could pay off my debt. It was a symbiotic relationship. They provided me safety and I scrubbed the dishes." He snatches the paperwork from Evie and heads for the stairs. "Come on, we can take these with us."

The bright sunlight outside provides safety from any further vampire encounters. The three of us divvy up the credits into our pockets and satchels. Bastian is in more trouble than I had originally thought. It's one thing to be a savior, but to be the son of the man you're aiming to kill is a entirely different story.

"Ezekiel mentioned the Canyon of Whispering Souls. What

is that?" With my bow on my shoulder, my hands are free to skim over the tall grasses in the meadow. Although it's a place of great tragedy, there's something that warms my heart about walking through a field where Bastian once walked. This was his home.

"The road from Moss Ford to the First City runs through the chasm. To go around it would add many miles to our journey." Grayson takes Evie's hand. "It's haunted by tortured souls." He stares straight ahead. "Proof that Arazian can use the creatures even after they're dead both near and far."

"That's horrible." In Avren, we believed that our souls passed to the other world, a place on another plane of existence. This was the only thing comforting me when my mother died. The thought of living the miserable life of a Miscrete, dying, and then being trapped in a canyon or a swamp to haunt for eternity made me feel for them.

"I hear it has good dental benefits." Grayson laughs.

Evie releases his hand and smacks him on the arm. "We don't know how many of our friends and family are Miscretes—Levi's parents, Lyden, *my* sister. The ones where we don't know their fate. They simply disappear. Do you know how difficult it is for me every time I need to kill them? The way they use her voice to haunt me?"

Then it wasn't just me. In Tenny Rocks, the creatures used Levi and Flynn's voices to confuse me when Bastian and I fought them in the storeroom. Facing them, or their ghosts, again isn't something I look forward to.

"I'm sorry, baby." Grayson wraps an arm around Evie and pulls her close. "I don't know why I'm always so damn insensitive."

She rests a head on his shoulder in an apparent act of forgiveness.

It makes me long for Bastian, and it twists my gut in knots knowing his fate is up in the air. I thought I understood love with Flynn—the brush of our hands, love notes, and heated kisses away from the cameras—but with Bastian it's different. It's not a juvenile crush. It's about survival. It's about family and loyalty and belonging. But more importantly, it's about a primal need for each other that has me in a cold sweat every time I see him. His safety and wellbeing are at the forefront of my mind as I'm about to march through a place called the Canyon of Lost Souls. Because as cliché as it might sound, I can't go on in a world without him in it.

Evie wraps an arm around my waist and stops to string a stray wisp of my hair behind my ear. "We'll find him, Mari. I promise you we won't leave until he's safely with us. We love him as much as you do."

CHAPTER SIX

Mari

HIGH WALLS of red sandstone reach upward, framed by the bright blue sky. A hawk screeches as it circles above, searching for its next meal. In the echoes formed by the canyon walls, our footfalls crunching on the gravel are deafening. Despite the eeriness of Grayson's story, the pathway doesn't appear too frightening in the daylight. The black spires of the First City rise like soldiers beyond the next hill which should scare me, but all I can think about is Bastian.

Grayson starts to whistle a tune I've never heard before.

Evie holds a dagger in her hand, ready for whatever we might face in this foreign landscape.

"How long does the canyon run?" I wipe the sweat from the back of my neck. The sooner we're out of this sunbaked wasteland, the better.

Evie kicks a rock at a snake sidewinding in our direction. "About another mile."

As we continue, a sense of hope creeps through me that we'll make it through with little to no confrontation with Miscretes or their ghosts. Until I see the bones. Human skeletons begin to litter the dusty path. Scorpions and snakes skitter and weave through ribcages as the hawk circles above. He's not waiting for his next mouse to catch. He's anticipating our deaths.

I remove my bow from my shoulder and draw an arrow from my quiver, nocking it.

Grayson continues whistling his obnoxious song. To my relief, he removes his dagger from his pocket. "Do you think they've met the likes of the Kindred Few?"

We both ignore him, scanning the barren landscape. Movement first comes from a hole in the canyon wall about a foot or two above the desert floor. A Miscrete drops to the ground, followed by another, and then an entire swarm. Without hesitation, I let an arrow fly in their direction, dropping one of them to the ground.

Voices call out behind us in a strange mixture of human and other-worldly tones. We turn to face our new foes, but no one is there. A freezing cold gust of wind sweeps down the canyon walls almost knocking us from our feet. Icy-cold fingers dance beneath my shirt and along my skin. The ghosts are working with the Miscretes.

Hoping the extent of their influence is to make me feel like a block of ice, I turn back to my flesh-and-blood opponents, raising my bow to take out another one. Evie and Grayson rush the swarm, slitting throats and driving their daggers into chests. We are outnumbered, but we must get past them to reach Bastian. I shoot an arrow at another Miscrete diving for Grayson's back.

Three Miscretes creep behind Evie as she removes her dagger from the monster she just killed. Without looking up, she drives her elbow into a face, leg-sweeps the second one, and implants the blade into the third one's skull. I quickly reload and help her take out the other two.

Grayson muscles a Miscrete to the ground, his hands around its neck, his dagger on the ground out of reach. Another Miscrete picks it up and flings it at my brother, who ducks, but not before the blade swipes his shoulder and he cries out. My arrow hits the creature directly in the heart. Grayson removes another dagger from his belt and kills the one beneath him before collapsing to the ground.

I rush over to him, kneeling, and pulling his shirt away from his shoulder. It's a deep gash. While not fatal, it must hurt like hell. I unscrew my canteen and let the cool water flow over his injury as I wait for Evie to finish off the last of the Miscretes.

The circling hawk is long gone. Must not have an appetite for Miscretes.

Evie brings over her pack and removes a swath of white bandaging cloth. I let her take over as I keep watch for more creatures. She wraps the cloth around Grayson's wound. Blood seeps through the pure white material. "It could use stitches, but with our new knowledge, we don't have a minute to spare. Bastian needs us."

"I'll get by." Grayson props himself up on his elbows, wincing. "If we play our cards right, we can get the young prince out of the city without bloodshed."

Prince? I guess if Bastian is Arazian's son, and he's the self-proclaimed Dark King, he'd call his son a prince.

Bastian would never go for it.

"We need to get to the city first." Evie helps Grayson to his feet. "There's more Miscretes where those came from."

The terrain changes as we exit the canyon and the road curves up a hill and through a forest. From this perspective, the First City no longer looms over us, but I can sense its threatening presence even against the backdrop of the clear blue sky. Arazian left Avren before I was born so my entire image of him is constructed from the stories of the elders of the city. Everything points to him being a deranged man deter-

47

mined to run things his way. Did he pass any of this on to Bastian?

Large black crows hop along the forest floor and stare down at us from the branches of trees. In the woods near the cabin, we see different types of small birds who sing comforting songs, not the caws and screeches of crows and hawks.

"We'll enter through the supply doorway." Evie digs into her pack and throws a tunic and a tan pair of pants at me. "Put these on over your clothes. You need the look of a worker. Once we're inside, we can blend in to find Bastian."

"Isn't the city full of Miscretes and vampires?" The way I see the First City in my mind is so different than Avren, with its clean streets and affluent shops. Arazian's city must contain dungeons, torture devices, and lots of spider webs.

Evie pulls her tunic over her head before helping Grayson with his. "It's a normal place, more normal than Avren, I would say. Humans live along cobblestone streets making a living with baking or carpentry or one of the other trades. The Miscretes live below in dark labyrinths. It's rumored that Arazian's pet vamp feeds them once a day with a stale loaf of bread and contaminated water."

"Is there no saving them?" Evie's comment about Levi's parents, Lyden, and her sister stuck with me. In the canyon, we killed people's family members. With our lives on the line, we didn't have a choice, but every Miscrete death will haunt me now.

Evie rubs the bridge of her nose with her fingers. I'm bringing up something she's probably tried to work out in her head for years. "Not that I've found."

I drop it, not wanting to hurt her more.

The uphill climb is tough on my thighs as we wind through the woods. As a mathematician, my mother would have been able to calculate the angle of the slope we're climbing to take her mind off the burning muscles. One glance at Evie keeps me from complaining. She carries both her and Grayson's packs on her back, never slowing down.

At the crest of the hill, I pitch forward and rest my hands on my knees, trying to catch my breath. Avren has made me soft. Over the past seven weeks of training, I've developed muscles only soldiers have in the city. But my endurance is lacking. If Bastian were here, he'd make me run up and down this hill ten times.

When I reach for my canteen and finally look up, the blood rushes from my body. Seeing the First City from high in the air and seeing it up close are two different experiences completely. The structure was erected to intimidate. The enormous black spires I saw from a distance, appear as if they are made of obsidian erupting from the ground in jagged angles. Soldiers holding spears across their chests guard heavy wooden doors at the front entrance of the city.

The prophecy states that Bastian and I will lead others to take down this city, but staring up at the massive stone structure, I'm not sure if I have the guts to step foot inside of it. How in the world can an ancient prophet see worth in someone so unworthy?

Evie snatches my arm. "Come on. The service entrance is closer to the rear." She opens her satchel to reveal a stash of yellow gemstones. "This is Rekja, a stone used by the First City to provide power to its residents. Because it is only found in the Elmriddens, they rely on merchants for their supply." She holds a rock in the sunlight. "One of these has enough power to light the city for a week."

"That's amazing." I watch how the sun rays dance through the facets of the stone, sending fractals of light dancing over the forest floor. Avren's power came from the giant furnaces in the Unseen, operated by the Undesirables.

"There are ways to do things better." Grayson takes the gem from Evie's hand. "For a city so hellbent on being the shining

49

pinnacle of progress, Avren is still stuck in the dark ages. As much as Arazian is a load of shit, he is on the leading edge of innovative ideas."

We skirt along the edge of the woods until we reach a small dirt road leading to an opening in the rock. A line of people wait as a soldier inspects each one. More than likely, they'll make me leave my bow and quiver outside. I'll have to rely on the daggers inside my boots.

The guard assesses the three of us when it's our turn. He stands at least a half a foot taller than Grayson and his shoulders are almost as wide as Bastian's. "Names and purpose."

"If you please." Evie gives him a flirtatious smile. "We'd like to sell our Rekja to a dealer in the city. We're siblings from the Kelvic family." Moving a step closer to him, she opens her satchel, revealing its contents.

The guard is like putty in her hands. He returns her smile. "Ferdinand will give you the best price. Be sure to stop by here on your way out and maybe we can talk for a while."

She trails a finger up his uniform. "I'd like that." Then she turns and saunters through the doorway as if she knows what she's doing and where she's going.

When we're out of earshot, Grayson hisses, "I hate when you do that."

"Jealous?" She raises an eyebrow.

"No." He furrows his brows. "But if I'm not with you and one of these massive dumb fucks decides to take advantage of you..."

She whips around and places a hand on his chest. "Seriously? You've known me long enough that you know I can take care of myself. If he or any other of your so-called 'dumb fucks' lays a hand on me, I'll slit his throat. Are we clear?"

Grayson rubs the lower part of his injured arm. It's obvious that he needs someone who puts him in his place. "Perfectly."

More than anything, I want to be like my sister. Never in my life have I met someone with so much confidence in her ability to not only take on a squadron of soldiers but to seduce any man she sets her sights on. She knows who she is, and she lives it.

The obsidian walls of the corridor lined with torch sconces, live and breathe my worst nightmares about the First City. It's not until we've walked about ten minutes that things begin to change. The passageway widens and the dirt floor is replaced with cobblestones.

We finally reach the end, which opens into a huge open space filled with buildings. People, not Supes or Miscretes, walk the streets, conversing and going about their daily work. Most wear clothes like ours—tunics, cotton pants, dresses. The best part is, they pay no attention to us.

"Where do you think they have Bastian?" Despite the surprise of the city, I have a singular focus.

"If Arazian knows he's one of the saviors, or worse yet, his son, there's no doubt he's locked away in his palace." Grayson tips his cap at a pretty blonde woman walking by, swiftly receiving an elbow to the ribs from Evie.

"Gray's right." Evie glances up at a sign on the front of a brick building. "Let's eat something and discuss our plans. One does not just waltz up to Arazian's front door and knock. His vamp keeps him sheltered."

Unlike the shops in Avren, the tavern we enter is simple. A long bar runs the length of a wall. Tables and booths fill the remainder of the space. A burly man with a black mustache and beard wipes down the counter as we enter. Several patrons sit at the bar, talking and drinking from steins.

"Take a seat wherever you'd like," the man calls out. He lifts a glass mug to a tap, filling it to the brim with brown liquid. "I'll be over in a few."

"No hurry," Gray calls back, leading us to the corner booth, away from other patrons. The topic we need to discuss isn't one for others to overhear.

The bartender drops three menus at our table, promising to return in a couple of minutes. Before looking at mine, I take a minute to evaluate our surroundings. Thankfully, it's not as busy as the streets outside. Most of the people appear normal, only more diverse than Avren. A woman, slightly older than me and with darker skin, signs to another woman at her table. A pang of sorrow hits my heart seeing someone use sign language again, so I turn my attention to the bartender. He's laughing and joking with the patrons, stopping for a second to rest his hands on the counter. With his sleeves rolled up, it's evident that his massive forearms are covered with black hair. This guy makes Bastian look small.

Evie leans close to me and whispers, "He's a werewolf."

A sheen of sweat covers my skin as images of Tanner's death flash through my mind. I shimmy along the bench, closer to the wall, before lifting my legs up and hugging them to me. If Evie knew, why did we stay?

She places a hand on my knee and squeezes. "He's working, not hunting, Mari. There's nothing to worry about."

When the bartender returns, I can't keep my menu from shaking in my hands. I'm sure his wolf senses pick it up. "Uh... I'll have your stew and an apple cider."

He grins at Evie as he taps the stacked menus against the table. "Not from around here, are you?"

She squares her shoulders with her usual confidence. "Nearby. I grew up in Moss Ford. Still work the bar there from time to time."

"Ah, a fellow bartender." His grin has grown so wide beneath his beard, it nearly reaches his ears. "What's your favorite mix?" As a person, this man is nothing like the werewolves I faced in the forest.

"Oh, I don't know." Evie taps her chin and furrows her brow

as if thinking hard. "Maybe the Frosted Yalum or the Fairy Feces."

The bartender sits down next to Grayson, making him move closer to the wall. "Both of those are great, but I really like the Death March. Just the right blend of sour and spice." He elbows Grayson. "And after one, they're out of my tavern, puking their guts out. Love it."

"Never made one." Evie folds her hands on the table, leaning slightly forward as if she's interested in this conversation. The complete opposite is true. Bastian has to be the only thing on her mind.

The man gets up, shaking the table as his massive frame squeezes out. "Finish your dinner, and I'll show you."

"We have plans." Evie pouts as if she's disappointed. "Maybe another time... uh..."

"Ralph." The bartender holds out his hand. "And you are?"

"Cerie," Evie says, taking his hand in hers. "It was wonderful to meet another mixologist. I look forward to learning from each other."

"Same here." Ralph walks back to the bar, shooting occasional glances in Evie's direction as he works.

"Laying it on a bit thick there." Grayson scrunches his nose. "I can still smell the fleabag. I think I've lost my appetite."

"Being nice is the only way you gather information." Evie removes a piece of paper and a pencil from her bag. "You're better at it than I am."

"True, but it's difficult to *be nice* to dogs who hit on my girlfriend."

"You'll get over it." She scribbles down a couple of things. "With Ralph's help, I think we can devise a foolproof plan for entering Arazian's palace undetected. A bartender hears and sees everything."

"And you think he'd give us that information?" My heart is still beating irregularly from Ralph sitting next to Grayson.

She looks over her shoulder and gives a little wave to the bartender, whose face flames bright red. "Mari, I've got this puppy eating out of my hand."

A LONE GUARD stands at the path leading to the gardens behind Arazian's two story home. After ten minutes behind the bar, Evie had learned from Ralph that his friend Zeke takes a lunch break around noon, leaving the other guard solo.

"This should be easy." Evie waltzes down the path like she belongs there. Her confidence must be high after using her often-hidden charm with two other men.

"Stop where you are," the guard calls out, drawing a large sword from his belt. "This is a prohibited area."

Evie takes a step closer, not intimidated by the guard's blade. "We're filling in for the regular gardeners. They're home sick today."

The guard narrows his eyes, making it evident that he's not buying what Evie has to sell. "The gardener already water and pruned early this morning."

"Yeah, well…" Instead of coming up with a different lie, Evie turns to her usual tactic. In two swift movements, she removes her dagger from her belt and lets it fly at the man. It buries deep into his chest. He falls to the ground with a thud.

Now I'm not so sure I want to be like Evie.

"What did you do that for?" Grayson stands above the guard, crouches, and removes the blade. He cleans it on the man's cloak and hands it back to Evie.

"Figured it was our best way of gaining entry." She steps over the body and walks through the gate to the garden. "When it comes to my brothers, I'm not playing around."

We round a group of hedges and find ourselves facing a tall

man with long, dark hair. His skin is deathly pale like the vamp Bastian, and I encountered in the meadow. Staring into his blood-red eyes, it feels like all the blood is draining from my body replaced by an intense cold in my veins. This must be Sterling.

"Welcome to the First City, Miss Windsong. We've been waiting for you."

CHAPTER SEVEN

Bastian

THE SKIN on my palm is raw from driving it into the pane, trying to get the window open. Sterling, who at first appears more as a butler than a second-in-command, is really the one running things in the First City. My birth father has a thousand screws loose. He trusted me in the care of the Hales then butchered the entire family.

I'm scanning the room for something to wedge beneath the metal to pry the window open when someone knocks on the door. Sterling back for another round of fighting?

Before I can open it, the door cracks, and Arazian pokes his head inside. "Good. You're still awake." He waltzes in as if he owns the place—which I guess he does. "I want to speak with you privately."

Oh goodie. Father and son bonding time.

He sits in an armchair beside the window and points at the other one. "Have a seat. This might take a while. Sterling's out on a hunt, so we have a little time."

I lean against the post of the canopy bed and cross my arms. "What do you want?"

He shifts uncomfortably in the chair before leaning on his knees and tenting his fingers. "Giving you up was one of the toughest things I ever had to do, but I couldn't raise a little boy, and it wasn't safe for you here."

The last thing I want to do is make him feel better in his pity party, but I need more information. "Why not?"

"Your mother sent her soldiers after you—thousands of them." He uses a finger to adjust his glasses. "Don't know how she planned to keep you a secret, but she wanted you. But there was no way I'd let that traitorous woman have you."

"So you dumped me with the Hales and killed them when they no longer fit into your plan?" I roll off the bedpost and begin to pace. This is too much. My parents can't get over their issues with each other, causing people to suffer for their insolent crap. "And you think shacking up with a dangerous vamp is a good idea?"

"Sterling and I have an understanding." He purses his lips, not seeming to want to expound on this *understanding*.

I stop pacing to sit in the chair across from the man who shares my eyes, although the character I like to uphold is lacking. "And what do the two of you plan to do once you have the two saviors? You realize it states that we will burn this place to the ground?"

He taps his finger on the arm of the chair and crosses one of his legs over the other. "Though Sterling wants her, the woman —or should I say, temptress—is of little interest to me. I do suppose we need her to follow through with the prophecy." The steel in his eyes as he speaks of Mari sends a shiver down my spine. "She's in the city as we speak, intent on rescuing you. Like father, like son, having the women wrapped around your finger."

My heart stirs with the thought of her coming after me in

the city. Since the prophecy was revealed, I'd thought she'd want nothing to do with me. Other than Levi's memorial, I'd avoided her until the night I slipped away. She spent the nights in her old room she had shared with him. The very sight of her set my skin ablaze with images of our night together in Tenny Rocks, but now that she knew I was from the First City, I thought her feelings for me had changed.

"I'll need you to convince her to stay." A slight smile creeps over his lips. "To seduce her into believing nothing matters beyond your touch." He glances away as if he's moved by his own words and trying to compose himself. "That you're happy here, and she can be as well."

"I'm not going to beg her to stay here." What in the world made this man think he'd manipulate me into telling the one person I loved that she'd be happy in this hellhole? "Sterling locked me in here. Now you want me to put Mari in the same position?"

"He plans to kill her." Arazian snaps his fingers, and the damn window I worked on for twenty minutes opens.

My mind races with where to go first. I rush over to the door, but it is still locked. "Is that who he's hunting?" Without waiting for his answer, I grip the handle and pull with everything in me. "Open this fucking door, *father*."

"I can't do that, Bastian." He stands and crosses the room, watching me like a caged animal. "Prophecies can change. With new information, you'll see who the actual enemy is and how urgently we need to build our army and defeat her."

"I will *never* stand with you. You're a fucking lunatic." I'd feel sorry for his disillusioned ass, but he's wallowing in his own manure. "Jaresiah Hale is my father."

Arazian places his hand on the doorknob and shakes his head. "I'm the one keeping Sterling from killing the temptress. As I see it, she's the one standing between us. If she's out of the picture, you'll no longer have your physical needs clouding your mind. I only thought I'd extend an olive branch." He clucks his tongue, turns the handle, and leaves before I can respond.

I pound on the door with both fists. "Come back! I'm ready to talk." After five minutes of slamming my hands against the door, I turn and slide to my bottom, gripping my hair. Arazian is mad enough to let the vamp kill Mari. And I could have done something about it.

Looking up, my gaze rests on the infuriating window, only to realize Arazian left it open. Not only is my father the Dark King, but he's the *magical* Dark King. It shouldn't surprise me. With all I've discovered about my life today, what's the difference if there's a little magic sprinkled on top?

I rush across the room, stopping to remove my dagger from my boot and clenching it between my teeth as I climb through the window. The room is on the second story. Below is a vast garden with white flowers dotting the bushes. Straddling the windowsill, I look for a trellis to descend. Nothing is nearby, so I'll have to drop down.

The door to the room opens before I have a chance. Sterling holds onto a person with a burlap sack over their head. His blood red eyes meet mine. Quicker than I can blink, he's thrown the squirming person onto the bed and is standing by the window.

"I brought you a present. Think of it as a cat bringing back a mouse for you to play with. I don't like it, but your father insisted." He grips the front of my shirt, yanks me from the window, and tosses me across the floor, slamming the window shut again. "Don't disappoint, Prince of Darkness."

And then he's gone, leaving me alone with the squirming person on the bed. The one person I believe can gut me with her words.

I kneel beside the mattress and carefully lift the burlap sack from her head, leaving her hair a tangled mess. Even like this, she's beautiful. "Mari." My heart aches with the sound of her name on my lips.

Tears stain her cheeks. When Sterling carried her away, blindfolded, she probably thought she was a goner. She looks at me warily, not moving an inch. It's been over three weeks and so much has transpired, it's a miracle to have her here in any form beside me.

"Mari, I…"

"Shhh…" She places a finger to my lips, her eyes searching my face for an unknown answer. "I thought you were dead. Let me take a moment to appreciate the fact that you are indeed, not."

As I muster every bit of courage I have, I touch her cheek, letting my fingers glide over her soft skin and wiping away a tear. I want to tell her that everything will be alright—I won't let Sterling hurt her. But I can't promise the world when I hold so little power of my own. So, I give her the one thing I have. "I'll die before I let that vamp touch you again."

A small smile crosses her lips. "So valiant. If I didn't know better, I'd think you had a crush on me."

Our circumstances should make our proclamations and flirtations hollow and weak. It has the opposite effect on me. It fills me with an urgent need to find our way out of this room. "Arazian placed a spell on the room, so it's impossible to open the window or door. I might have to work a different kind of magic to get us out of here."

"What's that?" she asks, leaning into my fingertips. Despite our captivity, our pull to one another adds a thick layer of desire to our beautiful cell.

"I could muscle my way past Arazian when he's in the room. The only problem is he'll use his magic to stop me." I tap my lip, playing out scenarios in my head. "I've killed vamps before. Sterling deserves a wooden dagger or two to the heart." Then it hits me. The idea might be crazy enough to work. He seems nostalgic for a real father and son relationship. "Or, I could convince the Dark King that I'm on his side."

She sits bolt upright, scooting back on the silken bedcover, her eyes drilling into mine. "I have information that might help, but I'm afraid to tell you."

"Arazian is my birth father. I know. He's keeping me here to convince me he's in the right. That we need to work together to take down Avren." I leave off the part about my mother. "He's convinced if he builds a stronger army, has possession of the two saviors, and has the Northern Duke on his side, he can defeat Avren's soldiers, and ultimately the Council."

Mari stiffens, and she looks away, her eyes trailing over a painting.

"I know it's a lot." I want to reach for her but keep my hands on the edge of the mattress. "It's as if my worst nightmare is dragging me under, and I don't know where to turn for help. Where are Evie and Gray?"

"I don't know." Her eyes meet mine again, but there's trepidation behind them. "He knocked them out before he took me. With the sack over my head, I couldn't see if they were alright."

Without asking, I pull myself up onto the bed and sit beside her, no longer cautious. "If we agree to work with Arazian, we might be allowed more freedoms. And if I go into this, I'll go all in. You can't believe the words that leave my mouth. It will take a lot to convince the Dark King and even more to convince Sterling."

She bites her lip, making me wish it was my teeth tugging on her plump rosy flesh. "We need to rescue the Miscretes."

"What?" Didn't she remember the way they swarmed us in Tenny Rocks? Or see the scar running across my face from when they took Lyden?

Her hand slips into mine, sending electricity all the way to my core. It's the first time I've let her touch me since the reading of the prophecy. "They're our friends and family. We must find a way to reverse Arazian's... your father's... What do you want me to call him?"

"The Dark King suits him just fine," I mumble. He doesn't deserve the respect of "father."

"We need to find a way to reverse the Dark King's magical engineering. It's complete mind control. And I think you're right." Her finger trails along my thumb, making me very conscious of how close she is to me. "We need to show them that we want to be here. That we've seen the light and want to work with them. It will give us access to the inner workings of this place. That way, when the time comes, we'll have all the information necessary to bring the First City to its knees."

"You have a devious mind, Maribel Windsong." I give her a sideways glance, imagining her on her knees from the hallucination I had when Sterling's fangs pierced my skin.

Her hand slips to my thigh, causing my head to spin. Then she removes her hand to straddle me, one thigh on either side of mine. She wraps her arms around my neck, her chest inches above mine, but I barely notice as she adjusts her core over me. I squeeze my eyes shut at the friction, trying to control myself.

A feather-light touch trails along my jawline, tucking a piece of my hair behind my ear, lingering. Her warm breath dances along my skin. "Isn't this what Sterling and the Dark King expect us to do locked up in here? What did the vamp call me? Your mouse?"

Mouse is not the word I'd use to describe the full-fledged woman straddling my groin. "Arazian also called you a seductress." I open my eyes as I lean my head back to give her better access to my neck. She peppers tiny kisses along my skin, stopping occasionally to suck it between her lips. "Won't these types of kisses leave a mark?" she asks innocently.

Yes. Sucking my skin between her lips and teeth will leave black marks all over my neck, and then the vamp and my father would know there was something between Mari and me. I grip her shoulder, massaging it as I push her back gently. "Do you think it's a good idea for them to know how much you mean to me?"

"It's a bit obvious," she says, using her hand to push me back against the pillows. "I think Levi, Gray, and Evie knew it before we did." Finding my hands, she lifts them above my head, pinning them against the headboard. She grinds against my hips as her lips find mine.

My imaginings come true as I suck her lower lip into my mouth, drawing my teeth over their fullness. If I could hold onto this moment forever, I'd die a happy man. When I release her lip, her tongue dives into my mouth, exploring mine. It's obvious she's dreamed about this as much as I have.

Shouts rise from down the hall. Releasing her, I reach over and snatch the dagger on my nightstand before I sit up and clutching her to me. I kiss her forehead. "I'll be right back."

Surprisingly, I find the door unlocked.

The noise is coming from the bottom of the stairs in the entryway. About ten Miscretes have Evie and Gray backed into a corner. My brother and sister have their weapons drawn, ready for action. Sterling observes from his perch on the stairs, stroking his chin with his long pale fingers. He glances up at me as if understanding the predicament I'm in.

Because if I race down the stairs to defend them, I risk ruining my new plan. If I don't do anything, well, who knows what could happen? And then there's Mari's desire to save the creatures, insisting there's a way to bring the monsters back. The growling of the Miscretes wakes me from my thoughts.

"Bastian," Evie calls, drawing an arrow from her quiver and hitting a beast square in the chest. "You are here. This lying bastard told us you left a week ago." Her eyes linger on the vampire on the stairs as she wrongly assumes he's what's keeping me from rushing down to help.

Two Miscretes charge toward Gray. He leg sweeps one,

ducks as the other reaches for him, then comes back up to drive his dagger into its chest. I feel like a proud father watching him use a move I taught him.

"What shall we do with the intruders, Prince Bastian?" Sterling doesn't even look at me, his hands behind his back. He's testing me, though I don't know under what pretense. It's not like Mari and I have put our plan in place to deceive the leaders of the First City yet.

Gray looks up at me as Evie fights back another Miscrete. There's confusion in his eyes mixed with another emotion I can't put my finger on.

"Lock them up. Their intrusion interrupted my time with Mari." I click my heels together and turn to go. "Father and I will deal with them in the morning."

CHAPTER EIGHT

Mari

OUTSIDE OUR WINDOW, the city streets reflect the flickering glow of torches, casting shadows on the ceiling that dance like specters in the darkness. Dawn seems hours away, yet the embrace of sleep eludes me.

My emotions churn. Bastian Hale, his very name a whisper of forbidden desire, lies beside me. His arms, strong and reassuring, still encircle me. The rhythm of his breath fills the silence of the room and echoes in my heart. He's the son of our enemy, a fact that looms over us like a shadow threatening to engulf our fragile sanctuary. But in this moment, in his arms, there is a warmth that defies the reality of our circumstances. Despite the dangers within this city, there's no place I'd rather be.

Last night, when he returned, a palpable tension hung heavy in the air, suffocating us with its weight. Emotionally drained, he sought solace in the simplicity of our embrace. His words faltered against the truth that lingered in the tremble of his arms. There was a hint of something darker lurking beneath the surface. He tried to shield me from the storm raging within him, but I could feel its ferocity, threatening to tear us apart at the seams.

As much as I want to turn to face him, to take in the pillar of a man I've come to respect and love, I don't want to wake him from the rest he deserves. If he takes on the role of the Dark Prince, it will take a toll on him. Instead, I close my eyes and think about my own father, the Northern Duke.

Daxon Barellis came home every evening from his job on the Council, carefree and ready to spend time with his *girls*. He'd sweep me into his arms and throw me into the air, catching me as I squealed. After dinner, we'd play a game of Magii or go for a walk to Sweet Street, the smells tempting my young nose. He didn't bring work home with him—until the one night I over-heard him talking to Mother.

"We need to get Mari out of here."

I huddled on the floor around the corner from the kitchen, clutching my legs to my chest. What did he mean "out of here"? Avren was our home.

I heard a familiar clicking noise. My mother tapped her long nail against the metal counter, a sure sign she was in thought or agitated. Most of her decisions were based on reason, not emotion, the total opposite of my father. It was a wonder the Council matched them. "You're not thinking about Mari, Dax. The city provides the best life for her. With our positions, she's sure to obtain a good job and lock in an advantageous match. There's nothing for us in the wilderness."

There was silence for a minute before I heard my dad's strained voice again. "I know things, Em. And you know I can't tell you what's really happening, but a future in Avren looks bleak for Mari."

I peeked around the corner to see my dad kneeling beside my mom, pleading as if my future was in her hands.

She took him in, not moved by his unfettered acts of emotion as her lips remained in a straight line. "You won't change my mind. Until the Council's soldiers start turning on the people, the city walls are the safest place for our daughter. You know what type of creatures lurk in the wilderness."

My father lowered his voice. "And I know what type of creatures lurk within these walls."

A week later, he brought home the music box for me, and then he left. At the time, I didn't really understand their conversation, but now that I'm on the outside, it's clear. My father wanted us all to leave the city—to make a better life outside the golden walls. Mother wouldn't give in to his emotional leanings, counting more on her rational side. Ultimately, it cost us her life.

Bastian shifts behind me, his face nuzzling into my neck. It sends a delicious shiver down my spine, and I lean into his warmth.

"Today's going to change things." His breath tickles my skin, and I squirm, so he wraps his arm around my stomach, his iron-clad grip locking me tight against him. "You might not like me as much."

The feeling of him against me has my heart pounding in my chest as our night in Tenny Rocks comes rushing back. "I doubt that." I can barely get the words out.

He splays his palm flat against my stomach to creep his fingers dangerously close to my undergarments. "What if I become the narcissistic son-of-a-bitch of Arazian's dreams? Treating you like a possession rather than a partner?" His fingertips trail along the edge of my panties, threatening to undo me. "Dragging you back to my room to fuck you at my will rather than making love to you? Arazian says he wants me to convince you to stay, but he needs to believe I can be as cruel hearted as the rest of them. Because if they believe we're working together our whole plan could unravel. We need to write the narrative, not them." One cool finger slips between my folds, making me see stars. "The Dark Prince you see outside this room would never give you pleasure like this because you're only good for one thing: his desires."

I hold a fist to my mouth as I moan. I try to concentrate on his words, but it's difficult as his finger moves in slow, deliberate circles. I want him to increase the speed, but he's not ready for me to be anywhere close to releasing.

"Sterling locked Evie and Gray in the dungeon tonight. That's what the commotion was about." He stops his finger, making me whimper as I try to grasp his words. "I'll speak with them later today. They're safe for now. But I need you to know that no matter what I say or do, I love you more than anyone in this world."

I turn to face him, his dark hair falling over his eyes. He leans in to kiss me, not in possession, but in love. As much as he might hurt me, I need to trust him and the plan. My role is the mouse—the plaything he uses at his will, to be discarded in public. But here, in our bedroom, we're on an equal playing field. The dual saviors of the wilderness who will take down the First City together.

His lips are soft against mine, and for a moment, the danger and the plan seem miles away. I lose myself in the warmth of his arms before breaking our kiss and resting my head on his chest. "I'll give you everything I have," I say, feeling the reassuring rhythm of his heart. There's a price we'll need to pay to succeed. The lovers must become something else: a manipulated pawn and a strategic lord. "We'll rebuild this world together, even if it means tearing everything apart."

"Well, not everything, drama queen." His lingering finger begins tracing circles again and I buck my hips, causing him to laugh. "Tonight, and every night, will be about you, about us. The Dark Prince and his will must go down with the First City, leaving you with Bastian Hale, son of a farmer. Do you think you can accept me this way?"

But I can't answer. His finger dives deeper within me, and I bite into my lip as I begin to shake. I don't want an arrogant, sadistic prince. Simple Bastian suits me fine. As his thumb strokes my sensitive spot and his other finger circles my channel, I cry out his name, sweat streaking my hairline. When I open my eyes, a satisfied smirk is on his lips.

He won't let me forget his name.

WITH THE MORNING LIGHT, I stretch my arms over my head, my body tangled in the silken sheets. I'm alone in the room. My heart pangs as I run through Bastian's words from the night before. When I see him, I can't run into his arms. I need to play my part. And what will become of Evie and Gray in the dungeon? I must trust Bastian to free them.

But I'm not going to lay around in this bedroom all day waiting for him to return. Though I fear how he'll act when he sees me, there's something I want to do. Evie had mentioned there's a way to reverse Arazian's spell on the Miscretes. If any place holds this secret, it's the First City, and I can't think of a better way to use my time. Without the strength of his mutant army, the Dark King has nothing but a single vampire on his side.

I pull on my trousers and shirt before searching through Bastian's bag and finding a dagger and a wooden stake to slip into my boots. Bastian's pendant lays against my chest. Between the necklace and talking silently to Levi, I know I can get through this. Although Bastian would never let anything happen to me, this is the most alone I've felt since my mother died.

The door creaks open and I pause, checking the hallway for signs of life—or the dead. Sterling's presence echoes through the halls of Arazian's mansion. I haven't met Bastian's father, but I can't imagine him being any more intimidating than the vampire.

"Your company is required in the master's dining quarters." His voice sends a chill through me as I turn to Sterling, no more than three feet away. "The king wants to meet you."

So much for remaining unnoticed. The First City will have to wait until later, though I'm not sure if they'll let me leave whenever I want. In Avren, when the Council called us, we dropped what we were doing and went directly to their chambers. Here, in the First City, defiance is my aim. "And what if I don't want to meet with him?"

A glimmer catches Sterling's eyes, so slight it might be mistaken for the reflection of the flame in the nearby oil lamp. "You are not in a position to refuse the Dark King's summons, Maribel Windsong." His lips part slightly to reveal his stark white fangs.

I've never felt the pierce of a vampire's incisor, but the blood drains from my body at the sight. "Where do I go?"

"Follow the scent of sizzling meat," he hisses, promptly wrapping his arm around mine and pulling me to him as he drags me down the hallway.

The dining room is downstairs. By the time we reach it, my arm feels like it might fall off from the strength of Sterling's grip. I use my other hand to rub it when he finally releases me.

"The prince requested you take your meal in the room, but his father insisted he meet the other savior." Sterling's gaze drags down my clothing. "Not that you're much to look at. Avren grows weaklings in its laboratories. I can't tell you how many of its *soldiers* I've had for a late-night snack."

As much as his words turn my stomach, it's true. People born in the wilderness seem a lot healthier than the Avrenians.

My sheltered life within the city walls only built my mental and artistic strengths. The Grove hardened my muscles, now hidden beneath my clothes.

I lift my chin but then think better of it. Facing Arazian as the confident person I've become with the Kindred Few's help will ruin our plan. The more I'm out of the spotlight, the more freedom he might allow me. As Sterling opens the door to the dining room, I keep my head down, trying not to react to my growling stomach from the scent of bacon.

I hear a chair scrape against the floor.

"So, this is the girl." His footsteps draw near. "Hardly savior material."

My cheeks flame, and I wish I'd worn my hair down instead of braiding it so I can hide behind the tendrils. I try to peek at Bastian, but his father's body blocks my view.

"Look at me, girl." The king's voice is gruff and demanding. It holds the air and authority of the Avrenian Council. "Another orphan tossed to the wolves by Raven and her lap dogs. Pity." Long fingers touch my chin, forcing me to look up at his face. Blue eyes, so much like Bastian's, stare into mine. His gray beard, stature, and aging skin differentiate him. "My son says when he took you in, you were nothing but a stick." Arazian places a hand on my hip and squeezes, and another chair scrapes against the floor. "Got a bit more meat on you now."

Bastian now stands beside his father, and there's a cold indifference I haven't seen since I first arrived at the cabin in his expression as Arazian continues to massage my hip. The last man who touched me this way in front of Bastian ended up dead. "She's scrawny as hell. Don't pretend otherwise. The only reason I keep her around is the damn prophecy. We need her to defeat Lady Raven's soldiers. As I said earlier, you were right about Avren. The sooner we burn that wretched place to the ground, the sooner we can bring peace to the land."

"Oh, come, Bastian." Arazian finally removes his hand from

my hip and shakes his son's shoulder. "She must be good in bed. All that repressed tension has all the rejected Avrenians seeking the arms of another. Even I have had my share since leaving the city."

Bastian shrugs and returns to the table, seemingly not interested in the conversation. "I've had better. But I guess I'm stuck with her until this cursed war is over."

Throughout the conversation, Sterling watches us. I can sense his stare. He's evaluating the validity of the prince's words and is a lot less trusting than the king. Like a fly, he hovers around us as we sit at the table.

"Tell me, Maribel." Arazian passes me a plate of bacon. "What did your mother and father do in the city? I knew a lot of people."

I need to lie. Because my father was on the Council, they had to know each other. "My mother was a seamstress, and my father taught philosophy at the school."

"Respectable jobs." The king strokes his beard. "I knew a Windsong once. Beautiful woman with raven hair and an aptness for mathematics. Top of her class at the university. She married a fellow Council member." His eyes drill into mine, and Sterling stops his flitting about.

"My aunt." I fiddle with the napkin on my lap and draw in a deep breath. "Emily Windsong. She developed the theory of mixed equational ringlets, making it possible to reduce the ratios of birth defects. My uncle, Dax Barellis, left the Council and his family behind for the wilderness."

"Is that what they told you?" Arazian leans back in his chair and crosses his arms, assessing me like I'm a germ in a petri dish.

"It's the truth." If I continue to play the role of the brainwashed accidental savior from Avren, it leaves room for Bastian to wedge himself between the king and his vampire.

Arazian leans forward as if ready to tell me the secrets of the universe. "Your uncle is alive and well."

I widen my eyes as if this is news to me.

"Dax was forced to leave Avren. He never would have left Emily or their daughter. Never in my life have I seen a man more dedicated to his family." He shakes his head and smiles. "Told him he needed a lover on the side. It was the practice of most of the Council members, although that was hidden from public view." He lifts his goblet, takes a sip, and then wipes his mouth with his napkin. "The man remains loyal to his wife even after her death."

His confessions make me long to see my dad. Too many years have passed. And he didn't leave us of his own accord. "You make it sound like a bad thing,"

"We all have needs and desires, Maribel." He leans in closer, and I swallow back the bitter bile rising in my throat.

I want to look at Bastian to see his reaction to the king's forwardness, but Sterling is watching for any indication that our relationship extends beyond the bedroom.

"I don't like to share," Bastian growls at his father. "You can have any woman in the city. This one's mine."

Arazian backs away from me and laughs. "You hear that, Sterling? My boy learns fast. He'll make a mighty fine king some day." He raises his goblet toward his son. "A toast. To Bastian Valeria, prince of the First City and future king of the entire land."

Bastian raises his goblet to clink against his father's. "To your health and prosperity, Father."

The lack of eye contact with the man I love is unnerving. I'm surprised at how much I need his reassurance to know that everything is going to be alright between us. His declaration of ownership, although appreciated, made me feel like a horse or a cow. Keeping up the charade is more difficult than I had imagined.

"I've arranged a ball in your honor, Bastian." The king glances at Sterling who nods. "My son has returned home. Perhaps it will provide you the opportunity to choose a wife from the city. Or a harem, whichever you prefer."

Bastian sets down his goblet and stabs his eggs with a fork. "Sounds delightful." He stuffs the eggs into his mouth and chews before washing them down with the wine in the goblet. "And despite my current company, I prefer blondes."

A knot develops in my stomach. *He's only playing a role.*

"Duly noted." Arazian points his fork at his son before eyeing me again. "I'm a brunette man, myself."

The dagger in my boot is begging me to take it out and drive it into this man's heart.

But I must play my role.

To save the Miscretes and the family I love.

CHAPTER NINE

Bastian

I HAVE YET to find a single redeeming quality in my so-called father.

Sterling watches us like a hawk ready to dive for its next meal. One wrong move on my part will give us away. The sympathetic look I want to give Mari could spell disaster. Pounding my father's head into the ground is out of the question.

I play my role as the indifferent prick.

"Blondes, brunettes, red heads... I'll take them all." I can't look at Mari as I stuff a half of a slice of bread into my mouth so I don't have to talk and hurt her further.

"I can't help but wonder about your sudden change of heart, Bastian." Sterling pulls up a chair and rests his hands on the table. His long slender fingers look like daggers. "Yesterday, you wanted nothing to do with your father."

Stretching my arms over my head, I say casually, "There's nothing that a good night's sleep and a roll in the hay can't cure." I wink at Mari, causing her face to flame. "Sleep has eluded me for weeks. I'm cranky when I'm tired. Besides, though my father is a bit sloppy with his methods of letting the Miscretes run amuck, I believe he's honest in his intentions."

Arazian beams at me like he's a proud, well, father. I want to smack the smile from his face, but instead, I grip a wad of the tablecloth in my hands between my legs. "I knew you'd come around. I didn't think it would be this quickly, but it pleases me to have the Dark Prince sit by my side. The ball will provide me with an opportunity to show you off to my citizens. News of it is sure to get back to Raven."

Lady Raven. My birth mother and leader of Avren. The fates sure had a sense of humor when I was chosen as the savior of the wilderness destined to take down both my mother and my father. "And what will she think about you keeping me hidden all these years?"

Arazian slaps his hands down on his thighs and laughs. "She'll be furious. When you resurface, people will wonder about your mother. With your age, you had to have been conceived in Avren. She cares more about her position and how she looks than she'll ever care about you."

"We expect an attack," Sterling says, his lips set in a firm line despite Arazian's laughter. "Not a full-on assault, but Avren's best infiltrating the First City to assassinate you."

I didn't expect that. My mother cares enough about her image that she'll send people to kill me?

"We have security covered." Sterling looks at the king. "Our sources say they will attack within the next few days." The vampire turns his attention back to me. "Your father has wards set up to keep them out. But if they do happen to slip through, they'll deal with our Miscrete army." He pushes back his chair and stands. "My belief is they will attempt the assassination before the king's announcement at the ball."

Makes sense. My mother doesn't want word getting out

about her fling with my father. If I'm out of the picture, there's no mystery to solve.

"Why announce it in the first place?" If I'm such a threat, keep me a secret.

"Because—" Arazian holds his hand out to me— "look at you. You're a pinnacle of strength. Who better to pull people and creatures from the wilderness to our side? Rumors have tarnished my image over the years, making them more reluctant to sympathize."

"And are those rumors true?" Mari's voice is pale, not like the strong woman I know her to be, despite the strength of her question.

"Shut up, Mouse," Sterling snarls, his pale dagger fingers wrapping around her neck. "You are here for two reasons: to please the prince and to keep you out of the hands of the enemy. Your questions and opinions are not needed or valid."

Someday, I will kill him. I will drive a wooden stake through his stone heart, sever his head from his neck, and burn his body to ash for the way he treats Mari. For now, I keep my mouth shut.

"It depends on the rumor." My father lifts his goblet and takes another sip of wine. "Do I recruit the downtrodden to join my army of Miscretes? Yes, that is true. It gives them new purpose; despite the hands they are dealt in life. But all are accepted in the First City. Unlike Avren, I don't discriminate."

Liar

"What if someone didn't want to become a Miscrete?" Mari is walking a thin line. If she really wants to find a way to save the people my father has turned into monsters, she shouldn't reveal too much. But maybe she's trying to find the humanity in my father. She'll be sorely disappointed.

Arazian gathers Mari's hands in his on top of the table. "My Miscretes were people with birth defects—a hearing impairment, blindness, a limp, or the wrong skin color. Rejects of

Avren. This means they were doomed to a life of servitude for the elect in the city. You know this as well as I do. In the wilderness, their lives aren't much better under the constant threat of the Supes. Here, they are safer and enjoy a higher purpose in my military."

"And what if they want to live as ordinary citizens in the First City? Do you allow them that option?" Mari shakes free from Arazian's grip.

He appraises her as he leans back in his chair. "They are given a choice before the transformation begins."

Fucking liar

Evie's sister and Levi's parents would never have chosen to become a Miscrete. I must believe they are dead because becoming a monster is a fate worse than death. I also need to do something about her questioning.

"Go back to bed where you belong," I grumble, resting my elbow on my armrest and leaning my head against my hand. "A woman's questioning is maddening, and I don't have the headspace for it. We have important matters to discuss."

Mari's face reddens as she looks from me to Arazian. He only shrugs, seemingly giving in to his son's demands of his *woman*. It kills me inside speaking to her this way, like she's a possession, but it puts a tiny smirk on Sterling's lips, and his approval is our end goal.

She leaves the room in a huff, which I'm sure I'll hear about later.

"Way to put your woman in her place." My father pulls a pipe from his robe and lights it, sending a puff of smoke in my direction. "I wondered, as a savior, if she was strong like your mother. Better to stamp out her spirit than to let it flourish."

"I'll continue to train her for the battle, but her opinions are not needed at this table." I swirl the wine in my goblet, letting the deep red liquid slosh over the side onto my finger. "If I'm to become king one day, I need to command respect, even of the wench who shares my bed."

"Especially of the wench who shares your bed." Sterling remains standing, holding a finger to his lips. "Loose lips have sunk many a man in the heat of passion. Though you hold the title of the Dark Prince, I'm not ready to let you into our inner circle yet. You need to prove yourself."

"And how do I do that?" Sending my girlfriend to her room in the rudest way possible had to have proved something.

Sterling looks at Arazian, then takes a seat before continuing. "The two prisoners the Miscretes captured last night. They lived with you in the wilderness."

How does he know that? My goal was to distance myself from any association with Evie or Gray.

"They were seen in the city with Mari. Ralph, the bartender at the Full Moon Tavern, was questioned last night. Mentioned three strangers matching their descriptions." Sterling circles the table like a predator ready to pounce. "I want you to go down to the dungeon and kill them. If you're ready to become the Dark Prince, this small task shouldn't be an issue for you."

"I trained them as two of the best warriors in the wilderness." I set my goblet on the table slowly and tent my fingers. Calculation is important in this situation. Sterling doesn't trust me. He's testing my loyalty to my father and the First City. "Their value in an attack on Avren would be invaluable." Pushing back in my chair, I stand and hold my hand out to the feast laid before us. "Instead of being fed stale bread and lukewarm water in the pits of the city, they deserve the finest."

"They broke into the king's mansion last night." Sterling's face is stone, waiting for me to make a mistake. "Their intention was to kill your father."

"Their intention was to find me." I rest my hands on the back of my chair, leaning forward. "Grayson has connections in Avren. He knows the ins and outs of the city as well as you do." I look at Arazian, knowing he's slightly easier to manipulate. "And Evie's one of the best warriors I've seen with a bow. Her networks within the Supe communities throughout the wilderness are vast. Killing them would be akin to throwing a valuable weapon in the trash."

"Sterling was a bit rash in his comments." Arazian holds his hand against the side of his face as if assessing me again. "Your wilderness friends might be an asset to us if you can convince them to join the fight. But I do understand Sterling's desire for you to prove yourself. Your demeanor is vastly different than the man we encountered yesterday."

Sterling rolls his eyes, crossing one leg over the other. "Night and day."

Arazian taps his lip with his pointer finger. Whatever he's considering has me nervous. Evie and Gray are off the table, but they didn't bring up Mari yet.

"Bring me back an Avrenian soldier. We'll make a spectacle of him in the city square. Let the rejected people of Avren show him what true humiliation feels like." Arazian lifts his fork and taps it against his plate—*clang, clang, clang.* It's reminiscent of the bell that tolls before a hanging or beheading. He wants me to torture and murder someone. Killing a person in the heat of battle is one thing, but I've never killed a defenseless person. A shiver runs through me, but I don't show my fear.

I killed the soldier who attacked Mari in the forest. If I picture his face, I can do this. "I'll leave in the morning and bring a soldier back by midnight."

"Perfect." Arazian rubs his hands together as a broad smile crosses his lips. He really is mad.

For the remainder of the day, I avoid returning to our bedroom. Mari needs her space to recover from my comments and to think through her plan to find an antidote for the Miscretes.

Not being able to stomach another minute with Sterling and

Arazian, I decide to find my way to the dungeon. Word has gotten out about the Dark Prince returning to the First City, and from my first conversation it's clear that an imaginary reputation precedes me.

Making sure I hide all my weapons, I enter a bakery not far from the mansion. The bell above the door doesn't have time to stop ringing before everyone inside stops what they're doing and stares.

A little girl with pigtails tugs on a woman's hand. "Mommy, is that the bad man you told me about?"

The woman shuffles the girl behind her, not daring to answer her question.

"Can... can I help you, Your Highness?" The man behind the counter's skin flushes beet red. He removes a handkerchief from his pocket and wipes his face, but it doesn't look much different. "I'm sure my pastries don't compare to the ones your chef makes, but I... I... I'm sincerely humbled by your presence."

I cross the room and everyone I pass takes a step back. "I need directions."

"Whatever I can do to help." The man places a notepad on top of the counter and removes a marking stick from behind his ear.

The fear the people of the city have of the Dark King, and now the Dark Prince, only further proves that Arazian is up to no good. It's as if they think I can change them into a Miscrete with the touch of my hand.

"How do I get to the dungeon?" I tap my fingernail against the glass case holding the baked goods.

"The dungeon?" The man raises an eyebrow.

Everyone stares at me like I'm about to reduce the baker to a pile of dust.

I square my shoulders, lifting them slightly to capitalize on my intimidating appearance. "Do I need to repeat myself?"

The baker holds his hands in front of him. "No, no, it's only that it's Sterling's realm. I never see the Dark King visit the squalor. He prefers to remove himself from such places. I thought his son might hold similar preferences."

"I'm nothing like my father," I say, relieved to speak my truth.

An older man, hunched over with age, parts the crowd of patrons. "I can see that, My Prince. The entrance is between the butcher shop and the livery. Keep your head up and you'll have no problem getting past the guards."

"Thank you." I nod my head in respect. Digging into my own pocket, I remove a handful of credits and place them on the counter. "Make sure everyone gets what they want and if it goes over, send the bill to Arazian."

People stand back as I leave, mouths hanging open.

Why stay here if they fear my father?

It's all they've ever known.

Like Mari in Avren, the people of the First City probably don't know about a better life not living under the thumb of my mother or father. Their son, and the woman he loves, are the two people destined to bring them to their knees.

It's laughable, really.

The guards at the gates of the dungeon are much larger than any of the men and women stationed in Avren. I hold my nose at the same angle as Sterling's.

"Prince Bastian." A guard near the front bows his head. "An honor."

How does everyone in this place know me already?

Don't ask. Demand. "Open the gates. There's a prisoner I need to question."

"I did not receive an order from Commander Sterling," the same guard responds. I assess him for the first time beyond his bulk: reddish hair, freckles, square nose.

I place a deep scowl on my face, narrowing my eyes. "The Dark King owns every square inch of this city, does he not?"

"He does, sir." The guard averts his eyes, apparently not liking the intensity of my stare. "But..."

"And I am his son, so the city is my inherited right." I'm tempted to remove the dagger from my cloak to intimidate him, but I keep it hidden. "With a snap of my fingers, you'll be scrubbing puke from the dungeon floors."

The guard chews on his lip, shooting doubtful glances at the others before removing his key from his belt and unlocking the door. "As you wish, Your Highness. The name's Ernest if Sterling asks."

"And your real name is...?"

He provides me a lopsided smile. "You can call me Sergeant Fergus Bates."

Dropping the charade for a moment, I slap him on the back. "Thanks, Fergie. I won't forget this."

The stairs leading down to the dungeon smell of mildew and rot. The air grows cooler and damper with each step, carrying with it the musty scent of Miscretes. Flickering lanterns mounted on the walls cast long shadows for creatures to hide in. The lights barely penetrate the darkness below, leaving my descent shrouded in obscurity.

A voice calls out from the far reaches of the depths below me. His shouts echo through the stone-cut passageway. I slide my hand into my pocket, wrapping my fingers around the cool handle of my dagger.

The man's shouts quiet when I reach the bottom of the stairs, leaving the sound of the trickle of water, or some other substance, traveling through a narrow channel in the floor. Foul odors turn my stomach as I inch onward past the cells, stopping at each one to peek inside.

When I'm halfway down the passage, the man begins to shout again, this time only two doors away from where I'm standing.

"And if you don't bring us quality food and drink, my friend, the *savior*, will hold you personally responsible for my depleting body." Gray's wit hasn't disappeared, even with his "depleting body."

Leaning a shoulder against his cell door, I cross one leg over the other and remove two squares of paper and a pouch of tobacco from my pocket. After rolling a cigarette, I strike a firestick against the stone wall and light it. "And what if this savior of yours is a royal arse who thinks it might be fun to keep you locked up for a week or so?"

Hands grip the bars in the small window in the door as Gray looks out at me. "Bastian, you'd better be here to let me out of this hellhole. Why'd you leave us hanging last night? With the three of us fighting, we could have taken out those Miscretes in no time."

"And what about the vamp?" I blow a stream of smoke in his direction. "He's not a garden-variety Supe."

"True, but you told him to lock us up."

"Would you rather I told him to slit your throats?" Tossing my cigarette on the ground, I use the second paper to roll one for Gray.

"No... but..." He slips his fingers through the bars to take the cigarette from me. "Tell me you have a nice juicy steak too."

If my plan works, I'll have them both eating at Arazian's table in no time. "Where's Evie?"

"Over here." She waves at me from the other side of the passageway. "Tell me you've got one of those for me."

"Only if you say please."

"Bastard," she grumbles, shooting daggers at me with her green eyes. "We come here to rescue you, and this is the thanks we get?"

I roll her cigarette between my thumb and forefinger, teasing her before handing it over. "I'm going to get you out of here tonight. Arazian, and maybe Sterling, think I'm on their side."

"You mean your dad?" Gray asks, surprising me with his question, as his fingers wrap around the bars.

"How do you know that?" It shouldn't surprise me. Mari already knew.

"We went back to Moss Ford." Evie takes a drag on her cigarette. The small village holds as many painful memories for her as it does for me. "Found your birth certificate in the rubble of the farmhouse."

"There's a birth certificate?"

"Listed your father, but not your mother." Evie flicks ashes onto the stone floor.

Lady Raven. This is not information I'm ready to reveal to anyone else yet. The woman who carried me for nine months, then rejected me because I didn't fit her proper image.

Gray glances down the passage and purses his lips. "The guard comes through every fifteen minutes. Tell us about this plan of yours."

CHAPTER TEN

Mari

My shaking hand lifts the quill tip to the aged paper. The swipe of the ink leaves a wobbly mess where I'd intended to inscribe a flowery S. With a huff, I drop the quill into the jar of ink and sink my head into my hands as I stare out the window. Since my mother died, I've wanted to use her journal to keep a proper record of my life with the Kindred Few. Besides a couple of failed attempts to honor Levi with my words, I'd failed miserably.

Emily Windsong had a way with words. One might think her talent with mathematics excluded her from a talent in both disciplines, but the opposite was true. The way she pieced words together bloomed from her expertise with numbers. When my father had to write up official documents for Avren, she was always there, rewording his jumbled messes.

To keep my mind off breakfast, I flip in her journal to an earlier entry, wanting to reread her words as if they can somehow bring her back to me in a small way.

The Matching dance looms before us like Maribel's future in Avren. You were supposed to be here to prepare our daughter for the event determining her future. The Council members will sit on their mighty perches, evaluating every young man and woman like live-stock. With a good match, Maribel might not face the consequences of your mistakes.

And yet, I cling to my anger which hurts me more than it will ever hurt you. Caron brought me news from the wilderness. Those who left Arazian follow a new leader, one they call the Northern Duke. His followers say he stands against the city and its leaders. I say he's as foolish as you, Dax, if he thinks he can tear down the scientific and technological advances of Avren. Lady Raven will have his head removed before he can think about marching against the city.

Did Mother know before she died? Nothing I've read in her journals indicates her knowledge of her husband becoming the Northern Duke.

I tap my nail against the paper. Mother didn't like the stringent rules of the city either, but she wasn't willing to leave with my father, risking our lives to the wilderness. And the Northern Duke took away some of Arazian's followers. What is different in what my father stands for compared to the Dark King? From what I know of him, almost everything from his gentle heart to his fierce love of justice.

But has he changed?

I flip through more pages of the journal, finally calming my nerves from breakfast. Bastian's cruel words are not something I'll ever get used to. They bring me back to our first days together when he saw me as a worthless Avrenian.

My mother continued journaling as long as she could after the sickness hit her. As it progressed, her handwriting became more difficult to read. I flip to one of her last entries, something I haven't had the courage to read before now. Reading about her pain wasn't something I wanted to endure. But maybe she knew things. Things she wasn't ready to speak aloud in the carefully monitored walls of Avren.

Her handwriting is almost unrecognizable in this part of her journal—angled the wrong way, letters stopping and starting again as if she had to rest halfway through her scribbling.

They'll probably burn this journal with the rest of our belongings, Maribel. But if for some reason you can keep it, I want you to know what your father told me before he left.

It takes me several minutes to decipher the first couple of lines, but it's my mother's final message to me, so I continue, my gut twisted in knots with both grief and anticipation. I wipe away a tear.

This life is not ours. The Council owns us. If I cannot hold out until your eighteenth birthday, they will not send you to the Unseen but to the wilderness. Seek out your father. He will protect you. As it was in Avren, he is a powerful man beyond these walls. He knew too much, and the Council threatened to kill us if he revealed their secrets.

I pause my finger tracing her script. The Council held secrets.

Shocker.

My mother presented herself as one of the most loyal citizens in the city, but she was matched with Daxon Barellis, the renegade member of leadership.

My strength won't hold out for much longer, so I want to give you as much as I can.

The rest of the page is a series of bullet points, more in line with the mathematical part of my mother's brain.

~ Babies born with defects, as the Council sees them, are delivered directly to the First City. It is there they are raised, transformed at the age of fifteen, and become part of Arazian's growing army of Miscreations.

~ Anyone (and it doesn't matter how high-ranking they are) who stands up to Lady Raven, becomes an outcast. Arazian and the head council member were closer than most people thought, and he was sent to the wilderness.

~ Matching has nothing to do with compatibility, only control.

~ Avren and the First City are working together.

Wait. What? I thought the entire purpose of Arazian's Miscrete army was to defeat Avren and bring Lady Raven to her knees. And if they are working together, to what end? The Supes in the wilderness live their own lives, so that only leaves the humans. Are the humans really a threat to the two cities?

If they believe in the prophecy.

A tiny smile crosses my lips as I imagine Lady Raven lying awake at night having nightmares because of me, the young woman she sent to her doom because she was a few credits short. It makes me feel as powerful as Bastian.

There's one last bullet point, slightly smudged but readable if I squint.

~ *The sickness is used as a weapon against the Council's enemies, both in the city and the wilderness. Because of your father, they unleashed it in our apartment in a low dose to prevent the spread. The intent is for both of us to die.*

I swallow back tears, unsure of how to process this new information. My mother was murdered in the most cowardly way possible. And when my body stood up to the sickness, the Council's punishment was throwing me to the Supes. Thankfully, Grayson was there, but if he hadn't been, I'm sure I wouldn't have survived the first night.

And my father posed enough of a threat that the Council saw the need to hurt him. My heart is racing. He's not an ogre working with Arazian to take over the wilderness, he's on my side and wants me to succeed. Does he know the prophecy? Is he working in the background to lay the foundation? I need to find him. But he's way up north, near a place called the Murky Swamps where ghosts attack you.

The tinny tune from my music box comes rushing back as I once again imagine the warmth of my father's arms, the man I thought I knew so well.

I lay on the bed and close my eyes, bringing images of Daxon Barellis to my mind, and hoping I get to see him again.

The door opens and closes quietly, but I keep my eyes closed.

The mattress bows with his weight, and a warm arm snakes around my midsection. He buries his face in my hair, his breath warm against my neck. "Can you ever forgive me?"

"For what?" Yes, Bastian's words hurt me, but he laid out his plan ahead of time. "You played the part perfectly. The pompous son of the king and a person I dislike immensely."

He gently lifts my hair away from my face and kisses my cheek. "As long as you know I didn't mean a single word. I love you, Mari."

I shift to face him. They've given him new clothes to wear—a black velvet long-sleeve shirt and fur-lined cape. With his crystal-blue eyes and ebony hair, he plays the Dark Prince role well. I cup his cheek in my hand, trailing my fingernails over his tanned skin. "I love you too."

"Will you accompany me to the ball this evening?" He gives me a lopsided grin. The boyish action doesn't match his manly face. "My father says he wants you there despite his intentions to find me a suitable wife."

"And am I not suitable?" I prop myself up on my elbow, already knowing the answer.

He runs a finger down my arm, sending a delicious shiver through me. "Not in his eyes. You're a distraction from my real purpose—to lead the Miscrete army to take down Avren."

"But I'm a savior too. We're both supposed to take down the cities together." It sounds whiny, but I'm tired of Arazian treating me like I don't matter.

"You scare me, Windsong." He leans in closer and gives me a light kiss on the lips. "You're the wildcard in all of this. With me, people know what to expect. With you, anything could happen. And you're included in the fae prophecy for a reason. You will have a profound effect on this battle."

My mother's words come rushing back to me, but I'm still unsure of their meaning. "While you were gone, I read parts of my mother's journal. In her last entry, she revealed interesting information." I sit up against my pillow, unsure of where this conversation will lead. "She said Avren and the First City are working together, and I think my father is leading the charge against both of them."

Bastian raises an eyebrow, seemingly as unconvinced as I am. "Working together? Arazian hates everything Avren stands for. An alliance to what end?"

"I don't know." I pull at the satin material of the bedspread as I think it through. "It doesn't make sense to me either. Lady Raven and the Council made a huge spectacle of removing Arazian from the city. An alliance doesn't seem possible."

He looks down at his hands, his long lashes hiding his eyes. "Raven is my mother. Arazian admitted it."

It's a bomb landing squarely in the middle of our plan and something I never saw coming. "That's not possible."

"Oh, it's possible." He smirks, then lifts his eyes to mine again. "Remember Tenny Rocks? Do I need to teach you about the birds and the bees?"

"I understand how a baby is conceived. What I don't understand is why the Council would exile the father of Lady Raven's child." My head is spinning. I'm not sure how to wrap my thoughts around this yet. I've built this woman up as my supreme enemy, not the one who gave birth to the man I love.

He gathers my hands close to him and for the first time I realize they're shaking. "Don't you see. It's the perfect cover up for her mistake. Get rid of the temptation. Live the rest of her life as a pious saint with no sexual desire. If the evidence doesn't exist, it never happened."

In Avren, if a woman is with child, there are ways to take care of it secretly before anyone else knows. "Why didn't she go to her healer?"

"Because as absurd as it sounds, she wanted me. At least, that's what my father says." He traces a fingernail along the lifelines on my palm. "But he hid me away with the Hales, partly to keep me from my mother and partly because he didn't want to deal with a child."

"And to reward them, he had their entire family killed by Miscretes." My heart breaks for Bastian. This is so much worse than having your father leave to lead a rebellion. His parents are the people we need to kill to save the wilderness. I can't begin to understand how he's feeling.

I grip his hand to pull him closer to me, resting my forehead against his. "I'm so sorry. Everything in me wishes the Hales were your parents. Knowing a loved one has passed on is better than knowing they're an evil dictator."

As he pulls away, a bittersweet smile crosses his lips, and it melts me. I want nothing more than to see him happy for the rest of his days, but that seems impossible now. "Come on, evil dictators have their perks: roomy mansions, lavish feasts, and cozy dungeons. Speaking of, I went down to visit Evie and Gray."

"Are they ok?"

"Obstinate as ever and ready for us to bust them out." He clears his throat. "I plan to talk to father about making them my bodyguards. It's not like they've done anything to offend him except for breaking and entering."

"And Sterling?" The more I understand the dynamics of leadership in the First City, the more I realize that the vampire is more in charge than anyone thinks he is.

"I really don't care what he thinks." He lays his head back on a pillow and stares up at the canopy. "I'm the prince, not him. Only one man's power supersedes mine in this city, and he's like putty in my hands."

"You've only been prince for about a day." As much as I hate that he has to play this role, it's important to get the information we need. "Don't let it go to your head."

He props himself up and pouts. "What's the matter? Can't

stand that you're sleeping with a prince?" His long fingers trace my jawline, making me squirm. "Royalty doesn't get you all hot and bothered?"

I reach up and grip his hand, stopping his trailing fingers. "*You* are important to me, Bastian Hale. Not the prince you're pretending to be. We could live in a cabin in the middle of the wilderness and I'd be happy."

"But we do live in a cabin in the middle of the wilderness." He lifts an eyebrow as he grips my hand tighter.

"Exactly," I say before he uses his grip to roll me on top of him.

AFTER LAST NIGHT, the indifference in Bastian's glance when I enter the dining room almost shatters me. Arazian and Sterling sit at the table, both not bothering to look up as I take my seat beside the prince.

"Eat your food and then return to your room." Sterling, the only one at the table who doesn't eat, glares at me. "We need to discuss things that don't involve you."

My role is the mouse. My role is the mouse.

But I really want to respond to him like a lion. Doesn't he understand a word of the prophecy?

The chef prepared the usual hard-boiled eggs along with fried bread. Bastian pours me a glass of juice.

"I trust you slept well, my dear." Arazian looks to Bastian and winks. The man makes me sick.

"Very well, thank you," I respond as a dutiful mouse. "And you, Your Majesty?"

He rubs the side of his neck and winces. "I woke with a terrible crick. Perhaps later you can swing by my room and massage it for me."

Bastian's fingers turn whiter as he grips the arms of his chair.

I lean my elbows on the table to block Sterling's view of them. "Whatever I can do to help the king."

"You have a fine woman here, Bastian." Arazian stares at me a little too long, so I take a sip of juice and hope someone changes the subject.

"She's alright. I'm looking forward to the ball tonight. The First City has some fine women." Bastian touches the pads of his fingers together, not daring to look at me. "I'll share my bed with one... or two... or perhaps three."

Arazian laughs and slaps his hands on his legs. "That's my boy. We'll find you a queen to birth my grandson in no time."

It's times like these that I draw upon our time alone in his room. His fevered kisses, gentle touches, and whispered secrets. His sweat-drenched body sated yet craving more. We fell asleep, a tangled and exhausted mess but more in love than we've ever been. His indifference and insults are deafening when my mere presence should shake him to his core.

"Go to the room, Maribel," Bastian almost growls, his knuckles still white from gripping the chair.

"But I haven't finished my breakfast," I protest, not willing to back down over food.

He turns his head to look at me, anger burning in his eyes. "I'll have the maid bring it up to you."

I push back in my chair and jut out my chin. The anger is not at me, but his dismissal doesn't sit well as my heart races, begging me to stand up to him. But I can't. Not for our plan to work and not if we want to put an end to the reign of Arazian and Sterling.

CHAPTER ELEVEN

Bastian

I HATE PRINCE BASTIAN.

But it doesn't come close to how much I hate my father.

Once Mari has left the room, I recline, crossing one leg over another as if I belong in this madhouse. "I have a matter I'd like to discuss."

Arazian leans forward and folds his hands on the table, eager to hear more from the jackass prince. "What is it, son?"

Sterling has remained dangerously quiet throughout breakfast, probably taking in anything he can use against me later. When my father propositioned Mari for a massage, I almost threw the table aside so I could strangle him. Mari and Sterling kept me in my place. Showing my true feelings would jeopardize my position.

I sigh as if truly bothered by the issue I'm about to bring up. "I'm concerned for my life. There are those out there that want a free wilderness, and I pose a threat to their cause. The prince of the First City could continue building a Miscrete army for many years" With my head tilted slightly to the side and my eyes averted, trying to feign reluctance, I ask, "Could I have two personal guards?"

"You have me." Sterling says, startling me. I almost thought the guy had taken a vow of silence. "What more do you need?"

"I'd like to have two guards by my door each night and to accompany me when I go into the city." Throwing in a half-lie can't hurt. "When I went to a bakery yesterday, the people were afraid of me. Fear can cause people to do crazy things."

"You have other priorities, Sterling." Arazian looks at his second-in-command as he responds. "We'll find you two guards before the ball tonight."

I bite my lip, unsure how to proceed with my next request other than to just ask. "There are two people unjustly locked in our dungeon. Two of the best fighters I know. I'd like to hire them as my personal guards."

"They were thrown in the dungeon for breaking and entering into your home, sir." Sterling's eyes burn with unholy light. There's no way I've gained his trust. "I was about to give the order to have the Miscretes tear them to shreds when Prince Bastian asked to have them incarcerated."

"Do you trust these two individuals, Bastian?" Arazian balls up the napkin from his lap and puts it on his plate.

"With my life," I say, not having to lie. "Their skills would be a great asset to our arsenal. If you want to defeat Avren, it's much better to have them with us than against us. And the only reason they were breaking and entering was because they were trying to find me."

"I still don't think it's a good idea, Your Majesty." Sterling pushes back in his chair and stands as if he knows he's outnumbered. "But I'm only the second-in-command. What do I know?" He storms out of the room like a spoiled teenager, slamming the door behind him.

Arazian waves his hand. "Don't mind him. He gets a bit temperamental at times."

"I've seen." My back still aches from when he body slammed me onto the dining room table.

"I'll have your two guards brought up to you by noon." He pushes back in his chair, wiping the leftover crumbs from his pants as he stands. "And you believe they won't need any specialized training?"

"Not much," I say, standing and adjusting another hideous black outfit a maid had left on my bed for me to wear. "Whatever they need, I'll provide them."

"Come for a walk with me through the garden." Arazian opens the door to the main foyer, and I follow him to the rear of the building.

Side by side, we walk through the hedge-lined backyard of the mansion. White flowers bloom, sending a thick fragrance throughout. Without the natural pollinators of the wilderness, it's a wonder these plants survive in this unnatural world.

"With both you and Maribel in our possession, Sterling believes we are almost strong enough to move against Avren, but I want your opinion." He walks beside me with his hands behind his back, father and son out for an afternoon stroll. His words imply that he sees me as an equal, ready to lead the First City into battle. "Our Miscrete army is two thousand strong. With a little more time, we can grow it to three thousand by taking in the people of the First City, Tenny Rocks and the Grove. Moss Ford would be too dangerous, of course."

"By 'take in', do you mean turn them into Miscretes?" I swallow back the bile in my throat, trying to keep my composure.

"They won't join us willingly, Bastian." He stops to face me, and I look into eyes so similar to mine. But there's something different—a wild recklessness that I'm noticing for the first time. My father is a bit unhinged.

97

"What if I could get them to join us willingly?" Anything to keep him from attacking the free people of the wilderness. "Give me a week. Tomorrow, I'll journey to the towns and convince them to join our cause. Tenny Rocks might be a little more difficult than the Grove, but I can be persuasive."

He strokes his beard, shaking his head. "It's too dangerous to send you out there. I have enemies in the wilderness. If word gets out that you're my son, they may exact their revenge on you."

"What kind of word can spread so quickly in a week?" Surely word that spread like wildfire in the city won't move past its walls? I need to throw the full arsenal of my convincing power at this man. "When I bring back the able-bodied men and women, I'll train them to join our already powerful army myself. Lady Raven will beg for mercy."

He begins walking again, rounding a bend in the hedges. "You may leave tomorrow, after the ball, but Maribel stays here."

"No." There's no way I'd leave the woman I love with monsters. "The saviors are not to be separated. If we are to take down Avren, I must always ensure her safety. Believe me, if I could find a way to sever our connection, I would. But for now, she needs to stay with me."

"You drive a hard bargain. And your guards? I'm sure you'll want them to travel with you as well?" A tiny smile crosses his lips as if he sees my requests as a joke. "What guarantee do I have that you will return after a week?"

"I will return, father, you have my solemn promise. With a full-fledged army, I will be back." The ironic nature of my oath is that the army will return to destroy everything the Dark King has built.

"I never thought you'd turn out so amazingly beautiful, Bastian." Arazian touches my arm in what should be a memorable father and son moment, but it fills me with dread. This is the man who killed my family and turned my friends' families into

Miscretes. As much as he wants it, there's no room in my heart for him. "Someday soon, we'll rule the First City and the wilderness together."

"YOU CONVINCED him to let us walk out of the First City with Evie and Gray?" Mari sits in the armchair with a book, her eyes wide. She closes the book and places it on the table. "I'm not sure how you did it, but you're amazing."

I tilt my head to the side and flash her a smile. "I've been told that from time to time."

"But we still have to go to this ball tonight?" She frowns as if I'm dragging her through the Murky Swamps.

"I need to meet the queen of my dreams." I lift my eyebrows. "Or possibly a queen and several concubines." Despite the joke, I regret my words the second they leave my mouth.

She rests her elbow on the windowsill and stares outside at the garden. "I don't know how long I can do this. I thought I was stronger, but Arazian lays it on a bit thick."

Crossing the room, I drop to one knee beside her chair. "I've known the man for less than a week. It's not like I can control him. It's no wonder my mother wants nothing to do with him." I slide my palms along her thighs before resting my head in her lap. "You are one of the strongest women I know."

Her fingers run through my hair, and I don't move, enjoying her gentle massage. "I'm nothing like Evie or Susan."

I lift my head and sit back on my haunches. "Maybe not in physical strength, but your mental toughness, emotional stamina, and fortitude are unmatched. You and Gray not only lost your loved ones, but also your entire way of life." Gathering her hands in mine, I touch my lips to the side of her finger. "I can't begin to understand what you went through, Mari."

Her chest heaves as she rests her head against the high velvet back of the chair. "I imagine you do now, *Prince* Bastian."

"Don't call me that unless you mean it." I pitch forward, grabbing her around the waist and pulling her onto my lap on the floor.

There's a knock on the door.

Damn it.

Mari scrambles from my lap, finding her perch in the high-backed chair as I go to answer the door.

Two women stand outside, each holding a formal outfit. The one closer to me curtsies. "Your Highness. Clothing for you and Miss Windsong for the ball."

I reach out and snatch the bundles without saying thank you. Word will get out quickly about any kindness I extend to the help. My outpouring of generosity in the bakery has surely reached many ears in the city.

Once the door is closed, Mari jumps out of the chair to join me beside the bed, where I lay my suit and her dress. Mine is standard royal dress clothing, complete with tails and a frilly black tie. It's almost as ridiculous as what I have on.

But Mari's dress makes my jaw drop. It's red with a low-cut neckline, a V-line waist, and an exquisite skirt covered in flowery lace.

She lifts the dress to her shoulders, spinning around. "It's a shame to waste such a beautiful dress on this sham of a ball. I need to share you with women who hope to catch your eye."

I grip her shoulders and draw her close, our faces inches apart. Her face is flushed as if I've caught her off-guard. "There is only one woman I have eyes for, and she'll be wearing red."

My lips meet hers, tasting the sweetness I'll never grow tired of if I live for seventy more years. Her mouth parts as my tongue sweeps along the ridge of her teeth, my hands roaming from her shoulders to her arms to her hips. If we had more time, I'd take her to bed, but Arazian expects me in the ballroom within the hour.

I back away slightly. "Mari, I…"

She runs her fingers through the dark hair falling over my face. "Shhh… my prince must perform his duties." She turns from me, picks up her dress from the bed, and disappears behind the changing curtain.

I remove the ghastly black jacket Sterling gave me to wear while I'm in the city and unbutton my shirt, letting them both drop to the floor. I shrug on the black button-up shirt made of a silk material. I've never felt something so soft on my skin. Finally, I change out of my pants. As I tuck the shirt into the waist, Mari steps out from behind the curtain.

The ball gown gives her the appearance of a seductress rather than a princess, but I'm not complaining. The front of the dress is open almost down to her navel, cutting perfectly beside her breasts. It's difficult for me to rip my eyes away to see what else the dress has to offer. Cinched in at the waist, the bottom moves fluidly with her steps. This is an outfit my father picked out for his own pleasure. In his eyes, I'm supposed to find a wife, not love the woman I'm with.

"What do you think?" She turns and looks at me over her shoulder as I take in the large silken bow hanging limply on her back. "Can you help me fix the ribbon?"

Lifting the cool material in my hand, I'm really at a loss never having tied a bow in my life. "Maybe one of the maids could help you. And as for the dress…" I sweep her hair from her neck and run my lips along her skin, causing tiny goosebumps to form. "I'd say I don't want to share you with anyone else."

She spins around. Standing this close, it's obvious her nipples are pressing against the thin material. I don't want to take her out in public for more reasons than one.

"Are you ready to go?" she asks, not seeming to care about

wearing a dress she wouldn't be caught dead in two months ago. She adjusts my lapels and brushes away a stray piece of lint. "You look very handsome."

"One last thing." I remove a hair tie from the pocket of my pants on the floor. I gather my hair at the nape of my neck to keep it from falling into my face. When I finish, I hold my hands out to either side. "Am I presentable?"

"The dark prince of my dreams." She smiles sweetly before opening the door.

I follow her into the hallway, taking her arm in mine. If she's my escort, I want to make it clear that we're together.

"When will Evie and Gray join us?" She wobbles a bit in the heels the maid left for her and clings onto me tighter.

"Look behind us." I noticed them the second we left the room, standing like statues at the end of the hallway. As my guards their job will be to protect me from any immediate threats.

"I'm still shocked you got Arazian to agree to let the four of us walk out of here tomorrow." She pinches my arm. "You had to break my heart several times to do it, but you've officially managed to play the part of the obnoxious prince."

"And I'll need to continue my role tonight." Treating her like shit is the worst part of the plan. When we leave the First City, I'll make it up to her tenfold. "I need to dance with women my father sees as worthy of my attention. I'll rely on Evie and Gray to keep you away from him." The knot in my chest still burns with hatred over how my father treated Mari at breakfast.

Vibrant music drifts up the staircase from the hall below. I hold onto Mari's arm, shaking slightly as we descend the stairs to the entryway full of Arazian's guests. Curiosity turns heads in our direction. The Dark King has a son, an heir to the throne of the First City. Women bat eyelashes at me as I pass but none are brazen enough to introduce themselves to the Dark Prince.

Mari remains quiet by my side. This must be as overwhelming for her as it is for me. Even in my role as commander, I don't enjoy being the center of attention.

Arazian holds up his hands as we approach, still clinging tightly to each other. "And here he comes now, my pride and joy, Prince Bastian."

For some odd reason, the guests around him applaud as if I did something grand. This whole fucking party is designed to show off his son. The son he abandoned as a baby.

My father hands me a glass of wine, totally neglecting Mari as he stands on his tiptoes to look around the room. He cups a hand to his mouth. "Sterling... Sterling! Come over here."

The vampire seems to appear out of nowhere, lurking beside me. "Yes?"

"Can you entertain Miss Windsong? I have some people I want Bastian to meet."

Sterling snakes an arm around Mari, gently prying her away from me and whisking her into the crowd.

My heart sinks. It will be difficult to protect her when I don't know where the vamp has taken her. But then Gray steps into my line of vision and holds two fingers to his temple, giving me a salute before he slips into the crowd, following the vampire.

CHAPTER TWELVE

Mari

DANCERS TWIRL AROUND THE FLOOR, making it difficult for me to keep track of Bastian. Sterling knows what he's doing as he zigzags his way to a long table lined with silver trays of food. We're clear on the other side of the enormous room from where we started.

"Fill your plate." The vampire appears bored as usual as he hands me a silver platter. "You have a long journey to Tenny Rocks tomorrow."

I scoop a heaping pile of mashed potatoes onto my plate, more interested in asking what he knows about my father than talking about my travel plans. "What do you know about the Northern Duke?" If he has worked with Arazian, Sterling must know something about him.

"What a strange question," he says, lifting a roll from a basket and setting it on my plate. He moves with supernatural grace, as if he's practiced every move he makes hundreds of times. "Where did you hear that name?"

I lift a shoulder and stick my finger into the potatoes for a small taste. "Bastian brought him up as someone we might want to recruit besides the villagers in Tenny Rocks and the Grove."

"Arazian and the Northern Duke have a love-hate relationship. They share their hatred for Avren but don't see eye to eye on a lot of issues." His eyes flick to the dance floor where Bastian twirls with a beautiful dark-haired woman.

My stomach lurches, but I keep my back straight, knowing it's all a show.

"If the two saviors show up on his doorstep, he might be persuaded to join the alliance. The more the merrier, right?" If we go to visit my father unsolicited, word will get back to the First City.

"You don't have to travel to the Murky Swamps." He pours himself a goblet of dark liquid. When he takes a sip, a mustache of red lines his upper lip.

I close my eyes to control the queasiness before responding. "Isn't that where he lives?"

The vampire wipes the blood from his lip with his sleeve, his eyes glowing with rejuvenation. "Yes, the Northern Duke lives there, but he was here two days ago. He's spending a week in Tenny Rocks before returning to his camp."

Bastian glides over the floor with ease, one arm wrapped tightly around his partner as they dance to the music. Beyond them, on the edge of the parquet, Arazian watches on with delight, a wide smile crossing his lips. He catches my gaze and winks. Heat rushes up my neck to my face. I don't want any attention from him.

"The Dark King fancies the younger ones. But I fear his son will grow jealous over the remarks his father gives you." Sterling leans in close, bumping his shoulder against mine like we're old friends. "If Arazian covets Bastian's possessions, any alliance, as unholy as they might be, will be called off."

"I'm afraid the prince doesn't pay much attention to a mouse." I lift a grape from my plate and plop it into my mouth.

"He pays more mind to you than you let on, Miss Windsong. Don't think I don't notice every flush of your cheeks, sheen of sweat along your neckline, and unfettered beat of your heart. Prince Bastian is wrapped around your finger despite his exhausting charade." Sterling holds out his hand, his fingers long and white. "Take my hand. Don't want you getting lost in the crowd."

The vampire leads me to a circular table with two chairs by the window. Grayson keeps his distance, chatting with a man in a dark gray suit. He glances nervously at us every minute or so, as if I'm his little sister on an actual date with a bloodsucker.

I use my fork to create a trail of brown sauce along the edge of my plate. It's as if Sterling can read my every thought through my inability to play it cool. I need to keep my mind off his intense stare. "How long have you known Arazian?"

An actual smile crosses the vampire's lips as he folds his hands on the table. "You're a fascinating little mouse, aren't you?" Out of the corner of my eye, I can see him twiddling his thumbs. "Think you can help out your band of misfits, brandishing your savior flag, but in reality, you're nothing more than a nobody from Avren. Questioning will get you nowhere with me, Miss Windsong."

His words sting slightly because I've also questioned my ability to help my brothers and sister, but I also know I've come so far.

I lift my goblet and take a swig of wine, letting the bitter liquid burn my throat. It gives me the courage I need to become the woman the prophecy claims I am. "You've got two choices, Sterling. Join our cause to free the wilderness from Avren's bondage or go down in flames yourself. If you choose the former, I want to know who I'm working with. Why did you leave your queen to work with a human? What's your interest in all of this?" I glance around the ballroom with my words sticking in my throat.

Near the center of the dance floor, Bastian laughs with two women, leaning in close to one, nuzzling her neck. His hand snakes around her back and pulls her close.

My heart races as I stab my fork into my mashed potatoes, unable to control my heated cheeks. If we're to pull off this plan, I need to get it together.

Sterling clicks his tongue, unfolds his hands, and lounges back in his chair, crossing one leg over the other. "It seems the mouse has fallen for the lion. If he's truly the Dark Prince, you are but a speck on the bottom of his shoe. He can have any woman or man he wants. You are but a way to pass a few nights."

"You forget who you are talking to," I say, straightening my back, done taking this degrading talk from him. "The ancient fae foresaw a female warrior rising from Avren. A woman destined to destroy not only her own city but its second-class spawn." I pitch forward, unafraid of his fangs and intrusive demeanor.

"I see." His fingers trail through his long hair, moving it away from his face. Blood-red eyes assess me differently than before—as if I've graduated from a mouse to a rat. "Perhaps the prince should make the trek to Tenny Rocks and the Grove without you. What assurance do we have that you'll return an ally?"

Damn my ego.

I draw in a breath. This conversation is as much of a battle as any fought with swords and daggers. "You have my word that we will return. The people of the wilderness distrust Arazian's intentions. The testimony of two saviors may make them sympathetic to your cause."

"And what about the mouse? What are her opinions on the Dark King?" He leans forward again, resting his elbows on the table and his chin on his folded hands. "He's taken quite a liking to you."

That he can burn in the deepest pit.

"He's doing his best to be hospitable to both myself and Bastian." The lie floats awkwardly between us, so I add, "I'd prefer him to tone down his forwardness."

Sterling smirks. "That's like asking a dragon to forego its wings. The man loves women, and he's not afraid to lay his intentions out there. My advice is to avoid being alone with him."

"Duly noted." I'm not sure if I've done enough to convince the vampire to let me go on the trip or that our intentions are to work with the First City.

As the exhausting night wears on, I watch woman after woman paraded before the Dark Prince, each one intent on catching his attention. I don't let it affect me anymore. The vampire must be convinced of my disinterest.

Arazian finally makes his way to our table, wearing a jeweled robe and a wide smile. From his stagger, I can tell he's had too much to drink, basking in the festivities.

He holds a hand out to me. "Do you mind if I steal her for a dance, Sterling?"

"Go right ahead," the vampire says, standing. "You can babysit her for a while. I'll retreat to my room."

The king takes my hand, leading me to the center of the dance floor. I can feel the heat of Bastian's eyes on us as his father wraps an arm around my back.

"You look ravishing." His eyes trail down the deep cut in the front of my dress. The scent of liquor fills the small space between us. "I picked this one out myself."

No surprise there.

"I hope Sterling has treated you well." Arazian's blue eyes finally move back to my face. "He's not always the best host."

"As well as can be expected," I answer honestly. "I ate dinner."

His hand slips lower on my back and I stiffen. I've done nothing to encourage this behavior, but the liquor and his position make him think he has the go-ahead. All I want is to get through this night and to leave this place behind in the morning.

Arazian lowers his head and whispers in my ear, "I'd love to see what's beneath your dress."

Everything within me screams to walk away, but I'm paralyzed. If I reject the king, I risk ruining our plan. With what we've seen and heard within the walls of the First City, nothing is more important than finding our forces. Once Avren is defeated with the help of the people and creatures of the wilderness, Arazian and Sterling will turn on them.

I give him a hint of a shy smile. "You flatter too much, but I belong to your son."

"Not for long, sweet Maribel." He dips me, his lips dangerously close to mine. "Once he's engaged to another, you're free, and I'll be there to scoop you up." With a strong hand on my back, he lifts me upright. "There's nothing I'd like more than making a savior my queen."

And Bastian would be my stepson. Awkward.

The music turns more upbeat, and the king releases me, leaving me alone in the center of the dance floor. I rub at my shoulder, which is tense from being on edge the entire night.

"Remind me to rub that for you later." Bastian's hand is on my waist. "May I reserve the next slower dance?"

"It depends." I turn to face him, taking in every inch of his handsome features: square jaw, dark brown hair, and crystal blue eyes that see right through me. "Have you proposed to any of the vultures that have circled you all night?"

"Not even close." His fingers dig into my hip, expressing his need to touch me despite the disinterested expression on his face. "There's only one woman I'm in love with, and she's driving me crazy in her red dress. I need to put on the appear-

ance of the bachelor prince. Do not dance with Arazian again."
He drops his hand and steps away. "I'll be back soon."

I wander aimlessly through the sea of people, trying to find
Grayson or Evie. One of them must have an eye on me, but the
amount of people in the room makes me dizzy. When I reach an
outer wall, I place a hand on it to steady myself, wishing for a
glass of water.

"I'd have gutted him with a dagger by now." Evie leans
against the wall about two feet away from me, disguised in the
uniform of a First City guard. Her red hair is swept up beneath
her hat, giving her the appearance of a younger male guard. "A
pervert, if you ask me."

"Are you referring to Arazian?" Not that I disagree. The man
shouldn't be pursuing a woman a third his age.

She crosses her arms and watches the dancers. "From what
Bastian says, the man has a fascination with your status as a
savior. Perhaps he believes if he has you and his son in his
pocket, it will negate the words of the ancient fae."

"The closer I get to him, the more urgent our task becomes."
I inch closer to her so I can lower my voice. "We need to leave
early tomorrow to gather our forces. This includes bringing the
Northern Duke into the fold."

"The Northern Duke?" Evie raises an eyebrow, clearly
unsure. "The guy's crazy as they come. We can't go into battle
relying on him."

I swallow. No one knows my truth, but I trust Evie and
Grayson as much as Bastian. They're my family. "Dax Barellis is
my father."

"As in the man who abandoned you?" She moves in close.
We're speaking in whispers now.

"Yes," I say, feeling my body shake and tears well in my eyes.
I didn't know it would feel this way to release my secret. "The
Northern Duke is in Tenny Rocks as we speak. I think we can

get him on our side along with his forces. He doesn't trust Arazian any more than we do. Probably less."

"You haven't seen your father in years." A gentle palm touches my arm as her eyes search mine. The terror of meeting him again, possibly changed from the man he used to be, is palpable. "How are you feeling about this?"

With my eyes closed, I swallow back the threatening tears, unsure if I can express the fear, worry, and elation of possibly seeing my father again. Either he will accept me with open arms or make me a true orphan with his rejection. "Like I need answers."

"That's the least you deserve." Evie squeezes my arm, then disappears into the crowd as Bastian approaches.

With my thoughts focused on my father, I didn't notice the change in the music from a lively reel to slow waltz.

He gives a slight bow, a formal gesture from the man who holds my heart in his hands. I loop my arm through his and let him lead me to the dance floor. Frowns of disapproval and raised brows of curiosity greet me from all sides as we shuffle through the parting crowd of partygoers.

Bastian stops near the center of the floor, slides a hand behind my back, and takes one of mine in his other. I touch his shoulder, the black silk soft beneath my fingers, and feel content once again in his arms.

"Arazian expects me to pick a wife tonight," he says as if casually speaking about the weather. "I need to think of a way to put it off."

Sterling is behind all of this. He senses the connection between us and fears our power. If he can get the king to break us apart, it will only strengthen the First City's position over the wilderness.

"If you feign sickness, you could slip away to your quarters and reschedule your 'Dark Prince wife tour' for when we get back."

He lowers his eyes and shakes his head. "This isn't what I want. You know that."

"The prince thing sure comes easy to you. A different woman dangling from your arm at every turn." It's a dig, and I hate myself the second it leaves my lips. "I didn't mean that. I'm sorry."

The corner of his lip lifts, causing my guilty heart to dive deeper into the caverns of regret. "It's an easy thing to let go to your head. But these women want me because I'm a prince, not because they know me. I'd rather be a poor man with you by my side than a rich man with any of them, Mari."

His words lift my spirits as we waltz around the floor feeling the weight of stares from every corner of the ballroom. The people of the First City don't know who I am, and their curiosities are piqued. I don't blame them. In Avren, he'd be akin to an unwed Council member. Although our matches are supposedly set based on a meticulous process, the same rules don't apply for those in power. Bastian is living, breathing proof of this.

The music stops abruptly though my head still spins from twirling about in his arms. I look to him, expecting a similar delighted smile, but he stares up at a raised dais with his brows drawn.

His father stands before the crowd of citizens, holding his arms out in welcome. "I want to thank all of you for joining us tonight. It has proved to be both entertaining and productive." Arazian's eyes rest on Bastian who drops his hold on me. Both fill me with ice-cold dread. "Come here, son. I want to introduce you to our people." He chuckles. "Although word spreads quickly here. Your intimidating yet dashingly handsome frame make you stand out, so it's no wonder the people are intrigued."

Without a glance, Bastian leaves me behind, walks through the crowd, who easily part for him, and climbs the stairs to join his father.

The older man embraces him before addressing his people

again. "We live in a dangerous world. These walls, the Miscretes, and Commander Sterling's expert leadership protect us, but I fear Lady Raven and her bloodthirsty soldiers are closing in. Just yesterday, the commander had to rip out the necks of five who wandered to close. The sooner I can get this one married, the sooner I'll have an heir." He rubs his hands together and turns to his son. "Have you chosen your bride, Bastian?"

Bastian's eyes flick to mine momentarily. The lump in his throat bobs as he swallows.

I know he can't say my name. It will ruin our plan.

"I guess if I have to choose," he says, his gaze sweeping the crowd in princely boredom. "Lady Raquel Masterdom meets the requirements."

Arazian claps his hands together. "Then it is settled. My son will marry tomorrow before he leaves on his recruitment campaign."

CHAPTER THIRTEEN

Mari

Bastian's lips remain in a firm line, the usual sparkle I've come to love missing from his crystal-blue eyes. He plays his role well—the son spurred by duty to the city—but inside, he must be crumbling. If he refuses, does he risk blowing a cover that's already as fragile as an eggshell in Sterling's assessment of our little role-play? Even an attempt to delay might draw suspicion.

"Fine choice." Arazian slaps him on the back as a gorgeous blonde woman climbs the stairs, reminding me more of Susan, Bastian's former girlfriend, than I care to admit.

Raquel wears an almost translucent dress, leaving little to the imagination. She holds her head up in rare confidence as she approaches the prince and slides a palm along his bicep. I want to look away, but I can't. It's not a betrayal. I see it on his face.

While a smile creeps over his lips as he rakes his eyes down her body, it's the nearly imperceptible things that warm my heart. His body is turned slightly away from her touch, his hands are in his pockets, and the fake smile on his lips is nothing like the way he lights up when I enter a room. I hope

Sterling knows so little about love that he misses these clues completely.

"It is tradition in the First City for the bride and groom to spend the night together before the wedding." Arazian tilts his head to the side, smirking. "A symbol of breaking our allegiance to Avren and their quest for utmost purity."

His proclamation sends a boulder to the pit of my stomach as I watch Raquel move her hand from Bastian's bicep to his chest, her fingers curling into the silky material of his shirt. She tugs the shirt loose from his pants before making quick work of the buttons holding the material together.

"What are you doing?" Bastian snatches her wrist, steps back and glares at his father. "Sexual relations are reserved for the bedroom, even in the wilderness."

"Not here, my boy. Our tradition lets Avren know we don't care about their rules and regulations." Arazian's attention is on Raquel as she lifts her dress over her head and drops it on the floor, leaving only tiny swaths of material to cover her lower parts and her nipples. "Here, we all delight in both the vows and the pre-wedding night. Proper consummation must be ensured. You're the prince. Besides, it gives others something to aspire to with their own partners."

Bastian bends down and picks up Raquel's dress from the spot it puddled on the floor and hands it back to her. "*This* will not happen. Send her to my room for the night if you insist on premarital relations, but I will not make it into a spectacle." In other words, he doesn't want to have sex with another woman in front of me. His proclamation does little to reduce the size of the boulder in my stomach.

Sterling steps forward. With all that has happened on the dais, I didn't notice the slithering snake in the background ready to strike. "Your morals, *my prince*, do not stand above the traditions of our society." He lifts Raquel's dress from her hands and tosses it to the crowd of onlookers. His long nails trail along the future bride's neck, leaving a thin trail of blood. He licks his lips. "Fuck this woman, or she'll suffer the consequences of your inadequacies."

Raquel steps back slightly from Sterling as her eyes widen.

Bastian doesn't look at me. He can't. It will tear both of us apart.

Stories of the First City's darkness spread to Avren when I was growing up, but I never imagined anything like this.

I can't look away as Raquel slips Bastian's shirt from his shoulders, his Kindred Few tattoo visible from where I'm standing. The fear of losing another one of the five rings hits me hard as I watch an almost naked woman run her tongue from the prince's bellybutton to his neck. The other guests transfix on this horror show. The boulder in my stomach flames and threatens to burn through the lining of my abdominal wall.

As I fix my attention back on the dais, Arazian sits in a throne-like chair with a front-row view of the action while Raquel shimmies Bastian's pants to the floor. I can't take any more of this. I want to squeeze my eyes shut as I work my way through the crowd, but it's impossible without running into someone. Coming from a city where sex with your spouse was only allowed in small doses, this is too much to comprehend.

An imposing figure blocks the door to the entryway, his fangs on full display. "What's the matter, mouse? Has the pussy cat hurt your feelings?"

"Let me by, Sterling." If he forces me to spend another second in this room, I might scream. My role is to play it cool so we can walk out the doors tomorrow. "I'm tired."

"I'll take you to the king's quarters."

"No!" I'm done with this place and anything that involves Arazian is out of the question. "Take me to Bastian's room. We need to get up early in the morning."

Sterling flashes me a rare smile and lifts a hand to my face, his thumb stroking my skin. "Oh, my dear little mouse. The cat has another pussy to play with tonight. The king left me instructions to bring you to his room."

Crap. Bastian and I might need to change our plans.

A shrill whistle pierces the air above my head as an arrow races toward the raised platform, hitting Raquel in the chest. She drops to the floor near Bastian's feet.

"Protect the prince!" Arazian calls out, holding an arm over his head as he ducks behind his throne.

More arrows whizz above my head, intent on their target. I turn to see the hooded assassin on the balcony of an upper room. They draw back another arrow and time stands still. Arazian warned of an attempt on Bastian's life, but I didn't comprehend the reality of it happening tonight.

An arrow flies into the wall behind the hooded figure, so they turn their attention to the far side of the room where Evie has another arrow nocked. She lets it fly just as the intruder sends one in her direction.

Grayson weaves through the crowd which is now dispersing in a panic. He draws back a dagger and flings it at the intruder, hitting them square in the chest. They stumble, holding the handle of the weapon, now covered in blood, before falling over the edge of the balcony. They land with a thud on the floor below.

Not bothering to check the body, Grayson rushes the stairs of the dais, handing a dagger to the almost-naked Bastian. They scramble down from the platform.

A flash of red draws my eyes to the side of the room as Evie nocks another arrow and lets it fly toward Sterling. But the vampire is too fast. With an arm around my neck, he drags me out of the room. In the entryway, he scoops me up and runs through the front door at a speed that has my head spinning.

Before I know it, we are descending stairs into a musty, cavernous space which I assume is the dungeon. The place where Sterling keeps the Miscretes as prisoners.

The vampire finally slows as he slams an iron door behind us and drops me on my feet. "Your little friends are no match for the First City, mousy Maribel. Bastian's act wasn't nearly convincing enough. When it came down to it, he'd never betray the woman he loves. It might be time to take you out of the equation. It's almost feeding time for the Miscretes. Perhaps you'd like to join them?"

Can you reason with a Miscrete?

They were once human. Like me, they had mothers and fathers, and some had sisters and brothers. In the armory, two tried to communicate using voices I knew well. If I could use their humanity as a connection, maybe I could convince them to join us in the fight against the First City. Without the Miscretes, what army would Arazian and Sterling have?

"You've already made up your mind," I state, running a stray strand of hair behind my ear. The dampness creeps into my bones and I shiver, crossing my arms over my revealing dress. I hate it. What I really want is the comfort of my linen pants and cotton shirt. They'd feel like home.

He taps his chin, assessing me with his ever-watchful eyes. "Yes, but I thought a warrior such as yourself would at least put up a fight." With calculated steps, he moves closer until I'm backed against the wall. He trails his fingers along my neck like he did with Raquel. "I had to fight to get this from the prince. Drawing blood from his neck gave me insight into your relationship."

Drawing blood?

What else did I expect? The guy's a full-blown vampire, and I already witnessed him drinking blood at the party. My fingernails scrape against the stones behind me as if I can claw my way out of this. "What does drinking Bastian's blood have to do with our relationship?"

"When I partake in a human's blood, the connection gives me glimpses into their mind." He's so close that our bodies are almost touching, making me uncomfortable. If I shift to the left or to the right, he'll only shadow me. "Young Bastian has an extremely dirty mind when it comes to you, Maribel."

A sheen of sweat runs along my neckline and over my palms. It is cold, making me shiver. The vampire senses my fear, lowering his head to pepper my neck with harmless tugs of the skin, first with his lips and then his fangs.

I'm not ready for this.

"What's in Bastian's mind?" I ask, hoping to stall the inevitable. "The male species can be so hard to read at times, so you must tell me."

Sterling lets out a light chuckle, moving back slightly to look me in the eyes. "Oh, dear mouse, the human male is not hard to read at all when women are concerned. My venture into his head involved his desire for you and a wish he has for that beautiful mouth of yours." One of his long fingernails taps my lips, sending a chill down to my toes. "I'll leave it at that. But I am curious as to whether you reciprocate his feelings." Without warning, he leans in, piercing the skin of my neck with his fangs.

My hands fly from the wall to his shoulders, trying to push him from me, but it's no use. He's too strong. I go limp in his arms, confident he will drain every ounce of blood from my body. As my eyelids flutter closed, vivid images fill my head, but I'm not sure if I'm creating them or if the vampire is planting them. Either way, through the excruciating pain, an erotic panorama emerges.

It is evening. Fireflies flick through the lower boughs and bushes, searching for their mates. The dark mouth of a cave opens before me. Moans echo through it, but I'm not sure if they're from creatures, ghosts, or simply the wind. I clutch my arms to my chest and realize I'm naked, exposed to whatever lurks in the cavern.

A figure emerges, large and imposing, dark hair loose at his shoulders. I shield myself behind a tree, not wanting him to see me like this—with my heart exposed. The body I've dreamt of for many evenings fills me with shyness and trepidation.

"Don't hide yourself from me, Mari," Bastian says as a tear slips down my cheek.

I'm not ready for him to see the deepest parts of me.

And I'm so sleepy. Curling up into a ball in the grass sounds like a tremendous idea.

"Mari. Come to me." He walks toward me, every inch of his loveliness on full display.

If I wasn't so damn tired, I'd drink him in, admiring his perfection. My eyelids droop as I desperately grasp at memories of his body that I've imprinted from our times together. Strong shoulders, the planes of his chest holding the beloved tattoo we share, narrowing to his stomach, where a patch of dark hair leads my mind's eye lower.

The pain radiating from my neck dulls as I lose myself in his arms, unsure of whose embrace holds me up. But then he drops me and my head knocks against something hard. I'm floating high above the First City in the clouds, finally getting the rest I need.

"Mari." A muffled voice comes from somewhere in the clouds. "Mari." A gentle hand shakes my arm, but my head hurts too much to open my eyes.

Go away. Can't you see I'm resting?

"You need to wake up." A splash of liquid hits my face, and I open my eyes in horror.

"What did you do that for?"

Evie kneels beside me. Her hair is a tangled mess of sweat

and dirt. Beneath her hairline, a jagged cut runs across her fore-head. "There isn't time to recover. We've got to leave."

I prop myself up on my elbows to take in the dungeon. Sterling was here with me minutes before—and he bit me. "Where's the vampire?"

"You've lost a lot of blood." She hands me her canteen. "Take a drink. I've got to carry you out of here in case he comes back."

I take a sip of the rust-flavored water and spit it out. "Ughh. It tastes like shit."

Instead of responding with her usual sarcasm, Evie wraps an arm around my waist and lifts me onto her shoulder like a sack of potatoes. "We don't have time for your princess tastes. Bastian and Gray can only hold the vamp off for so long."

I wiggle trying to free myself, feeling nauseous hanging upside down against her back. "I can walk."

She starts up the stairs as if I weigh nothing. Her grip around my thigh begins to ache. "You don't realize how serious this situation is."

Blood rushes to my head as she jogs up the stone steps.

"You lost a lot of blood. If we hadn't intervened, he would have killed you." A door near the top of the stairs creaks open, and we're in a hallway, our surroundings passing us at a dizzying speed.

Even with the discomfort of hanging over Evie's shoulder, my thoughts turn to my brothers. I'd watched Bastian kill the vampire in the meadow, but from what I know of Sterling, he is too powerful and cunning to be destroyed by ordinary means.

In what I consider an act of mercy, Evie shifts me into her arms and carries me like a baby. It's more comfortable but slightly more humiliating.

Sconces dimly light the hallway, which must run parallel to the city through the walls. It makes sense that Arazian would install safeguards against an attack on the city where he could avoid capture. When did Evie and Grayson have time to find the leader's escape route? They never cease to amaze me.

As we near a heavy black door at the end of the hallway, Evie sets me down. My legs shake, so I lean against the wall, not realizing how weak Sterling left me.

"Five stand guard outside." She removes a dagger from her boot and hands it to me. "Two males, two females, and a wolf." A jagged blade in her hand reflects the light from a nearby sconce. She nods to the weapon in my hand. "If I don't make it, don't hesitate to use the blade to defend yourself. You're better than you think, sis."

Sis? As in sister? That one three-letter word gives me all the confidence I need to make sure we both leave the city alive.

Evie inhales sharply before turning the handle to open the door. In the few seconds it takes the guards to register that it's not Arazian or Sterling at the threshold, my sister has buried her dagger into a guard's gut, shoving him to the ground. The other four watch, wide-eyed, but are quickly reaching for their weapons.

Before one of the female guards can draw her bow, I fling my dagger end over end, hitting her squarely in the chest. I rush forward, relying on adrenaline to keep me upright, and snatch my weapon.

Evie is engaged in hand-to-hand combat with two of the guards, utilizing leg sweeps and punches to knock them down. While she's occupied with the male, the other female reaches behind my sister and yanks her back by the hair. She screams out in pain.

The third guard walks slowly toward me before dropping to the ground on all fours, shaking his body and transforming into a wolf. He's a sandier color than the other two wolves I've encountered, but his teeth are just as long and sharp.

"You're the one they call a savior," the wolf growls, moving closer. "The one who will tear down this sanctuary so the humans and purebred Supes can live more comfortably." He's so close that his massive paw nudges my shoe. I glance down at the red heels Arazian gave me to wear to the dance before swallowing back the lump in my throat. "And I'm the one who will stop you."

Nearby, Evie's managed to put the woman who grabbed her hair into a headlock. In a swift move, she lifts her opponent and throws her into the other guard, sending them both over the edge of the cliff. She turns her eyes to us.

A snarl curls the wolf's lips as he lunges for me, knocking me to the ground and the dagger out of my hand. Images of Tanner locked beneath the werewolf when I first entered the wilderness pass through my mind. I brace myself to have my throat ripped out.

Shouts rise nearby as the wolf's teeth snap at my face. A sharp pain stings my cheek as I shove at the creature. The intensity of his growl vibrates through my entire body as he draws back to attack again. His stench is almost too much to take as I'm surrounded by a mass of heat and fur. I close my eyes, knowing I'm not strong enough to push the creature away.

Suddenly, with a shout, the air clears around me. I open my eyes to find Bastian wrestling the wolf beside me. With impossible speed, he removes a dagger from his boot and drives it into the wolf multiple times until it slumps to the ground.

I close my eyes again, this time out of exhaustion, ready to leave the First City behind.

CHAPTER FOURTEEN

Bastian

MARI SLEEPS IN MY ARMS. I hold a clean cloth to the deep gash in her forehead from the wolf's bite. But it's the two puncture marks in her neck that have me seething.

The vampire got away.

I wanted to rip his fucking head off and tear him limb from limb, but he was too fast. And he sensed this. He knows about the protectiveness I have over Mari and will use it against me with my father. There's no way we can wait until morning to leave. Arazian will never let me go willingly. It's too much of a risk now to stay any longer. And Tenny Rocks is the first step to unlocking a victory over the First City.

Exhaustion runs through every muscle in my body, but Mari needs a healer. Gray and Evie drag along beside me, both nursing their own wounds. Our escape didn't go as smoothly as we had planned thanks to the vamp.

"She's going to be ok." Gray smooths back a wisp of Mari's

hair, worry lines creasing his forehead. "There's no other option."

No, there's no other option. Because if Mari dies, I die. The damn prophecy ties us in every way possible. We're in this together.

We trudge through a stream, knee deep in water to keep the Miscretes from picking up our scent. It's not as cold as I had anticipated this early in the season, but it slows our progress and keeps me from deciphering the sounds I hear within the deeper folds of the forest.

"Where are we?" Mari's eyes remain half closed as she shifts in my arms.

With my intense focus on our surroundings, I didn't notice she was awake. I adjust my arm to draw her closer to my chest, thankful she's coherent enough to ask the question. "About an hour out of Tenny Rocks." I furrow my brow, not wanting to lay any of my current worries on her. "We'll have you with the healer in no time."

She touches the bandage on her forehead with her finger-tips. "It doesn't hurt too much."

"No, but those beasts carry all kinds of disease. It's best to have you checked out before we rally the people." I wink at her causing her cheeks to redden. At least some of her blood flow is returning. "Can't have the people thinking either of the saviors are weak. We must display dual pillars of strength."

She chews on her lip, sending all kinds of feelings through me. "What if they don't see it in me? I only learned to shoot an arrow a month and a half ago. One look at my twig arms and they'll shout 'fraud'."

She has come so far in the time I've worked with her—quicker than most students. I close my eyes and inhale before looking at her again. "Strength isn't always measured in muscles. It comes from the inside. Leaving your life in Avren, facing a world you never dreamed of before, and changing your worldview takes more mental fortitude than most use in a lifetime."

"I'd still rather have the muscles when convincing a crowd of strangers." She squeezes my bicep and smirks. "You're like a walking advertisement for the cause." Her gaze rests on the dark recesses of the woods, but it's difficult to read her expression through the shifting shadows. "The Miscretes still haunt me."

My boots slosh through the murky stream. We're several yards behind Evie and Gray, both with their trained eyes watchful for Arazian's creatures. "I know they do." Seeing the monsters as the enemy is easier for me. To reach my goals—trying to save Lyden, taking down the First City—I must dismember as many of the creatures as possible. Then I think of Evie and Levi. What if their families can be saved? Or... My heart sinks. What if I've already killed them? "There's someone in Tenny Rocks who might know the answer, but he's difficult to track down."

"Not a people person?" She shifts in my arms. "I think I can walk now."

"Are you sure?" I grant her wish and release her slowly into the stream. It's not the best reintroduction to walking after being bitten by both a vampire and a werewolf.

She clutches my shirt to steady herself as she sloshes through the water.

"The person I speak of is a shifter, a very rare condition in these parts, though I've heard it's common beyond the great sea.

I first met Xeno when I was thrown out of a tavern after a drunken brawl. It was over a woman I can't recall and really don't care to. Huddled in the corner of an alleyway, I emptied the contents of my stomach, facing the lowest moment in my life. After the deaths of my family, drinking and fighting were medicinal. A scrawny rat scurried over the dirt path in my direction. It smelled my puke, probably sensing the pathway to an easy meal. As it drew close, I kicked at it with the heel of my boot. "Get away."

Without warning, the rat's body grew until a full-blown man stood before me, just as skinny as the rodent. "Do I look desperate enough to fill my belly with your secondhand slop?" He scrunched his nose as he glanced at the remnants of my dinner. "The tavern tosses its leftovers when the night is through."

Never having seen a shifter before, I've backed myself against the clapboard wall, fearful. "You can change into a rat?"

"How else do you think I get my expansive knowledge of this world?" The man crouched to look through the sack I'd dropped when he startled me. He removed a half-eaten loaf of bread and ripped a piece off with his teeth. "Remain hidden. That's what I say. You learn all types of juicy secrets." He held up a finger, still on his haunches. "For example, the men who attacked you in the bar coordinated it hours before."

What? I'd bought the lady a drink. The bartender kept the drinks coming, refilling my mug at least ten times. Eventually, a man pushed his way through the crowd of patrons, claiming the woman was his fiancée and drew back his fist. I was too wasted to use my usual reflexes, and his fist grazed my cheek before I grabbed his neck and had him in a headlock. That's when they descended on me. Three, maybe four men knocked me free from my attacker, punching and kicking me onto the floor, but at that point, I was too drunk to care.

A man's voice rose above the shouts of the onlookers, angry and authoritative. Strong arms lifted me from the floor and the next thing I knew, I was on the ground outside the tavern, alone and wasted. I had only assumed the other men were defending their buddy from a stranger who had him in a headlock. A coordinated effort didn't seem likely.

I looked at the rat man. "I doubt it."

"Have you checked your sack? Still have the credits you

came in with at the start of the night?" He nudges my bag with his toe. "They were all in on it—the woman, the bartender, the five men. A gang that scouts out strangers to the village."

With one eye on the man, I lifted my bag and rifled through it. He was right. My pouch of credit was gone. "How do I know you didn't take my money when you stole my lunch?"

"As a rat, I live like a king. I fill my belly with an abundance of leftovers and my mind with a wealth of knowledge. I didn't steal your credits." He leaned against the wall and crossed his arms. "The name's Xeno, and I've got the names and addresses of your attackers."

That was four years ago. Other than my last trip to Tenny Rocks with Mari on the way to Frostacre, I've always made time to seek out my friend when visiting. If anyone has information about how to transform a Miscrete back into a human, besides the leaders of the First City, it's Xeno. "You could say he prefers the company of rodents."

Mari loosens her grip on my shirt. Even in the pale light of dawn, I can see her wide eyes. "What's that supposed to mean?"

"It means he's a shifter. That's how he gets his information— hiding in the walls and beneath the floorboards of residences. The more knowledge he gains, the more he knows how to be at the right place at the right time." I often wonder if his abilities as a shifter outshine my strength in a secretive, non-public way.

"I'd love to shift into a fly and attend a closed-door Council meeting in Avren." She hangs her head slightly, as if imagining the things she'd hear. "No one in the land holds more secrets than Lady Raven."

Her name makes me shudder. I've never met my birth mother, but after her cruelty to Mari and Gray, she'd better hope she never meets me. "How are you feeling about seeing your father?"

She drags her lower lip between her teeth, and it all but shatters me. This will be difficult for her, but if her mother's letter holds any truth, the man has the same end goal as we do.

"I'm nervous." She takes my hand, and it feels so small in mine.

I want to protect her, not only from the monsters—both human and otherwise—but from her demons. She's lived too long thinking she wasn't good enough for her father to stay. That he didn't want her. She knows otherwise now, but her past thoughts have done their damage. "I'll be with you. After what happened to your mother, he'll be thankful you're alive."

"What if I'm not enough? When he left, I was so young. With the prophecy, he'll expect a warrior to walk through his door." She touches the puncture marks on her neck. "And I know you say I have strength from within, but without the three of you, Sterling would have drained me dry."

I close my eyes, wanting her to feel the worth I see in her. When I open them again, I see smoke rising from among the trees ahead. We're almost there.

Evie and Gray pick up their pace, more than likely spurred on by Gray's empty stomach. Early morning in Tenny Rocks means a full breakfast at the tavern. The singular focus, along with the sounds of the water, make me miss the sinister plot brewing in the forest.

Movement on the edge of the forest draws our attention. Hundreds of Miscretes step out from behind the trees, heading in our direction.

I unsheathe a sword from my belt and hold it in front of me. "Go, Mari. Get to Tenny Rocks."

She hesitates as the swarm of monsters approaches. Gray and Evie run along the grass beside the stream, weapons drawn.

"Get to Tenny Rocks," Evie says as she hands Mari a dagger. "Find a woman named Freya. She'll hide you until we get there."

Evie's directive seems to hold more clout than mine. Mari

steps out of the water and rushes along the bank and thankfully doesn't look back.

The three of us face the Miscretes. We scramble onto the far riverbank, and Evie draws back her bow, the first arrow hits its target as one of the beasts falls to the ground. What if it was Lyden? Are we really facing the enemy? What if we can save them?

"Stop!" My voice echoes through the small valley. "Don't kill another Miscrete." It goes against everything I've stood for in the past. Unfamiliar tears sting my eyes. "I won't ask you to do this anymore, Evie."

She holds her bow at shoulder height, but it shakes slightly as if she's fighting an internal battle. "They'll follow us into the village. They obey Sterling's direct orders."

I toss my sword onto the gravel, where it lands with a loud clang as I move closer to the Miscretes.

This startles the ones near the front of the pack, who release low growls, pushing at the others. More than likely, my plan won't work, but it's worth a try.

"We will not harm you. You are a human, not a monster." My voice is clear, hiding the fear I feel deep within. If they sense it, all is lost. "Sterling uses you as an end to his means. He doesn't care how many of you die because he'll just create more." I make eye contact with a male creature near the front of the pack. "We intend to help you."

The eye contact seems to help because he steps forward. "You are the enemy of the First City. You must be eliminated." There's something familiar with his voice.

I hold up a finger. "Or we could find out how to reverse what has happened to you, and you could help us defeat the real enemy." My legs shake. The sword lies ten feet away, and I have no recourse should the swarm decide to attack.

Another Miscrete steps forward, this one slightly taller than the rest, possibly the leader. "There is no cure. Sterling made sure of this."

"Lyden." I look back to the first Miscrete, sure I recognize him. "We're your friends. Mav, Laurel, and your father are back in the Grove. Let us help you so you can go back to them."

Puss oozes from his eye and most of his dark hair is gone, most likely from pulling it out. He's missing two fingers on his right hand, and like any other Miscrete, open sores cover his skin. He stumbles forward, landing one foot in the river. "Liar. Sterling warned us about you. That you're the Prince of Lies."

"Nothing is further from the truth." I take two steps toward the river, not taking my eyes from my friend, no matter how painful it may be.

I glance back at Evie and Gray. They walk forward to stand beside me.

"The ancient fae prophecy declares that two saviors will rise up to defeat both the First City and Avren." Gray looks at me before kneeling with the hint of a smirk on his lips. "One of the two saviors stands before you. Bow to him, let him help you, or be destroyed."

Evie follows suit, kneeling to my left. It is both mortifying and empowering. I'm not a king, just the son of simple farmers. My birth parents mean nothing to me.

The Miscretes, including Lyden, look to the one I assume is their leader. The one who believes there is no cure. He's missing an ear and half his nose, but through the window of his eyes, I can still see his soul. It's the one thing Arazian is not able to take away from these creatures with his wicked experimentation. There's true fear behind his green irises that's desperate for rescue.

Without warning, the leader drops to his knee and bows his head, shocking me enough that I stumble back a step. The others do the same, either following his lead, or miraculously believing that somehow, I can save them. My body continues to shake, no longer out of fear but with the groundbreaking potential of my position. It humbles me to the point that my legs almost give out.

I rest a hand on Gray's shoulder, encouraging him to stand. "Together we will find a way to reverse what the vampire has done to you. Then together, we'll defeat the evil forces of the First City."

Instead of the rousing applause I expect from my speech, the Miscretes stand and return to the woods with a flurry of grumbles. Most of them are just following their leader.

"That was a hell of a risk you took." Gray lifts my sword from the ground and hands it to me. "If they'd ripped you to shreds, Evie and I wouldn't stand much of a chance."

"Thanks for saving my neck, brother." I wrap an arm around his shoulder, pulling him close before using my knuckle to give him a noogie. "The whole savior spiel was effective, though underwhelming on my part."

As we walk beside the stream to Tenny Rocks, Evie says, "You were born for the role of the savior of our world. Don't ever let me hear you downplay yourself again, or I might have to kick your butt."

CHAPTER FIFTEEN

Mari

MY HEART RACES as I reach the outskirts of the village. While I had planned to follow Evie's orders to find Freya, I've decided to seek out my father instead. This has me filled with uncertainty and almost as much fear as facing the Miscretes. I have so many questions to ask him about our past and about the man he's become. The man the wilderness calls the Northern Duke.

In the early morning light, I take a moment to catch my breath in an alleyway, running my fingers through my hair. I stoop to wring out my pant legs. The water forms tiny streams through the dirt path. Pain radiates from the bite mark on my neck as I touch the two concentric circles with my fingertips, instantly brought back to the dream Sterling planted in my head. My face flushes with the memory, not wanting to dwell on it. Instead, I step out from the alleyway and search the almost empty village square for the local tavern. A stranger of my father's stature with red hair and a beard shouldn't be difficult to find. People talk in places like Tenny Rocks.

The door to the Rusty Plate squeaks on its hinges as I push it open and cross the stone threshold. Like other taverns I've visited, it contains tables, chairs, and a bar where patrons can sit on high stools. Ornate wallpaper, lace doilies, flower vases on the tables, and padded pink seat covers stand out as differences from those establishments. As I had hoped, people dot a few of the tables around the tavern, eating breakfast. It's nothing like the crowd Levi and I faced in Rumsford, but I might pick up a lead.

A large woman with blonde curls sticking out from under her white mobcap rounds the corner carrying a tray of delicious smelling food. "Sit wherever you'd like, hun. I'll be right with you." With ease, she doles out the plates of food on her tray to three men and a woman sitting at a round table.

I scoot onto a stool at the bar and close my eyes. This is not what I want. As a savior, I should be strong enough to fight alongside my comrades, not shuffled off to safety. And here I am, worried sick about what's happening to them. If I can get my father and his forces on our side, I might add to the worth I bring to our team.

"What can I get you?" The blonde woman stands on the other side of the bar with her hands on her hips. She's applied color to her eyelids which is a practice I've only seen in Avren. Is she an Undesirable?

"Uh… I'm actually looking for someone." I brush some of my hair over my neck to hide my scar. "A man they call the Northern Duke."

The woman's lips fall into a straight line. "Oh, honey. Why do you want to get yourself involved with him? I hear he conspires with the First City. That's why he's out here and not back in the Murky Swamps where he belongs."

I don't want to provide too much information to someone I'm not sure I can trust. "Heard he's looking for recruits. Thought I'd see if I have what it takes."

Her eyes rake over my tunic before landing back on my face. "I thought he preferred his soldiers a bit... larger." She takes a mug out from under the counter and pours steaming liquid into it from a kettle before setting it on the counter in front of me. "Take my advice. The man uses people to advance his own demented schemes. Run the other way."

I take a sip of coffee and set the mug down. "I still want to find him."

She shakes her head and lets out a nervous laugh. "To each her own but here in Tenny, we live and let live. It's better not to get involved in the politics of the cities." She wipes down the counter with a rag, pausing to look me square in the eyes. "But if you insist, word has it that he's staying in the Ranis Cabin on the outskirts. Comes into town to meet with other riffraff." She begins to wipe again. "Like I said, I stay out of it and mind my own business."

The Ranis Cabin. I commit the name to memory while I finish my mug of coffee, leaving a credit on the counter to pay for it as well as the information.

More people fill the streets as I exit the Rusty Plate into the main square of the village. A man leads a horse pulling a wagon of metal pots that clank as he hits potholes in the dirt. Two women beat laundry hanging on a line with paddles, sending billows of dust into the air. A young boy with a scowl on his face carries an empty metal bucket to the well in the center of the square. No one carries a weapon. No one seems the least bit concerned about the two cities looming over them like monsters ready to swallow them whole.

I approach a woman propping the front door to her shop open with a chair. "Excuse me, can you tell me how to get to the Ranis Cabin?"

She spins around, the heavy skirt of her dress almost knocking me down as she appraises me with disbelief I received from the woman in the tavern. "The Ranis Cabin? Now why in the world would you want to go there?"

Do I really need to state my intentions every time I ask for directions?

"I'm to meet a friend there after breakfast." I peek into her shop, hoping my feigned interest might bend her sympathies my way. Until I see what she's selling. "You sell journals?"

"Journals, books, writing instruments... Plenty to catch the eye of a young scholar. Have you attended university?" The woman steps into her store, and I follow, no longer feigning my fascination with her stock.

"Me? No." I prefer not to tell others about my Undesirable status. While the people of Avren consider everyone in the Unseen and the wilderness to be an Undesirable, a direct exile from the city might garner more disdain. "But I pursue reading and writing. They hold a special interest for me." I miss my shelf at home in my room with the books Bastian collected for me.

While the woman arranges displays on a counter, I browse the titles, not wanting to waste too much time. But curiosity holds me captive. The books in Avren's library were carefully selected to advance the views of the Council and what they wanted the Citizens to believe. Here, there is a wider selection of ideas. My finger runs along the spines—*The True Benefits of Supes on our Society*, *A Farmer's Almanac*, *The Mixture of Species*, and *Redeeming the Undesirable*.

"Follow the stream to the south past the miller's bridge. The cabin has blue shutters." The shopkeeper doesn't look up from the cloth she folded on the counter. "I assume you know who is staying there to ask me such a question."

Without answering, I lift a brown leather journal from its spot among other books in a basket. I trace the soft skin with my fingertips and read the inscription. "You bring light into darkness. Is this a motivational phrase?"

"Hmm...?" The woman turns to see the journal in my hand.

"In a way. That's an old saying used to describe the saviors." She laughs and lifts the book from my hand. "There are some who believe that two warriors will rise from the cities to free the wilderness from bondage. Over the years, writers have penned books and books about them." She traces the cursive script with her fingernail. "Thought I'd do my part to spread the propaganda."

"And what if they're real?" I say, absentmindedly, trying to grasp the idea that I'm included in any book.

"Then I say you're a silly-headed girl who needs to find herself a husband and get your head out of the clouds." She snatches the journal out of my hand and tosses it into the basket. "Nothing like a half-dozen children to knock down your romantic notions."

"How much for the journal?" I remove the pouch of credits Evie gave me from my pocket.

"Five credits." She raises an eyebrow, most likely assuming I could never afford it.

As I'm digging through my bag for the right amount, I see someone else enter the store out of the corner of my eye.

The shopkeeper stops what she's doing but remains behind the counter, keeping the barrier between herself and the customer. "Can I help you, sir?"

"I'm looking for a book on Miscretes," a deep voice says.

I freeze with my back turned to the man. It's a tenor I know within the recesses of my soul. His laugh, his stories, and the soft melodies he'd sing to me before I'd fall asleep made me adore him until he left us behind.

"Nasty creatures." The woman walks over to a shelf and pulls out a book. "I'd stay away from them if I were you." Her voice trails off as if recognizing the man in her shop for the first time.

I breathe in deeply, knowing I can't keep my back turned forever. I must face my past to move on with my future. When I turn, he's digging through the books in the basket. My father was always a reader, a trait he passed on to me. His red hair has grown out and is tied at the nape of his neck with a ribbon. He no longer wears the distinguished clothes of a Council member in Avren but a long-sleeved cotton shirt, leather trousers, and boots. He carries a crossbow strapped to his back.

The shopkeeper moves behind the counter again, the skin on her face pale as the curtain billowing in the window. Maybe she thinks the Northern Duke might shoot her instead of paying for his purchases.

"Daxon Barellis." I state his name aloud as if it might add validity to our reunion.

He turns his attention away from the woman and looks at me. A flicker of pain crosses his eyes as he desperately searches mine for an answer. The lump in his throat bobs as he drags his lower lip between his teeth. "Maribel?"

No longer caring that he left us or that we have an audience, I throw myself into my father's arms and cry. His chest heaves beneath my face as he smooths my hair.

Resting his hands on my shoulders, he moves me away slightly. "You look so much like your mother." He shakes his head, tears still glistening in his eyes as his hand slides down to mine.

"I didn't think I'd ever see you again." Here, in a place I consider relatively safe, the warmth in his eyes almost undoes me. I associate my father with Avren and the apartment we shared with my mother. I associate him with the Council. With the pain of losing him to the wilderness.

"Come, we have much to discuss." With a quick glance at the shop owner, he tugs on my hand.

"Wait." I release his hand, find the five credits in my pouch, and lay them on the counter before taking the journal from the basket. "Thank you." I nod to the woman who clutches the counter as if she's holding on for dear life.

Outside, I stuff the journal under one arm and take my

father's hand again. "What have you done to earn yourself such a reputation?"

He lets out a hearty laugh and glances around. "Made up a bunch of shit. Keeps people out of my real business."

"And what is this real business?" I can't imagine anything more important than his family. In his absence, my mother died and the Council exiled me. It's not like he'll get a father of the year award.

"Getting you back." He squeezes my hand. "Mission accomplished."

"You created the persona of the Northern Duke to rescue me from Avren?" It seems far-fetched. Why work with Arazian to plot the takedown of the other city?

"No, I…" His voice catches and he hangs his head. "There are much bigger forces at work than what I can handle as a simple man, Maribel. If you haven't noticed, the wilderness is a dangerous place. You need to find your foothold or greater powers will drag you down."

This is true. The Kindred Few saved me.

"When Raven exiled me to the wilderness for speaking against her harsh rules, I was devastated. She separated us and later used our connection as a weapon." He scratches at his nose with his free hand, a nervous habit. "As I gained more and more followers as an alternative to the cities, Raven grew nervous. She sent orders to cease and desist our preparations or she'd have to take drastic measures. If I have to say one thing about the Council leader, it's that she's not a liar."

"And the drastic measures?" A lump grows in my throat.

"She unleashed a sickness from her lab on the wilderness and then on her own citizens, or at least any she suspected of disloyalty." He leads me over a bridge to a cabin with blue shutters. "My people were able to get one protection capsule into the city and slipped it into your drink. It saved your life. People died finding that capsule, but they knew your life was worth saving."

"And then Raven exiled me, assuming a Supe would finish the job for her." Forces worked behind the scenes to protect me, adding another layer of guilt for the people who died.

My father unlocks the cabin. "A close confidant told me about the Kindred Few living near the Grove. To keep up the façade of the Northern Duke and my close ties with Arazian, I needed to find a safe place to hide you until it was safe for us to be together." He rests an arm on the doorframe. "Listen, I know this is a lot. Your exile wasn't a random following of the laws by the Council. Raven knew, not only that you were my daughter but a prophesied savior. You've already survived two assassination attempts."

It all makes my head spin. When Lady Raven sent me to the wilderness, it was a death sentence. But to know she unleashed the sickness as a weapon against my father is almost too much. "And it's safe now?" I rest my hand on the doorframe where his had been moments earlier before I follow him into the cabin. It's tidy, the way my parents always kept our apartment in Avren. Two twin beds sit a few feet apart, one with a bag on the end of it. Dishes are drying in a rack beside the sink. A table with two chairs rests against the far wall, clear of any clutter.

"It's imperative now." He holds his hand out to a chair at the table, so I settle in, ready to hear my father out. Not sitting himself, he crosses his arms. "You are one of the two saviors destined to destroy the First City and Avren. With his son in his possession, he believes he can control both of you." He flips the other chair around close to me and leans in. "Why would his son have any influence over you?"

My heart flutters in my chest. In finding my father, I've barely thought about what the others are going through with the Miscretes. I chew on my lip, unsure of how much I should reveal. It's an awkward teenage-daughter-and-father conversation. "He's the other savior, and I..." I don't know how else to put it. "I love him."

"You love Arazian's son?" He closes his eyes and exhales. When he opens them again, they drill into me like I've just stayed out past a curfew. "Do you understand who we're dealing with, Maribel? The man is as crazy as they come. I've had to lie through my teeth to keep him on my good side. If we help him take down Raven, he'll set up a regime stricter than the one in place now."

I drag my fingernail along the woodgrain of the table. "His son is nothing like him. In fact, he's only known his birth father for a short time. He was raised by a good family in the wilderness."

"That doesn't mean he hasn't inherited the man's ludicrous tendencies." He runs his fingers through his beard. "He can't be trusted."

"I trust him with my life." I shove back in the chair, knocking it over, and cross the room, not sure where I'm going. "Bastian Hale has more invested in this resistance than anyone I know and would never betray the Kindred Few."

He folds his hands on the table, his reddish hair showing strands of gray peppered throughout. The weight of what he's endured is apparent in the bags beneath his eyes. "I've lived long enough in this world to know that even the most trustworthy have their limits."

CHAPTER SIXTEEN

Bastian

SIXTEEN TIMES.

I can count on my fingers and toes the number of times I should have died but by some miracle survived. It's like some divine force protects me from the inevitable. As much as I put myself in harm's way, I'm here to stay.

For now.

Evie's friend Freya lives in an apartment on the second floor of a clapboard building in a section of town called the Washout. Ten years ago, a flood wiped out half the town, leaving behind only the stone structures. Everything made of wood floated away with the rushing waters of the river. And instead of learning their lesson, the people rebuilt in the quickest way possible, leaving the town susceptible to another cataclysmic disaster.

A stair creaks beneath my weight as we climb to the second story, passing two flats along the way. The number *24* hangs on the door with the *4* hanging slightly askew.

Evie knocks twice and stuffs her dagger into her jacket. "Wait to be invited in. She's not fond of men."

Gray rolls his eyes. "It's not like Freya's on my list of top ten humans either. We're collecting Mari and leaving."

The door cracks open, and a hazel eye peeks out, flicking from one of us to the other. "What do you want, Everleigh?"

"Did my friend Mari come by here?" she asks, sticking a toe into the opening of the cracked door. "I told her you'd help her out."

Freya snorts. "You think our childhood friend status makes us buddies until death do us part?" She narrows her eyes, never bothering to acknowledge Gray or me. "The Reckoning changed everything. I categorize my life into *BR* and *AR* now, and you definitely come before the Reckoning—a part of my life I'd care to forget about. And don't bother to tell me you did everything you could because I've heard that way too many times from the other survivors."

"I lost people too." Evie's jaw juts out as her eyes tear up. "Your brother was special, but they carried my sister off. And my parents..." She turns and barrels down the stairs, leaving us staring at Freya.

The woman snorts again and slams the door in our faces.

"You know what they say about women from Moss Ford." Gray elbows me as we walk beside each other down the stairs.

I remain quiet, knowing he'll tell me either way.

"Can't live with them, can't chop them up and bury them in your yard." Gray smirks.

I raise an eyebrow, not sure where this is going, and glad that Evie is nowhere in earshot.

"If you do, the other women in Moss Ford will hunt you down." He runs his fingers through his hair, then shakes his head. "I love Evie with everything in me, but the Reckoning did something to all of them."

"Do you talk about it?" My conversations with Mari about Avren help her heal.

"Never." He opens the door at the bottom of the stairs and lets me pass through. "She keeps it locked away in a closet, never to be discussed. The only time she's ever talked about it was when we passed through there to reach the Hale farm."

"Trauma can bring on intense memories." Just the mention of the Hale farm evokes vivid images of the night my family died. It's not a memory I like to revisit. "Where do you think Mari went?"

"Not sure." Gray crosses the square to the spot where Evie sits on the rock wall beside the fountain. "Maybe to a place you went on your date when we were here last?"

Evie remains quiet as Gray slips an arm around her back, pulls her close, and she lays her head on his chest. As much as my friend likes to talk, he has a silent understanding with his girlfriend and knows when to stay quiet.

"We went to get tattoos, to the river for the festival, to the armory, and..." My cheeks flame, conjuring our night by the pond. "And to this square. We could also check the inn where we stayed."

"It might help to ask around." Evie lifts her head, surprising me with how quickly she can come out of her funk. "If she had followed my directions, we'd be well on our way to Moss Ford by now."

"It's not Mari's fault." Gray stands and stretches his arms over his head. "Besides, Bastian wants to find his friend who might know more about the Miscretes. We need to assume that wherever our sister is, she's safe."

I remove a dagger from my jacket, letting it glisten in the sunlight of mid-morning. "I think we need to assume the oppo-site. Who knows where she is. Sterling may have dragged her back to the First City." I lean in close as I lower my voice. "We find Xeno but look for Mari along the way. He's not exactly well liked around here."

Surprisingly, it's not tough to find the rat. He sticks to the usual dark places with his kind. The bright sunshine exposes their secrets, so a dank watering hole down a less-traveled alley provides the right backdrop for sinister intentions.

Grumbles rise from the patrons as we open the door to the *Lucid Dream*, an unmarked tavern, intended for regulars only. Dim lantern light touches key spots in the room—the entryway, the bar, a pail in the corner used for urination. Otherwise, the booths sit in total darkness. On my previous visit, and according to conversations with Xeno, it's to provide privacy for backward deals, evil intents, and prostitution. This time, I only want to find him and get out of here.

"What do you want?" the bartender growls, handing a glass of brown liquid to a man with a black hood.

I leave Evie and Gray at the door and approach the bar. Stains cover the surface that appear to be someone's blood. "I'm looking for Xeno."

The man stands a head above me, built more like a bouncer than a bartender. His head's shaved bald and covered with tattoos of ancient symbols I can't decipher. A defected fae. Their long locks mean everything to them. "Rat boy. There's a human here to see you." He plops an olive into another drink he's poured. "Make it quick. I don't have a lot of patience today."

A figure emerges from a dark corner. He's wearing a brown robe with a hood over his head and carrying a pipe with a stream of smoke billowing out of it. He latches his arm in mine to shuffle me to a booth. Evie and Gray follow.

Beside me, Xeno's face glows in the light from his pipe. A jagged scar runs from his left eye to the corner of his lip. "I told you not to come here. What do you want Bastian?" His blood-shot eyes dart to my companions.

"Don't worry about them." I shift in the booth, giving my

attention to Xeno. "I need any information you may have on Miscretes."

"There was a horde of them moving this way early this morning. Heard they turned back for some reason." Xeno takes another puff off his pipe, sending an unnatural smell in my direction. "Sterling on your tail?"

I drum my fingers on the table, knowing I'll have to pay for the information I need. Digging into the pocket of my jacket, I remove a healthy bag of credits. Xeno's eyes widen when I plop it on the table and shove them in his direction.

"I need an antidote or a lead on who might have it." Most people assume the change is permanent, so I'm rolling the dice that Xeno's even heard talk of a reversal.

"Do you hear what you're saying?" He sets his pipe on the table and leans closer to me. "They're monsters, Bastian. No longer human."

"Bullshit," I call his bluff. With Arazian controlling this portion of the land, creatures like Xeno live in peace. They're free to do whatever they want without regulation. The Council in Avren doesn't bother to pull the riffraff into their well-oiled Undesirable machine. It's too risky to bring this type into the city. "Tell me what you've heard"—I close my hand around the money—"or miss out on three hundred credits."

"Three hundred?" Saliva dribbles from his lip. "Where does an orphan like you get that kind of money? You dealing in the underground, Hale?"

"There are many who believe in our cause. Ones who donate credits to help us succeed." I rest my elbow on the table and pitch forward, done playing games. "Tell me what you know about the Miscretes."

"Not here." His eyes flick to my brother and sister. "And not in front of them."

"Anything you can tell me, you can tell them." I'm willing to change venues, but isolating myself from Evie and Gray isn't

smart in a place like this. "Meet us by the dock tonight." I slide
out of the booth and tip my chin to Xeno. "Don't disappoint."

"YOU HAVE any reason to believe he won't be there?" Evie asks as
we walk through the alley to the village square.

I'm focusing my thoughts on Mari and finding her before we
meet Xeno tonight. "Huh?" I shake my head. "Um… no. He's a
man of his word. Some call him a dirty rat, which is understandable, but he's never failed me."

In the square, I scan the crowd for Mari's auburn hair,
wondering if she got lost looking for Freya's apartment. With a
bit of asking around, she should have easily found it. Unless
something distracted her.

"We need to find the Northern Duke." I quicken my pace
through the crowd, convinced that if I find him, I'll find Mari.

"You're talking crazy, Bastian." Gray jogs to keep up with me.
"Unless you think the Duke wants her for her savior status. It
seems every other leader around here does."

"The Northern Duke is Mari's father." I stop to let my words
sink in. It's a lot.

Gray grips his hair and glances at Evie who appears
unmoved by this revelation. "You knew this too?"

"Mari talked to me recently." She walks between us. "There's
no way I'd have considered working with the guy before she
filled me in. Maybe we misjudged him."

"We can't keep secrets from each other." Gray takes on his
older leader role, crossing his arms. "This is mission-critical
information."

"It wasn't our secret to share." Although he's older, it doesn't
mean I have to do everything Gray says. "She revealed it when
she was ready. I still feel guilty about letting you know now, but

it's the only way for you to understand why I think that's where she's located."

"This changes everything." Gray marches ahead and spins to face us. "There's real hope of having the Northern Duke's forces help us defeat Arazian. We might not need the Miscretes."

"We need the Miscretes." Evie glares at him.

He holds his hands in front of him as if she might attack. "Ok, ok, we need the Miscretes. But you must admit that having a former Avrenian Council member on our side flips our odds."

"Who says he's on our side?" In my brief encounter with Dax, he met with Arazian to talk about their plans to attack Avren. "We know nothing about his relationship with the Dark King before they were exiled. Perhaps he has every intention of working with the First City."

"He's her father." Gray stumbles over a rock causing several women to laugh as he lands on his ass.

I lend him a hand to help him up, drawing him close. "And Arazian is my father. Not like that made much of a difference."

We stop at several stands set up to sell wares from blankets to bread and ask about the Northern Duke. Although the keepers have heard he's in town, they don't know of his whereabouts.

We leave the bakery stand with a fresh loaf of bread to share, and a younger man chases after us.

"Wait!" he calls. "You said you're looking for the Northern Duke?"

"Yes," Evie says, hands on her hips. "Do you know him?"

"No, but I know where he's staying." The man flashes her a smile, lifting his eyebrows. "The name's Billy."

"I didn't ask for your name." Evie keeps a frown firmly planted on her lips. "Just give us the information." My sister is an expert at turning down male attention. It's a wonder Gray ever wormed his way into her arms.

Billy removes his hat. "Uh... I've heard he's in the cabin past miller's bridge." He points to an opening in the buildings. "Follow the river to the south, and you'll be there in no time."

"Thanks for the info." Gray flashes him a smile then throws a possessive arm around Evie's shoulder. "We appreciate it."

I don't fault him. I'd do the same thing if I were in a similar situation with Mari. But we don't have time for games. If she's with her father, he might turn her back over to Arazian and Sterling. "Let's find this cabin."

CHAPTER SEVENTEEN

Mari

"I HEAD BACK to the Murky Swamps in the morning, and I'd like you to come with me." My father gathers supplies from the table —a tin cup, a map, a razor—and packs them in a canvas bag. "The information I gathered from Arazian on this trip is valuable to the resistance."

I watch him move about the room, adding more things to his bag. My heart's heavy as I think about losing him again. Closing my eyes, I release a stream of air through my nose. "Why did you leave us?"

He pauses and looks at me. His eyes no longer hold the light from our evenings together in our apartment. They're almost defeated and definitely beat down. "I'd never intentionally leave you, Maribel. I wasn't given a choice." He sits down in the chair beside me and rests a hand on my knee. "Raven had me tailed. She'd pieced together my connection with the resistance from outside the city. We stopped meeting in secret out of fear of her soldiers sniffing us out. Opposition from within the walls of

Avren held grave consequences. When my exile was imminent, I left on my own, escaping through the Council tunnels and finding my way to the resistance in the wilderness."

I don't look at him as he keeps his hand on my knee. It's familiar but in a fuzzy kind of way like a memory you can't fully recall.

"It was the hardest thing I've ever done. And if I'd known..." His voice catches. "If I'd known what Raven had planned to do, I never would have left. I would have found a way to fight. As much as I want to right the injustices in this world, your mother and you meant more to me than any cause."

It's his plea for forgiveness for leaving me behind and for not being there when my mother came down with the terrible fever. Many nights I held a cool washcloth to her forehead, hoping my efforts would help her fight. But it was too much.

"Do you trust me, Father?" I need to let the past live in the past. The question is who will Dax Barellis be today? "Because the Kindred Few are my family, and I trust them with my life. Yes, Bastian Hale is Arazian's by birth, but he's far from his child. The man I know and love would die protecting me. So, if you say you trust me, you must accept the other savior."

He strokes his beard. "Arazian wants to use you to lead the Miscretes into Avren. You're nothing more than a convenient pawn to him. It is true that if you both lead the charge, he'll have more at stake if he loses Bastian. I think the man cares about him in a warped kind of way. He's his heir to the throne."

"And what's your role in all of this?" I lean my elbow on the table, resting my head on my hand. It's different having an adult conversation with my father. Most of my life he's been the fun parent, dreaming up ways to entertain his daughter.

He sighs and stares out the window at the meadow beyond the stream. "To play the part of the cruel duke to the north. The wilderness is a game of chess, each of the kingdoms kept in check by the others. The fae in Frostacre don't bother the vampires in Crestone. The werewolves in Rumsford stay clear of the dragons living high in the Elmridden range. And all of them limit their hunting grounds to the wilderness, staying clear of both Avren and the First City." He turns back to me and tilts his head to the side. "Who wants to cross the Murky Swamps to a place called the Outpost of the Damned to hunt humans?" With his hands in front of him he wiggles his fingers. "My wicked reputation is spread through rumors I created myself. The people who follow me help fan the flames to the far reaches of the land." He removes rolled up paper from inside his jacket. "But to answer your question, my current role is to keep Arazian in check. You say he doesn't trust me, but I hold the battle plans right here."

I take the rolled papers from him, spreading them out on the table and holding the ends with a rock and a candlestick. It's a map of the land from the First City to Avren. Red stars mark key villages—Tenny Rocks, Moss Ford, and the Grove. "What important about the red star towns?"

"I'm to convince leadership that they should join Arazian and fight with us against Avren." He runs his finger along the river from Tenny Rocks, passing the other two villages. "The forces will travel by water." Shuffling the papers, he takes out another which appears to be the inside of a large structure. "These are the blueprints of Avren." He points to the aquifers entering the city at the base of the cliff walls. "Raven won't know what hit her."

"Don't guards oversee the water supply?" I circle an entrance with my nail. It doesn't make sense that a former Council member wouldn't know this.

"Yes, but they're not the most heavily guarded areas. The Council is more concerned about a direct attack. It's the way Avren has always played when it comes to battle. When I sat on the Council, we discussed ways to prepare our guards to fight in a war, one Raven highly anticipated. It was a war that Avren would initiate against the Undesirables and the Supes, not the other way around." He places both palms firmly against the table as his shoulders heave. "Arazian trusts me with this information because we were friends in Avren. It wasn't until Raven exiled him that he lost his grasp on reality. I'm here in Tenny Rocks under the pretense that I'm recruiting for the battle."

A knot grows in the pit of my stomach. This is a turning point. Either I trust Dax Barellis, or I turn away from him and work with the Kindred Few on my own. "We are here to recruit as well."

There's a heavy knock on the door. I stand and remove a dagger from my boot, holding it in front of me.

My father motions for me to hide behind the bed.

Crouched beside the mattress, I hear the door creak open. Seconds tick by as a trickle of sweat drips down my neck. If it's the Miscretes, will my father handle them alone?

"Where is she?" *Bastian.* He's alive.

I rush across the room and throw my arms around his neck, and my legs around his waist. Breathing him in, I look up to see Evie and Grayson behind him.

He runs a hand along my thigh, unfazed by our current company. "Why can't you follow directions?"

"Because then I would have missed my father." I wiggle out of his arms and hold a hand out to the other person in the room. "Bastian, Evie, Gray... meet Daxon Barellis, the Northern Duke."

My father bows his head to the other three with a tiny smile on his lips. "I must thank you for looking after my Maribel when I wasn't able. It means the world to me."

As outside observers, their initial unbiased impression of him is important. My judgement is clouded by years of this man tucking me into bed and telling me stories of heroes and fair maidens. He's the one who always saw beyond the walls of Avren into the possibilities of the world beyond, giving me glimpses of this place through his stories and music. But can the

Kindred Few see the magic in my father, or will they only see the intimidating duke the rumors make him out to be?

As the leader, Grayson holds a hand to my father. "Very pleased to meet you sir. I'm Grayson Elrod. My parents were Nor and Minny Elrod. Did you know them?"

"Very well." A warm smile lights my father's face. "They were wonderful people who understood what the world could be if we had the courage to change it. Nor introduced me to the resistance. I'm sorry we lost them so early into this battle."

"Thank you." Grayson purses his lips and his eyes glisten, showing an unfamiliar lapse in his usual upbeat personality. I've come to know a man who hides his sadness behind a wall of humor. "Dad always said there were good people on the Council. He never told me who they were, but he said that one day, we'd gain the momentum to set things right."

My father takes Grayson's forward nature as an in to approach Bastian. "Arazian's son and heir to the First City's throne." He holds his hand in front of him, sizing up the commander. "And the man my daughter has given her heart to —another man to take my place in her life. When we met in Arazian's drawing room, I didn't know your connection to Mari. If I had, I may have pummeled your face into the ground."

Bastian takes his hand, assessing him in his role as the commander of the Kindred Few, not as the man in love with his daughter. "We're in Tenny Rocks to recruit soldiers to take down the First City. Will you stand with us or against us?"

My father smirks and releases Bastian's hand. "The Dark Prince wishes to take down the kingdom he's only just inherited? Why do I find that difficult to believe?"

"Because you don't know him." Evie steps forward with the usual steel in her eyes. "Bastian stands for family, not titles. Loyalty, not power. From what I've heard from Mari, you used to uphold the same values."

"And you are?" Evie's raw edges don't faze my father. He must be familiar with other strong females in the wilderness.

"Everleigh Knox of Moss Ford." She keeps her arms firmly crossed. "And if you think of double crossing us, I'll be your worst nightmare."

My father chuckles. "I'll remember that."

"What happened with the Miscretes?" None of my companions appear to have any new scratches on them or tears in their clothing.

Bastian eyes my father then looks back at me, probably willing to trust him—for now. "Told them I was the savior and plan to find a cure."

"And they all bowed down to him. You should have seen it, Mari." Grayson elbows Bastian. "This guy's charisma is off the charts."

"And do you have any leads on this cure?" My father pours three glasses of water from an earthen pitcher and sets them on the table. "Because in my time in the wilderness, and with Sterling, I've only reached dead ends."

Bastian picks up a glass, drinking most of the water before responding. "We're getting close, I hope."

"Did you find your friend?" It might be crazy, but when my father says he's working against Arazian, I believe him. His insider knowledge of the First City can only make our side stronger.

Bastian glances at Grayson before answering. "We're meeting him tonight. I'm hoping he has more information because I'm not sure where to take this after him."

"Well, the sages of Shiloh are a waste of time. Grenderhol, who claims he knows all things up in the Elmriddens, is a sham. Couldn't tell me where to find my lost dagger, let alone how to reverse what Arazian's done to the Miscretes." My father rolls up the map of Avren and stuffs it into a side pocket on his bag. "The dead ends make my head spin. That's why I go to the source himself, but he doesn't trust me enough yet to release mission-critical information. If I prove myself, I might obtain more insider knowledge."

"I thought he gave you the battle plans," I say.

My father purses his lips, and his cheeks redden slightly. "I stole them." It's probably not the best thing to admit to your teenage daughter.

"And how do you intend to prove yourself? I thought you and the Dark King were buddies." Grayson leans against a doorframe. As our leader, he seems to hold a sense of responsibility for not guiding us down crooked paths.

"Arazian trusts me in a limited capacity. We agreed to work together, joining forces in the fight against Avren, but a man like that expects acts of loyalty. A key assassination, pulling forces from multiple cities..." His gaze falls on me. It reminds me of the way he looked at me the day before he left Avren. A hint of a smile crosses his lips and his eyes water as if he's proud of who I've become. "Convincing the saviors to lead the First City into battle."

"Does Arazian know I'm your daughter?" I think back through conversations I had with the Dark King, searching for any hints I might have laid.

"It states your father's last name in the prophecy." Evie sits on the edge of the bed, taking in every word Dax says and observing his body language. Her ability to read people astounds me. "If Arazian or Sterling have caught wind of what is in that document, they know."

"Besides the fae, we're the only ones who have read it for many years." Bastian rinses his glass in the sink.

"And where is this document now?" My father lifts his packed bag onto the table. Does he plan to leave me again?

My battered heart thumps against my chest.

"Right here in my pack." Bastian pats the side pocket of his bag before opening it. He reaches inside, coming up with noth-ing. "Shit! It was right here. Someone must have taken it."

"And if that someone was Sterling, the First City knows you are my daughter, and we'll have to work with that." My father straps his pack to his shoulders, looking ready for a long hike. "I have the cabin rented until tomorrow morning, so you may stay here tonight."

I stand, afraid of losing him again. "But…"

He steps forward and pulls me into a hug. "This isn't good-bye, Maribel." His familiar palm strokes my hair as tears sting my eyes. "You have your quest and I have mine. I must prove myself to Arazian, and I refuse to compromise my daughter." He kisses the top of my head. "I promise we'll see each other again." Releasing me, he nods to the others. "Take care of each other. Family is a beautiful thing." The door to the cabin opens, and then he's gone, taking part of my heart with him.

A warm hand rests on my shoulder. Bastian's breath against my skin reassures me. "He wants to prove himself to you. You're all he has left."

I don't want proof. All I want is my father back in my life. With the long road ahead, I'm no longer sure if that's possible.

CHAPTER EIGHTEEN

Bastian

THE WEATHERED DOCK reaches halfway across the river. Upside down dinghies sit along the bank, nets strewn over them. A single oil lamp on a pedestal lights the dock and surrounding area. Besides the evidence of the fishermen of Tenny Rocks, we are alone.

"Guess your buddy doesn't want the credits." Gray tosses a stone into the air, letting it flip several times before catching it again. "Did you really trust he'd show up?"

"He'll be here," I say as I walk out onto the dock and scan the opposite bank of the river. This town never had a very active nightlife. Not like Moss Ford. The night Mari and I went to the dance, we happened to be here for one of the two festivals they hold all year.

The dock creaks beside me, and Mari lays a hand on my elbow. She's remained quiet since we left the cabin, clearly upset about her father leaving. "Do you think he'll really have a lead on how to help the Miscretes?"

"Maybe. Maybe not. The real variable is whether he overheard the right conversation at the right time." I place a hand on top of Mari's, wanting to reassure her. She's had enough bad news for tonight. "If he doesn't know, he might point us in the right direction."

A hooded figure emerges from an alley close to the armory where Mari and I faced the Miscretes not that long ago. Xeno pushes the heavy cloak back, revealing his face.

Mari inhales sharply.

There's a reason he keeps the hood up most of the time. The twisted toll of transformation has left scarring and tufts of rat hair on his skin and along his elongated jaw. He's one ugly dude. But aesthetics aren't what I need him for.

"Do you have the credits?" Xeno's eyes flick to the small bulge in my jacket pocket. "You better keep to your end of the bargain, Hale."

"I've always been a man of my word." I jangle the bag in my pocket, enticing him with the sound of greed. "What do you know about changing the Miscretes back?"

He runs his fingers through the limited hair he has left on his head, draws on a bit of saliva in his mouth, and spits a wad of it onto the dock.

Evie groans and turns away.

"Never cared for women myself," Xeno mumbles more to himself than to us. His beady eyes take Mari in. "You going to turn your nose up at me too?"

Still holding onto my arm, she looks at him directly. "It is not my place to judge you, shifter. Where I'm from, the Council measures you not for who you are but for your outward appearance. My plan is to change this, beginning anew in the wilderness."

"You didn't tell me you travel with the other savior, Bastian." The shifter circles us, probably sizing Mari up. "Not the mighty warrior I anticipated when I overheard the talk of Maribel Windsong."

"How did you know?" She takes no offense at his words, letting her curiosity win out.

"You're the talk of the wilderness. Bastian Hale and Maribel Windsong are destined to free us from bondage. And look at you." His eyes widen as he holds up his hands to form a picture frame. "A very handsome couple. It's too bad one of you must destroy the other."

My heart races, not over his taunting but at the reminder of the end of the prophecy. Never in a million years would I hurt Mari. When I heard it the first time, it was easy to push that aside and focus on the part about working together. But as much as I try to blot it out of my memory, it's still there haunting my subconscious.

"Tell us what you know about the Miscretes." Evie pushes her red braid over her shoulder and removes an arrow from her quiver. "I'm done with the stalling."

"You travel with interesting folks." Xeno scurries behind me in a very *rat-like* motion. Peeking out from behind my shoulder, he hisses at Evie. "All in good time."

"We don't have time." Evie taps the arrow against her palm. We should have left her in the cabin. Unlike Gray, her negotiation skills are lacking. "My sister could be alive, living in a deformed body, and you want to sit and talk like we're catching up on old times?"

I give Evie a wary look, not convinced I can keep her emotions from bubbling over. This means more to her than anyone here. "What have you heard, Xeno?"

He twitches his nose before scratching behind his ear. "Honestly, not a lot. News from the First City doesn't flow into the wilderness very often."

Evie's shoulders slump. I built this into a viable lead, and the shifter has done nothing but disappoint.

"But for three hundred credits, I'm willing to enter the city and see what I can find out. If I keep within the walls and sewers, I might overhear or see something." His eyes glisten in the lamplight as I remove the bag of credits from my jacket.

"I'll pay you half now and half when you return with usable information." Although we're on friendly terms, I don't trust anyone who works the black market to return after he's pocketed three hundred credits. "And by usable, I mean information on how we reverse whatever Arazian or Sterling did to the Miscretes."

Xeno nods his head, holding out his palm as I count the credits. "Meet me back here in a week's time at midnight."

"A week?" Gray pipes up, running his fingers through his hair. "We've got places to go and people to recruit. We can't hang around here for a week."

"We don't have to." I drop the remainder of the credits into my pocket. "We speak to the people of Tenny Rocks tomorrow then travel to Moss Ford and the Grove. It shouldn't take that long."

"I will see you then." Xeno turns, jogs along the riverbank, and suddenly disappears among the tall rushes lining the water.

"Where did he go?" Mari stands on her tiptoes to get a better view.

"Transformed." Evie stuffs the arrow back into her quiver. "I don't trust that man. A rat brings nothing but trouble—filth, disease, and the ick-factor."

"The ick-factor?" I raise an eyebrow, knowing exactly what she's talking about but wanting her to explain further. "Please enlighten us on whatever in the world you're talking about, dear Everleigh."

She swings around, whacking me in the shoulder with her quiver. "Imagine you're back on the Hale farm and your dear old dad hands you a shovel and asks you to muck the stalls. The slimy fresh manure he's asked you to shovel out is paradise in comparison to where that man's been as a rodent. The ick-factor."

"It's not like he can help it. He was born that way, right?" Mari looks to me.

"Some are born with the shifter genes while others develop them through magical processes. I don't think anyone would intentionally pick a rat as their animal of choice." I lead the others along the riverbank to the cabin. "Xeno's family lived in a land where the shifting gene is much more common so more than likely he was born that way."

Back in the cabin, I roll the spare mattress out on the floor, letting Gray and Evie take the bed. I snuggle under the quilt behind Mari, wrapping my arm low across her stomach and pulling her close. It's incomprehensible how protective I feel of this woman. I want to guard her heart, her emotions, and her body from harm. The interaction with her father had me on edge as I analyzed his every move. Betrayal by this man might crush her.

Her soft breathing tells me she's asleep. I let the rise and fall of her back lull me to an unconscious world as I dream of many tomorrows.

WE LEAVE the cabin at sunrise, hoping to find the best place to recruit soldiers for our battle. By midday, the taverns will be busy, but we're hoping for a bigger gathering.

"It's not like a lot happens here." Evie kicks a rock as we navigate another empty alleyway. "People go to work, take care of their families, and go to bed. They live to serve Avren like little worker bees. This is a waste of time."

Gray pinches her cheek before she can slap his hand away. "There's my optimistic ray of sunshine. We can't give up, Evie. If we need to canvas the taverns, we will. Losing our battle to the First City is not an option."

"And why are you so cheery all the time?" Evie's eyes flash with familiar fire, making me back away from her. "You've lost your parents to Avrenian guards, friends have turned against you, and now Levi's gone. What the hell do you have to be so happy about?"

Gray's lips settle into a straight line and his eyes no longer hold their usual humor. "Nothing. Absolutely nothing. But if I don't trick myself into believing everything will be alright, I won't be able to go on. It's my coping mechanism, you know that. I keep going because of what I have, not what I've lost." He takes hold of Evie's shoulders, forcing her to look at him. "You and Bastian and Mari mean everything to me. This is the reason I don't give up and keep fighting."

As we enter the village square a small crowd gathers around a younger man on a wooden box. He holds a red garment in his hand, waving it above his head as he speaks. The four of us squeeze in among the people listening to the man.

"And if you think the Council in Avren has your best interests in mind, think again." He hops down from the box and weaves through the crowd, stopping to look people in the eye as he emphasizes his points. "Lady Raven only cares about the wares we send to the city in taxes. She'll use your sons and daughters as numbers in her army if this conflict rises to war. It's time to wake up."

This man's doing the work for us. At least he's giving them a reason why. Now the Kindred Few must show them how.

"We're not soldiers, Phillip," a man holding a cage of chickens calls out. "The Council offers us protection in exchange for goods and services. It's not that bad living in peace far from Avren's gates."

"No, Sage, we're not soldiers. But I'm willing to lay down my fishing nets in exchange for a sword if it means protecting our way of life." Phillip looks earnestly from one villager to the next. "Just yesterday, three soldiers marched into our home and took my Katherine." He raises the red garment above his head. It appears to be a sweater. "Told my neighbors that Lady Raven needed a seamstress. You can imagine my shock when I returned home from a long day at sea."

"And what of the First City?" Gray marches forward and hops onto the box, facing the crowd. "How many of you have lost loved ones to Arazian?" He points to the three of us. "My brother and sisters have come here to recruit people to not only rise up against Avren but the First City as well."

"Do you have the means for this fight?" Phillip asks, reflecting the previous question from Sage.

"The commander is an expert in training warriors. He's worked with us and others in the Grove to prepare us for this day. In one week's time, we'll begin a training camp outside the village to prepare for the long battle ahead." Gray looks at Sage. "We want to see all your able-bodied people there. Maybe you're comfortable in your way of life, but what happens when your family member is dragged off to become a Miscrete?"

There's murmuring in the crowd, people turning to discuss this with their neighbors.

Sage steps closer to the box. "We've all lost someone to the First City and for too long we've accepted it as inevitable. Who are we to stand up to a magician and a powerful vampire?" He strokes the goatee on his chin, staring at the dagger attached to Gray's belt. "But maybe it's time."

Several voices rise from the crowd in approval of Sage's statement.

Phillip stands beside Gray, taking his hand and raising it above their heads. "Tenny Rocks won't stand by any longer. We fight!"

Cheers rise from the crowd as they look to me as the one who can save them from the cities. I can teach basics in a short amount of time, but it's the numbers we need. If we can turn the Miscretes before attacking the First City, it gives us even more of an edge.

Philip and Sage join us as the crowd disperses.

"We'll go door to door this week. I think we can get two to three hundred men and women before you return." Sage has really flipped his stance on fighting. Maybe my 'savior factor' affects more than just Mari. He stares up at me in awe as if I'm a king or Council member. "Can you join my family for dinner tonight? It would be an honor."

I look to the others who nod or shrug their shoulders. We had planned to set out for the Grove, but another day in Tenny Rocks might give Mari more of a chance to recover before setting out on the long road ahead. She's regained most of her strength and the gash from the wolf is slowly healing. Also, pretending to be the Dark Prince of the First City has taken more of a toll on me than I had originally thought. It was emotionally and mentally draining.

As we walk to the inn to rent a room, Mari takes my hand and draws in close to me. "Are you ok?"

I smile at the simplicity of her question. There's an entire realm of possibilities wrapped up in that one two-letter word— *ok*. It's not something I can answer truthfully. In the past week, I learned my birth mother and father are alive and control the two most powerful cities in the land. Not only that, but I am destined to destroy them. Am I *ok* with this? I'd rather bury my emotions inside. It's safer that way. "Why are you asking if I'm ok when you're the one who was almost completely drained by a vampire?" I jostle her and kiss the top of her head. "How are you doing?"

"My strength is back." She spins out of my arm, still holding onto my hand, and flexes her muscles. Before coming back to me, she bites her lip as if contemplating whether she wants to bring up the next thing. "I miss my dad."

I pull her close again as we enter the inn. "We'll see him again. I promise."

Katiana, the innkeeper, is in the sitting room, dusting various knickknacks with a feather duster. Her dark hair sits in a ponytail on top of her head, and her face is red with exertion. The last time we visited, she wanted to kill me. I don't blame her. I beat up two of her brothers in a drunken brawl two years ago, leaving one with a broken arm and the other with a busted face.

She straightens from her hunched position when she sees us and rushes over to the counter, gathering all the keys and dumping them into a basket on the floor. "There's no availability. I hear there's a farmer on the outskirts who might have a barn you can sleep in filled with fresh manure. The men of the Kindred Few deserve much less. Where's the third?"

Very observant. I keep a straight face, looping my fingers through my weapons belt. "He was killed about a month ago. Too bad you didn't know him well enough to call him by his name."

Gray leans on the counter, his hands folded as if in a silent plea to pardon my rude comment. "Kat, darling. I didn't mean to stand you up for the dance. I came down with a terrible flu, and I was too sick to make it down here and let you know. Can you ever forgive me?"

"You're just like the rest of them." She narrows her eyes at Gray. "Nothing but a bunch of troublemakers preying on everyday people. You disgust me, Grayson."

He leans on one elbow, flashing what he calls his 'irresistible smile'. "Do I disgust you enough to turn down a date with me tonight? I'll take you out to a real nice place." His eyebrows raise. "Like the all-you-can-eat place by the wharf."

She absentmindedly fiddles with a key she's pulled from her apron. His bullshit is really getting to her. Never in my life have

I met a smoother talker than my brother. "Can you get us a bottle of wine?"

"I insist on it." Both elbows are on the counter as he flashes his dimple-filled smile and leans in close. "Got to loosen you up a bit, Kat. You're stuck in here all day serving customer after customer. It must be maddening."

I glance at Evie who sits on a high-back chair, flipping through a tabletop book. If it bothers her, she doesn't show it. We all know it's a way to get what we need, as much as an offensive tactic as breaking down a door to rescue a comrade. He's getting us a place to lay our heads.

"The penthouse is taken. You'll have to rent two rooms." She takes two keys from the basket and lays them on the counter. "What time will you meet me down here?" She bats her eyelashes at Gray.

"Seven on the dot." He taps her on the nose with his index finger, causing her to release a fit of giggles.

In the hallway outside our rooms, I pull Gray aside. "Do you plan to follow through with it?"

"Dinner. Yes." He inserts the key into the door to his room. "A quick peck on the cheek, a goodbye, and then a night in the arms of the woman of my dreams."

Mari has already unlocked our room. She looks over her shoulder at me and bites her lip again.

Six hours until dinner.

"See the two of you downstairs tonight."

CHAPTER NINETEEN

Mari

THE ROOM IS dark as we enter, with the curtains drawn, blocking the outdoor light. I have to let my eyes adjust. I stop in the entryway as Bastian closes the door.

"Do you need a nap?" He removes his weapons belt and drops it on the floor, producing a loud clang. It makes my heart stutter. And then, his breath is hot on my neck, and I close my eyes, breathing in the scent of him. "Because I find them terribly overrated."

I tilt my head to the side as he brushes away my hair and his lips find the sensitive skin on my neck. "We could talk stratagem for the upcoming battle. The Supes in Moss Ford will expect a clear plan before they agree to join."

"We could." His lips continue their casual assault on my neck, making me squirm.

I've missed this. We had time alone in his room in the First City, but it was under the constant threat of his father and Sterling. Here, it's just the two of us. And as much as the world around us makes demands of the two saviors, to each other, we're just Bastian and Mari.

Without another word, I twist around, burying my fingers deep in his dark hair and kiss him. His mouth opens to mine as he pins me against the wall of the entry, his hands resting on my hips. Although part of my attraction to him is purely based on the pull of our connected souls, it doesn't make me want him less.

His tongue explores my mouth as his hands roam my lower back and ass, lifting me as I wrap my legs around him. He pushes me harder against the wall, his core lined with mine, ready and waiting. "Mari," he groans as he rests his forehead against mine.

Over a month ago, we made love by the pond outside this village. The vivid images of him above me come rushing back as he carries me to the bed. He lays me down but remains standing to remove his shirt. His chest muscles flex slightly as he tosses the material into a pool of linen on the floor.

He crawls over me, brings his lips to mine, and locks my arms above my head with his hands. This time, it's a slower kiss as if he's trying to savor the moment. His teeth tug on my lower lip before he releases my arms and takes hold of the thin material of my shirt, ripping it down the center.

My eyes widen as I stare up at him, but there's no amusement on his face, only hooded lids focused on my naked chest. My heart hammers beneath it, never having seen this look from him before.

He brings his mouth to my breast, swirling his tongue around my bare nipple. I buck my hips in response as my core cries out at his touch. His hand works my other breast, mirroring his tongue. The burning need I have for him begins to build below my navel as beads of sweat grow slick against my brow. He works his free hand over my mound through the canvas material of my pants.

The hot air of his breath is jagged in my ear as he says in a low voice, "Come for me, Maribel."

It's enough to send me over the edge as I grip the bed covering, twisting it in my hands, and cry out.

Bastian's hand covers my mouth as he grinds against me. "Thin walls, Mari. Your goal today is to take your cries out on me. Bite me, claw me with your nails, but I don't want to hear a peep out of that mouth of yours."

Sounds like a challenge.

He's crouched over me again. This time, he sweeps down my body with his tongue, starting with my neck, where he's careful to avoid my vamp bite. He then spends a little more time around my sensitive breasts, trailing down my stomach to the hem of my pants. "I have a talent only a few people know about."

I prop myself up on my elbows so I can see him, his head positioned between my legs. "What's that?"

"I can remove you pants in less than a minute." The corner of his lip rises into a smirk.

"Big deal. I can remove my pants in fifteen seconds." I love seeing my boyfriend's playful side and am more than willing to invest in it.

He dips his head to the top button of my pants and pushes the metal through the eyelet with his tongue, leaving my bellybutton exposed. "But I can do it with my mouth."

From our time in his room in Arazian's lair, I know he has a talented mouth, but this is next level. "Timer's running."

Bastian successfully unbuttons the four attachments on the front of my pants in fifty-one seconds. He shimmies the pants and my undergarment from my legs the rest of the way, removes his own pants, and then lays beside me on the bed. He cups my face with his hand, stroking my cheek with his finger. "It will be different this time."

"It will?" The pain from our first time together drifted away with the excitement of our dangerous liaison. Sexual relations outside of marriage are strictly forbidden in Avren. But this isn't Avren, and I am finished letting Lady Raven tell me what to do.

I take in his features in the dim light. The first time I saw him, he was both terrifying and beautiful. This hasn't changed. The Dark Prince takes what he wants, using his size and skills to intimidate. But he's also my Bastian. The man who sees past my Avrenian prejudices to my heart and who I am truly meant to be. "You're no longer a virgin. That was the painful part. And this time, I want you on top."

"We can do that?" My inexperience shows, and my cheeks heat with embarrassment. I thought it was done the same way every time.

He chuckles, drawing me closer to him, and rests his forehead against mine. "I'm ready to open you to a world of possibilities, but I won't push the boundaries until you're ready."

I swallow, unsure of what that means but beyond ready to try. Instead of waiting for him to take the lead, I place one leg on either side of him and run my hands along the planes of his chest. He watches me as if he can't get enough. I'm afraid I might combust from the flames licking my skin. Positioning myself over him, I lower slowly, feeling the tip of him inside of me. Not wanting to wait any longer, I take him all at once, sitting flush against his hips.

The fullness almost makes me want to cry out, so I bite down on my lip, and grind against him, wanting to satisfy the growing need deep inside me. We move together as he reaches for my breasts, kneading them and occasionally flicking my pebbled nipples. My body responds to his touch as my heart pounds and my body warms.

He wraps an arm around my waist, flipping us so he's on top, one arm beside my head as he pounds into me. I lift my legs to clamp them around his waist, wanting him deeper. The thrumming inside has reached a fever pitch, and we're both slick with sweat. It's difficult to find the spot where I begin and he ends as we meld together. It makes me love him more than I ever thought possible.

Right before his release, his hot breath whispers in my ear. "I love you, Mari."

We're a tangle of arms and legs as he collapses beside me, holding me tightly to him. My entire body hums with pleasure. My heart swells with the fullness of my love for Bastian Hale.

SAGE LIVES in a cottage on the edge of town with his wife and three children. The smell of freshly baked bread makes my stomach growl as we approach the front door. Grayson has already left for dinner with Katiana, so it's only the three of us. We need to make a good impression, but without our charismatic leader, I'm not sure how we'll do.

Bastian knocks on the door and steps away, hands behind his back. We're both still coming down from our time together. If Evie's aware of anything, she hasn't said a word.

"Welcome." Sage holds the door open for us, shaking our hands as we enter. "We're so pleased you've accepted our invitation. I've also invited Phillip, if you don't mind."

"Not at all," I reply, feeling the need to step up with Grayson gone. "We're honored you invited us."

A warm fire glows in the hearth beside a wooden table, where Phillip and three children sit. They're eating soup from ceramic bowls and look up when we enter. A woman, I assume is Sage's wife, stands by the hearth, scooping another bowl of soup.

"Nessa… children. These are the guests I told you about." He nods in my direction. "Mari is a savior. Imagine that, Fawn. A female warrior."

The older of the blond, pig-tailed children inspects me and then Evie with her mouth open. My sister is quite impressive. "Why did the fairies pick her? If anyone's going to save us, I want her." She points a dirty finger at Evie.

"Beggars can't be choosers." Sage walks past his daughter and ruffles her hair. "Now be a good girl and eat your dinner. Children are better seen and not heard."

Sage's son hasn't taken his eyes from Bastian, whose head barely clears the ceiling of the cottage. "Can you teach me to kill a vampire?"

Bastian laughs, taking a bowl of soup from Nessa and inhaling the steam. "Thank you. This smells wonderful." He sits beside the boy at the table, appearing massive next to his small frame. "You want to be a vampire hunter?"

The boy lifts his butter knife and holds it in his fist, eyes wide. "More than anything."

"Fitz, we'll have none of that nonsense in this house." Nessa sets her bowl of soup at her place at the table and takes a seat. She holds her spoon up at Sage. "I told you all those fantastical stories would do nothing but fill his head with crazy notions."

Sage shrugs and looks to Bastian as if expecting an answer as much as his son.

Bastian leans in close to Fitz and plucks the butter knife from his hand. "I'll tell you something." He looks to Evie and me and smiles. "You see these two beautiful women?"

Fitz wrinkles his nose and sticks out his tongue, clearly not expecting anything like this from the mighty savior.

"Someday, you'll understand what I'm getting at. Anyway, these two women and I are here to recruit people like your dad and Phillip to help us fight a battle. If we win, we hope to live in peace with the vampires."

"You mean, no killing?" Fitz scrunches up his face, apparently disgusted with Bastian's answer as much as his comment about *beautiful women.* "But what if they're a bad vampire like Sterling?"

"Well, then you drive a wooden stake through his heart and burn the body." Bastian tears a piece of bread in half with his teeth and chomps away.

Nessa's lips twist as she shoots a wary look at Sage.

He clears his throat. "That's why we invited you here tonight. We want to discuss strategy and plans for defeating the First City. Phillip and I will recruit while you're away and have a small army ready when you return."

"The citizens of Tenny Rocks are reluctant to get involved, but once they determine something to be a worthy cause, they are loyal and hard workers." Phillip spreads a pad of butter on his bread. "I can't tell you enough how much I appreciated your timing this morning. People get tired of hearing the same voices. Your presence sparked excitement."

"Realistically, what are our numbers looking like?" A knot grows in the pit of my stomach, making it impossible to eat. For the first time, sitting around the table with Sage's family, the reality of putting real people's lives in danger hits me.

"Two to three hundred if we pull in from the outskirts." Sage walks over to the hearth and cuts a slab of meat from a carcass rotating on the spit. It adds to my nausea. "Word of the saviors will unearth those who haven't cared in the past."

"When I bring back my crew from the Grove, we should have at least seven who can train. Do you have anyone here who might help with that?" Bastian cuts a piece of meat from the slice Sage has dropped onto his plate. "Any experts in archery or with the sword?"

"We might." Phillip scribbles on a piece of parchment beside his plate. "Some have accepted their fate as workers supporting Avren's operations. The First City is a different story. Many have lost loved ones to the Miscretes."

"Then we focus our efforts on the First City and deal with

Avren later." As the commander, Bastian is usually content to let Grayson handle negotiations, but he has a natural gift for it. "We'll return in a week with more forces and our trainers ready to prepare."

"And what of the Miscretes?" Phillip taps his pencil against the wooden table. "We can't lose more people to their unconventional ways. And others are superstitious about the creatures still holding onto the souls of their lost loved ones."

"The Miscretes are their loved ones." Evie doesn't look up from her plate, shoving her vegetables around with her fork. "We will not initiate battle until we find a way to reverse Arazian's dark magic or whatever is binding them to the cursed bodies."

Sage sets his fork down, looking from Phillip to Nessa. "Do you really believe that?"

"When I lived in Avren, there were many things I believed because the Council told me they were true: the Undesirables deserved less than Citizens, the wilderness is a place where only the worst criminals are sent, and babies only stand a chance if they grow in test tubes." I push back in my chair to stand, walking around the table to emphasize my point. "You follow a similar narrative here. Avren controls you and the First City writes your story. Our lives are too short to let someone else dictate how we live." I pound my fist into my palm, more than ready to change the lives of the people of the wilderness. "It's a clever plan really. Morph your enemy into an army to turn against itself. The Miscretes are not our enemies. They're your family, your friends, and your neighbors."

Nessa has tears in her eyes. She rests her hand on Sage's elbow. "I *always* knew. We thought they were dead. Surely the Miscretes tore them limb from limb."

Sage bows his head, scratching behind his ear with his free hand. "She's talking about our twins—a boy and a girl. We assumed both were killed when the Miscretes attacked their group of friends while they swam in the river. The ones in the water got away because the monsters hate to get wet, but the ones on the bank, including Frederick and Felia, were dragged away."

"I'm sorry." Evie's words echo through the silent room. "I lost my sister and parents in Moss Ford. Like Mari said, I followed the narrative the First City fed me, assuming she was lost in the body of a monster forever."

"We're working on a way to get them back." Bastian pushes his plate to the side and wipes his mouth with his napkin.

"Really?" Fitz pipes up, eyes wide as saucers, and staring at Bastian as if he's a god. "You can bring back my brother?"

Bastian twists his lip, possibly regretting a promise to the children. "That's the hope."

"And that's all we have now, isn't it?" Nessa collects several empty plates and sets them in the sink. "Hope that an ancient fae prophecy brought us the two of you." She offers us a weak smile as if she's afraid we might let them down.

CHAPTER TWENTY

Bastian

THE STARS through our window glimmer against the black backdrop of the night sky. On the farm, I'd often sleep outside to take in the beauty of the heavens above me. Their soft twinkles reminded me that I was free. Our farm sent food to Avren as a tax, but unlike those who lived closer to the city, we never had to work there. And in a way, I felt bad for those trapped within the city's walls, never experiencing what the natural world had to offer.

I shift my head on the pillow to look at Mari in the starlight. Her face has changed. When she first came to the cabin, I'd sneak down to Levi's room to watch her, fascinated by the woman from Avren. She'd have bad dreams, her brow revealing her inner agony. Her eyes captivated me, quickly replaced by her wit. As much as I wanted to say it was the magnetic pull of the prophecy that drew me to her, nothing was further from the truth. Maribel Windsong was unlike any woman I had ever met.

When we returned from our dinner at Sage and Nessa's home, we sat down to discuss our next steps. Gray was in a foul mood from his dinner with the innkeeper, and I took every opportunity to tease him incessantly about it. But in the end, my brother made me pay for it.

"I think you and Evie should go to Moss Ford, and Mari and I will travel to the Grove." He leaned his elbows on the table with a smug smile on his lips. "Splitting up makes more sense if we are to make the best use of our time."

My brother had stirred a bee's nest inside me, ready to strike for mentioning such a ridiculous idea. "I'm not going to leave Mari."

"Come, now." Gray removed a piece of parchment from his breast pocket and spreads it out on the table. "I'm the leader of the Kindred Few, and I say Mari and I go to the Grove. To convince others, it will help to have a savior present. More than one of the vamps has a vendetta against Sterling. Besides, Evie knows Moss Ford better than any of us."

Evie reclined in her chair, boots on the table. "I agree with Gray. Stories of the mythical saviors have circulated through the wilderness for years. To have one present is enough to make people stop what they're doing and follow you. If Gray and I go to Moss Ford, it will take a lot of convincing based on faith. Word spreads like wildfire through the wilderness and most probably know by now that Bastian and Mari are the saviors. Proof always stirs embers, igniting the fire we all know needs a bit of stoking. Living the status quo is easier than upending one's life."

I closed my eyes and exhaled. My chair scraped against the wooden floor as I stood up and let it fall to the ground. My balled-up fists might have connected with Gray's face instead of the front door of the inn if I hadn't left in that moment.

In the fresh evening air, I found my way to the square and sat on the rock wall, wallowing in my thoughts and fears.

"It's not your job to protect me." Mari walked up beside me and leaned against the wall. "Don't you have confidence in your training? For weeks, you had me shooting arrow after arrow until I could hit the tree every time. We'll meet back here in less than a week, hopefully with an entire army."

I lifted my hand to her face, taking in her features in the torchlight of the square. "This is our fate, Maribel Windsong, and you're embracing it with more grace than I could ever dream of." Hot tears filled my eyes. "I'm fearful of what the future brings. What does it mean that we'll destroy each other? Never have words taken such a hold on my heart. I want to place you in an underground bunker and come back to get you when this is all over." I wiped at the tears with my sleeve, feeling vulnerable and wrecked. "What if I lose you?"

She settled between my legs and wrapped her arms around my back, laying her head against my chest.

This. This was what made life worth living.

She sighed, not moving an inch. "We must trust in what we're called to do. What kind of life do we live under the constant threat of the cities? And someday, maybe we can live free from the shackles binding us."

I kissed the top of her head. Her very essence filled me with hope of what her words meant. If she held onto this, I would need to muster the courage to support her, together or apart. "You're right. But letting you go feels as if I'm losing part of myself."

She shifted her head to look up at me, her eyes filled with what I'd describe as love.

My lips met hers, soft and inviting, as I savored the warm evening.

Hours later, sleep eludes me as I lie awake beside Mari, still unsure about our decision to separate. It's only a week.

Probably the longest week of my life as every minute I'll

wonder if she's alright. I do trust her skills, and having Gray with her will give me a bit more assurance.

The problem is, I know he's right. As much as I want to tuck Mari beneath my wing and protect her, she needs to continue the process of finding herself. For too long, Avren stifled her growth.

She shifts, turning her face in my direction, the light of the moon illuminating her face. With gentle fingers, she touches my arm. "Can't sleep?"

"I was about to shut my eyes," I say, not wanting to keep her up. I roll onto my elbow, lean in, and touch my lips to hers. "Get some rest."

With a slight sigh, she closes her eyes.

Dread settles in my stomach, keeping me restless. Morning will be here soon.

KATIANA LEANS into a rag she uses to scrub the counter in the small dining area of the inn. That spot on the wooden counter must be the cleanest surface in the entire wilderness. She glares at Gray as she does it, slamming her hand down from time to time in an obvious attempt to get his attention. But he ignores her, chatting away about seeing the gang in the Grove. He has his arm slung over Evie's shoulder, seemingly without a care in the world. He has his methods, but I don't always agree with them.

"Can't wait to get back there. Mav owes me ten credits." An enormous smile crosses my brother's lips. "Had a bet about how long it would take the two of you to get together."

"You did not." I tilt my head to the side to roll my eyes at Mari. "It was probably a bet to see how long it would take her to turn an arrow on me."

Evie lets out a rare snicker.

Gray waves a hand at me dismissively. "She'd be more likely to do that to Rafe, but either way, I'll collect my credits."

Mari and Gray have the easier of the two jobs. The people of the Grove are well-trained and ready for this battle. There are fifty, maybe sixty villagers to join our cause. And many of them can help train the others.

Moss Ford will be more difficult. I haven't traveled to that backwards town since the Miscretes killed my family. There are too many painful memories. Maybe that's why I'm glad Evie is going with me. We can face our demons together. We also need to convince free vampires to turn on one of their own. True, they probably despise Sterling's cold, black heart, but like them, he's rogue. His life appeals to those wanting fresh blood served to them without the chase.

A plate of food clatters against the table, interrupting my thoughts. Katiana glares at Gray, clearly having had her heart torn out and stomped on. Full glass of water in hand, she throws its contents at his face, wiping away his smirk.

He jumps up, using his sleeve to brush away the water, and looks down at his wet clothes. "This is the only clean outfit I have."

Katiana is gone. She's made her point, and Gray probably deserves every drop of it.

A man from the back delivers the rest of our food, and I reluctantly take a bite, hoping it's not poisoned. The sooner we can leave this place, the less likely Gray will face true consequences for his actions.

"Did you sleep with her?" I lean closer, out of earshot of Evie.

"Hell, no." Gray tilts his head to the side, his eyebrows drawn in with disgust. "Took her out to dinner and went for a pleasant stroll around the plaza." He lifts his shoulders. "Gave her a quick peck on the cheek before heading up to my room by seven. In her eyes, it must mean we're eternally bound to one another."

"You can't control what another's heart feels." I slice a sausage into smaller pieces on my plate. I'd like to think I'd never do that to Mari in the name of *acting a part* to achieve a goal, but my stunt with Raquel in the First City comes rushing back. My sins are far worse than Gray's, and I can only hope Mari has forgiven me. We still haven't had time to talk about it.

The sky outside is heavy with rain, ready to burst. A low rumble of thunder echoes in the distance in the direction of the First City. Despite our inevitable soggy hike to our respective villages, I pull Mari aside into an abandoned alleyway, refusing to rush our goodbye.

With her back against the wall, I rest my hands on her shoulders, sliding them down her arms. It's too much, looking into her wide eyes, so I rest my forehead against hers and inhale. She probably thinks I want to kiss her one last time, but I'm not ready to let her go.

"I'm sorry if I hurt you." I hang my head, so our noses touch. "Allowing me to play the role of the Dark Prince was not just degrading, but it also exposed you to sides of me I'd like to lock away in a closet. In the past, I'd have had no issue taking advantage of a beautiful woman." My palms are clammy against her arms. I drop them to my sides but refuse to move away from her. "Maybe not on a public stage. I've done many things I'm ashamed of."

She takes my face in her hands, her thumbs caressing the stubble on my cheeks. What did I do to deserve this woman? "Leave it in the past. I agreed to let you play the role of a prince. I knew the terms. The only Bastian who concerns me is the one with the last name *Hale*, not *Valeria*." She tilts her head upward, so we're looking into each other's eyes. "Your parents died in a Miscrete attack, and you've lived your life to avenge their deaths. You stand for honor and truth, not backstabbing and lies." A sad smile tugs at her lips as she brushes a strand of hair behind my ear, letting her fingers linger there. "I know you. You won't betray your family or my heart."

Her faith in me is almost too much to bear. I want to crumble to my knees with the weight of her words, a puddle of mediocrity, but instead, I take her face in my hands and kiss her. It starts off slow, but the raw emotions rolling inside like the thunder above us intensify my need for her. I graze her lower lip with my teeth, gently tugging, teasing before plunging my tongue into her mouth. She eagerly meets mine with her own as I slide my hands behind her hips to draw her closer. With her chest against mine, a soft moan escapes her mouth, making me wish we were back in our room. Her fingers plunge into my hair, yanking and pulling. I lift her, and she wraps her legs around my waist. I only break the kiss to suck on her neck which garners more sweet moans. This is not a goodbye kiss. It's a *I may never see you again* kiss. And with Arazian and Sterling after us, we must treat every parting this way.

Someone clears their throat at the entrance of the alley. Evie and Gray stare at us with their packs on and ready to go. Mari drops to the ground, cheeks flushing.

"I'd say to get a room, but Mari and I have stuff to do today, and I'm the jealous type." Gray snatches Mari's hand and leads her out of the alley. He calls over his shoulder, "I promise to bring her back in one piece. We'll meet back here in six days. Hopefully Xeno will have the information we need by then."

I wipe away the sweat on my brow with my sleeve.

Evie watches Mari lift her quiver and strap it across her chest. "She doesn't need him. You taught her to use her bow. And as difficult as it is to believe, whatever inherent DNA you both have that makes you saviors, gives you a layer of protection I haven't figured out yet."

"What makes you say that?"

She lifts a shoulder, her orange braid cascading over her

black shirt like a river of fire. "When we found her in the vampire's clutches, she was deathly pale. No one survives that, no matter what stock they come from. The fates want both of you to live, at least long enough to fight in this war."

Whatever the purpose I hold with Mari, it energizes me more than revenge ever will. It must. I'd never go back to Moss Ford of my own volition. Images from the night my family died still haunt my dreams, and the village makes them more vivid than any memories I can recollect. Evie and I need to get in and get out with as many recruits as we can before the mountain of our sorrows comes crashing down on us.

"Bastian?" Evie's hand slips into mine.

"Yes." I keep my eyes on the trail ahead, not wanting them to betray me.

She squeezes my fingers as if trying to drive home what she's about to say. "We can't bring back your family or my parents, but we can rescue those long forgotten. Never forget who you are and where you came from."

"You mean from the seed of a lunatic king and the womb of a heartless leader?" The path to killing my parents is laid out before me.

"No, from a farm where a family loved you enough to keep you from your birth father. Your family is in Moss Ford, not the cities we seek to destroy" She squeezes my hand again. "Remember that, and it will keep you from losing your mind."

"Easy for you to say." I drop her hand, stop, and close my eyes.

"You have no idea," Evie spits out as I picture her arms crossed over her chest. "Open your eyes and look at me."

I let out a breath and comply, not wanting a fight.

"Every time I kill a Miscrete, it could be my sister. Think about that." Her green eyes glare at me with the fiery passion I only see on rare occasions. "A very thin thread keeps me tied to the harsh realities we face. It's drawn tight, so tight that one gentle breeze might snap it. The Kindred Few keeps me from hurtling out of control. And I trust that you will help me get Ferrish back."

I rest a hand on her shoulder. "There's nothing I want more, Everleigh."

CHAPTER TWENTY-ONE

Mari

THE WELL-WORN path between Tenny Rocks and the Grove is familiar now that I've traveled it a few times. Stray raindrops make it past the canopy of leaves above and hit my face. A snaking stream runs beside the path, dipping, turning, and bubbling where it flows over small ledges. Its melodic flow is enough to keep me lost in my own world as Grayson strolls in front of me, hands in his pockets, humming.

The first night I entered the wilderness, he was on edge, his hand hovering over his weapons. One warrior to protect two teenagers who didn't know up from down. Now, with my quiver strapped to my back, we both are fully confident in our ability to face any creature that comes our way.

"What makes you more nervous?" Grayson slows to walk beside me, his hands behind his back as he continues his leisurely gait. "Facing a werewolf or Susan?"

"Definitely Susan." I've tried to forget about Bastian's former girlfriend. "If she finds out about me and Bastian, I might find myself flat on my back again."

"A werewolf can do that," Grayson points out.

I lift my bow, pretending to take aim at an imaginary enemy. "You forget I've already felled the mighty beast."

"Quite true, fair maiden." He bows and tips an invisible hat. "Or should I say, battle-proven savior."

Both Susan and Rafe scared me most when it came to reunions. Rafe's forward behavior was a bit unnerving, and I wasn't quite sure what to do with it. Using him as a pin cushion for my arrows wasn't an option, so I had to reject him in more subtle ways.

"We're about thirty minutes away. I'd like to stop at the cabin on the way to the Grove to gather a few supplies." Grayson resumes his humming, making me wonder if it's a nervous habit. He can't be afraid to talk to me. The guy's never at a loss for words.

"What are you humming?" I bend down and scoop up a rock. I toss it into the air, catching it again on the way down.

"A song my mother used to sing to me when I was young. I've forgotten the words." He removes a small ledger from his jacket pocket and flips through the pages. "As I piece any together, I jot them down in here." Squinting, he looks at the scribbled handwriting. "There was something about unity in the star. And then a bunch of garbage about holding hands and peace after the rivers run red."

I chew on my lip, running the words through my head again. "You said your parents were part of the resistance inside Avren. Maybe there's a message in the song. Why else would your mother teach you about bloody rivers? She knew she had to pass it onto you somehow. It was as if she saw the end drawing near." I remove my mother's journal from my pack and hold it in front of me. "My mother did the same thing. In the throes of her sickness, she let me know through her writing that the two cities are somehow connected and working together."

"She said that?" Grayson takes the journal from my hand and scans my mother's words. "You sure it wasn't the delirium talking?"

"No," I say, snatching back the only piece of my mother I have left. "Think about it. They have a bigger purpose than acting on their hatred of each other. Two saviors threaten their very existence. With Bastian and me out of the picture, they take away the symbolic hope that the wilderness can win."

"Arazian stole Bastian from Lady Raven and hid him away for twenty-one years." He raises his eyebrows. "There's nothing like an angry mother."

"Raven is too smart for that." I drop my journal back into my bag, not wanting it to get too wet, and attach the strap. "She'll never let her personal feelings get in the way of her desire for control. For her, nothing is more important than keeping the Undesirable in check."

"Why do I feel like the closer we draw to this battle with the First City, the more complicated our task becomes? If the two cities are working together, will we need to fight the battle on two fronts?" He taps his lip, staring ahead of us. "More importantly, will Bastian have it in him to kill either of his birth parents?"

"Without hesitation." I lift my pant legs as we wade through the stream we've followed which is now gurgling and meandering through a meadow.

Grayson raises an eyebrow with a telltale glimmer in his eye. "So sure for one blinded by love. I think we have a fifty-fifty chance of the commander carrying out the deed. Might go better if one of us is assigned the task."

I don't want Bastian remembering me as the one who shot an arrow through his father's chest.

By the time we reach the cabin, the sun hangs low in the sky, casting shadows among the trees. It exudes a warm feeling of home and acceptance—and a desperate ache for Levi.

Grayson glances at me as he unlocks the door. "His presence is strong here."

It's as if he can read my thoughts.

"Why did he leave us?" His infectious smile fills my memories, laughing from the other mattress in our bedroom.

The door swings open to a room left the way it was when we parted. "He knew how important you were to our cause."

I place my bow on the table and toss my bag onto the floor. "Pretty shitty thinking." Levi should still be here. Not me.

"You can't fight a prophecy, Maribel." He hangs his jacket and pack on a hook by the door. "Many have tried to no avail. You might as well kick up your feet and ride the current. As a fae, Levi knew this." Key ring still in hand, he tromps across the floor to the fireplace. He wraps his knuckles against several stones, wrinkling his nose each time. When he knocks again, a hollow sound resonates from a gray triangular one near the base. "There it is."

I slump into a chair, resting my face in my hands. "What are you looking for?"

He looks at me over his shoulder with his arm elbow-deep in the wall. With a grimace, he shifts and removes a canvas bag from the hole. "There you are." He replaces the stone before walking over to me, dumping the contents of the bag on the table. "Our insurance policy."

A pile of ordinary-looking rocks lays by my hands.

"Rocks? We came back to the cabin to get a bag of rocks you keep hidden in the fireplace?" I lift an eyebrow at my brother.

Maybe he's losing it with the stress we've been through over the past month.

Grayson pinches a rock between his thumb and forefinger and holds it up to the light. "This isn't a rock. It's shivilox, the rarest mineral in the world. Many years ago, the fae owned Undesirable slaves who worked a mine high in the mountains, but it's long since dried up. It's said to have magical properties, but I have no clue what they are. All I know is someone is stockpiling it because it's worth a ton. One ounce of shivilox is worth five hundred credits." He moves the mineral around on the table with his palm. "We must have ten thousand credits in our stash."

"What do you plan to use it for?" While I trust my family, they've been known to do questionable things.

"To win this war, Mari." He pushes the mineral back into the bag, closing the strings tightly before dropping it into his pocket. "If Xeno comes back with information about the Miscretes, it's not like he'll provide it willingly. Sometimes you need to grease someone's palm to loosen their lips."

We gather several other supplies from around the cabin and readjust the items in our packs.

"Ready?" Grayson pulls on his jacket. He lifts his pack from the hook and straps it over his shoulders. "I want to reach the Grove before the sun goes down and it looks like the rain's let up a bit. Mav, Rafe, Laurel, and Susan will help us gather the trained forces. At last count, it was a healthy number."

My stomach flips at the mention of their names. It's my pride nagging. They'll be too busy gearing up for this battle to worry about me like they did before.

As we walk along the path, the forest is quiet except for a bird or two in the trees above. The fresh feeling after a rain fills the air as I swat at a bug landing on my arm. Grayson takes to humming his song again. I walk beside him, lost in my mixed emotions. Within several hundred yards of the Grove, the distinct smell of smoke drifts through the trees. It's stronger than the normal haze from the cottage chimneys and campfires.

Grayson stops humming. "Do you smell that?"

"Yes. Do you think they had a bonfire?" Unless there's a forest fire burning nearby, it's the only explanation I can think of that makes sense.

His face falls right before he drops his pack and unsheathes his sword. "Stay here," he orders and takes off for the village.

Like that's going to happen.

I place my pack beside his on the ground and then draw an arrow from my quiver, ready for whatever danger lurks in the sleepy village. As I run along the trail, images of a doomsday scene fill my head, but nothing can prepare me for what lies before me as I step into the meadow.

Charred bodies litter the field, some still smoldering. The smell is almost as thick as the smoke. I choke on the bile in my throat. The stench of burning flesh is too much to bear. The quaint cottages of the Grove no longer stand to the right of the training grounds. Someone, or something, decimated every-thing. And that predator might be close by. Shaking—I raise my bow, not out of fear but out of grief and rage and whatever other jumbled up emotions make me want to turn the perpe-trator into a pincushion.

Grayson appears along the path meandering through the spot where the cottages once stood, his face as white as snow. It's something I've only seen in picture books and high atop the Elmriddens, but it's the whitest thing I can imagine.

I stare at him across the expanse, unsure of how long my legs will hold me up. They shake beneath me as if I stand on the sea and not solid ground. Deep in my gut, I know this is Arazian's doing. He's punishing us for leaving the First City.

Mav, his family, Laurel, Susan, the young pregnant woman and her husband, and even Rafe with his flirtatious smile and never-ending attempts to get my attention. If Bastian and I hadn't left the First City, they'd all be alive right now.

Finally, my legs give out, and I crumple to the ground, no longer caring about, or fearing, the First City soldiers. The mud beneath my cheek is cool. It soothes me slightly as I close my eyes, trying to block out images of the carnage surrounding me.

"Mari." Grayson's voice sounds miles away as I let the hopeless thoughts take over. My father once told me we come from the soil and one day we'll return there.

"Mari." He shakes my shoulder.

I let my eyelids flutter open to stare up at my brother. Some color has returned to his cheeks. He runs his fingers through the long brown hair hanging over his forehead. I see it now—what Evie admires in him. His calming presence, his boyish smile, the way my name pulls his lips back to form the *eee* at the end. The otherworldliness of the moment makes me think there's a possibility we're both already dead, released from the burdens of the world.

Something hard strikes my cheek. It stings and makes my eyes well with tears. I blink twice, trying to comprehend what happened. "Did you hit me?"

"You've got to snap out of it." Crouched beside me, he glances over his shoulder. "This was an intentional strike on a resistance stronghold. Arazian, or worse yet, Lady Raven."

"Lady Raven?" The thought hadn't crossed my mind. We left the First City on less than stellar terms with Arazian and Sterling, sending back a herd of their Miscretes empty-handed.

"You're the one who said they were working together. If the Miscretes believed us outside of Tenny Rocks, they might be more reluctant to follow the vampire's orders. Avren's soldiers outnumber the people of the Grove a hundred to one." He scans the field, then hangs his head. "They didn't stand a chance." He waves a crumpled parchment in his hand. "The First City is taking credit for it, but I don't know if I believe anything

Arazian says." Clearing his throat, he reads the official looking document. "'Due to illegal training of resistance soldiers in the village, the First City had no option but to decimate these residents. Any further building of forces in other towns and villages will result in the same action. Sterling Idris, commander of the Dark King's forces.'" With his head down, he says, "This has Lady Raven written all over it. You know the Council as much as I do."

The graveness of his statement hits my heart. "I'm not ready to face Avren yet. The First City is one thing, but killing our friends, our neighbors. It's too much."

He rests a hand on my knee, more like an older brother than I've ever seen him before. "You'd think years outside the city walls would desensitize me to those feelings. That the unjust murder of my parents might wipe away any sense of future regret. But it doesn't." He swallows and the lump in his throat bobs. "You and I are different than the others, Mari. They'll never understand how heavy this is for us."

I sit up and draw my knees to my chest, keeping my eyes on Grayson and away from the bodies. "Do you think you'll be able to do it? Kill your neighbor? Your uncle? Your childhood friend?"

He scans the meadow where I once learned to fight with a misfit group of strangers. "If they choose to take up arms against us, I'll have no choice. There's more at stake here than the freeing of the wilderness. If we succeed in taking down Arazian and the Council of Avren, we open a new world for the people of the city. In their current world, choices are limited and ideas are planted in children's heads that this is the right way to live. No one understands this better than we do, Mari. People have died and will continue to die in this war, but we can't go on as if the shadows of the cities don't suffocate us."

His conviction gives me courage. The thought of facing Flynn on the battlefield is my worst nightmare, but I need to see him as the enemy if he tries to stop us from reaching the Council. Looking out at the blackened meadow, my future path morphs from a murky distant landscape to a clear present. Bastian and I are the saviors the people of the wilderness have waited for and it's our job to rally our troops. Without us to present a path to victory, they take false comfort in their present situations.

I stand and brush the dirt and charred ash from my pants. With my quiver on my back and bow on my shoulder, I cross the meadow to the south.

"Where are you going?" Grayson calls, the sound of his feet behind me.

"To Rumsford." I don't turn around, set on my mission. "We still have several days before we need to be back in Tenny Rocks and I'm not returning empty-handed."

"Werewolves?" He takes my arm to turn me toward him.

I stop and tilt my head to the side, ready for him to try to talk me out of it.

"Are you out of your mind? They can't control their own behavior half the time, and you want to train them to fight against the First City?" He drops his hand, crossing his arms. There are times when he seems to think he's so much better than me because he's older.

"No," I say.

His face falls in relief as if he thinks the very act of his objection would change my mind.

"I want to train them to fight against the First City and Avren." I continue down the path that leads to the Lake of Glass. "It's as much their wilderness as it is ours."

Grayson falls into step beside me, remaining quiet. He's probably trying to come up with some way to change my mind about my impromptu trip to the werewolf capital of the wilderness. Not one of them harmed me while I was there with Levi. And as the savior, I need to believe they won't harm me now.

We scramble down a stand of rocks to the path below. The trees thin as we get closer to the lake.

"I'm supposed to protect you." Grayson's voice is quiet as if he's revealing a secret I'm not allowed to know about. "I promised Bastian that I'd bring you back in one piece. But I thought I was only taking you to the Grove, not on a suicide mission to Rumsford."

I whip around, undeterred. The stirring inside of me that started in the meadow has grown. Everything is laid out before me. I don't let him in on the secret that if I had time, we'd also travel to the Crestone Caverns to speak with the vampire queen. "You can turn back."

"I'm not going to leave you alone to face the wolves. Bastian would rip my head off. As it is, he's going to have my ass for letting you go." My brother pouts, pleading with me to change my mind. "The prophecy states two saviors will take down the cities, and you're going to get yourself killed before we can let it play out."

"That's not true." I climb over a rock, starting along the path that circles the lake. Out of the hazy smoke from the Grove, sunlight skitters over ripples on the water. While my mood has improved slightly with the new focus my brother gave me through his thoughts on Avren, images from the Grove still haunt me. As I crossed the field, I recognized two of the corpses lying side by side: Mav and Laurel. The picture won't leave my head. It's made me more determined than ever to take down the bastards who murdered them.

"You think the prophecy provides you supernatural protection? Because it doesn't." He skips a rock over the surface of the lake, breaking the surface. "A werewolf's jaws will rip out your throat as easily as mine."

I face him, tired of his attempts to change my mind. "I'm going to Rumsford, Gray. The wolves will give us a better chance to win. This is their land as much as it's ours and they need to know that the two cities are working together. That alone is enough to keep us up at night, but who knows what other secrets they're holding. Bastian's parents let him be raised by complete strangers. His father's a madman and his mother's more concerned about keeping her power than any familial ties she might have. Even if you say you have the Miscretes on your side, which may or may not be true, we're relying on a criminal to come up with a way to change them back into humans." I tilt my head to the side and close my eyes, not ready to put all my faith in a plan with so many variables. "Can we at least try with the werewolves? After what happened in the Grove, I'm sure Sterling has a bounty on our heads, whether it was carried out by the First City or Avren."

"Or it was a message to you and Bastian." Grayson tosses another rock, scaring two ducks from their spot on the lake. They fly away along the surface.

"Either way, we need to get to Rumsford and convince the wolves that their very existence is at stake."

CHAPTER TWENTY-TWO

Bastian

THE STORM HAS STAYED to the south, and I no longer hear the rumble of thunder. The forest, a place where I'm normally at ease, sends trepidation through me. It's abnormally quiet, lacking the normal chatter of the birds and rustle of the wind through the treetops. It's as if the wood itself knows the immensity of what is to come.

This is the first time I've traveled to Moss Ford since the night my family died.

I glance at Evie, who appears lost to her own demons as she clutches her hands together, her eyes darting in response to the occasional sound. She's the perfect travel companion for this trip because I don't want to talk about it. We have a mission to convince the Supes of Moss Ford to join forces against the First City.

I gave Mari the easy job to protect her. And I trust Gray to bring her back in one piece. But this damn prophecy connection makes every cell in my body long for her presence. It's as if I can't guarantee her safety unless she's with me, and whatever magic's behind our bond won't let me forget it.

Evie is the first to break the silence. "We'll go to the tavern first. Most of the locals hang around there at this time of day."

Knox's Place. The watering hole where Evie takes on her other persona, Everleigh Rose. In Moss Ford, she'll take the lead because she's earned the respect of the residents, especially the women. My fierce sister knows how to handle the Supes in the sophisticated manner needed to gain their trust. Most of the ones I encounter face my dagger, but she's not as quick to draw her weapon with them. Her words can be just as convincing.

As we enter the village, the streets into the square are cobbled, uneven, and lined with buildings that lean inward, their wooden beams and stone walls darkened by centuries of weather and magic. Though it is the middle of the afternoon, lanterns flicker, lighting the dim alleys between the buildings.

My sword remains strapped to my back, though I keep my hand close to my silver dagger. Evie carries a pair of short swords at her hips and moves with a predatory grace, her senses on high alert as her eyes dart from one sound to the next.

As we step into the village square, Supes mingle in the open, spilling out from the tavern. These creatures, rejected by their own kind, seem to have taken to drowning their troubles. Were-wolves, in their half-human, half-beast forms, stand around in groups, their fur glistening in the afternoon sunshine, sharing guttural laughter and swigs from crude mugs. A few of them look our way, appraising us with a mixture of curiosity and caution. Evie is well-known here, but I'm a newcomer, something they don't take too kindly to.

Fae flit about the square, avoiding the packs of werewolves. Some have wings that shimmer like stained glass while others move with other-worldly grace. Unlike the werewolves, they converse in hushed tones, and if they drink, it's from long, fluted stemware. A few perch on rooftops, eyeing us, their presence both enchanting and unnerving.

Shadowy hooded figures, too indistinct to identify, move silently among the gathering, their forms flickering in and out of view. The few humans who gather among the Supes are weathered with loss and pain, no longer caring that the beings among them use them to satisfy both their sexual and physiological cravings.

And despite the tension in the air, the atmosphere of the square is surprisingly festive. The beings socialize as if this is a place where the rules of the world outside don't apply. For the most part, they've effectively blocked out the First City and Avren like they don't exist.

"Stick close," Evie whispers, looping her arm through mine. "Fresh blood stands out here."

I'm not worried about a fae seducing me to his or her lair. I've dealt with their kind before. My trusty iron dagger is buried in my boot, and I'm not afraid to use it the second they take the conversation off the topic I deem appropriate. "We stick together. Keep each other in line."

She removes a bottle from the lining of her jacket and takes a small swig of the liquid inside before handing it to me. "This is what I use when I come to work. It helps unmask their glamour."

I take the tiny brown bottle between my fingers and drink the remainder of the potion, hoping I don't feel any side effects. Magic and potions always make me leery, but I trust Evie's judgment.

"We'll start inside the tavern. My parents named it when they took over, when I was young. The new owner kept the name in homage to my parents." She turns the knob on the heavy wooden door and takes to shoving it with her shoulder. "It's always stuck which isn't convenient for human patrons."

As light spills in from the outside, the dark atmosphere of

the tavern makes it difficult for my eyes to adjust. Lantern light and a hearth on the far wall are the only illumination in the dank place.

"Everleigh Rose!" The voices come from multiple places around the bar.

My companion salutes them and provides a rare smile. "Hey fellas. I'm not here on a pleasure run, I'm here on business."

My eyes slowly adjust to the faint light, and I can finally make out faces. Most of the patrons inside are human, the walls of the tavern providing some segregation between them and the Supes. Like the humans outside, they are time-worn and hold the weight of living among the supernatural beings, even the young. Most wear ragged clothing and their faces are dirty and wrinkled.

Evie marches over to the bar, her actions commanding the attention of onlookers. She uses a stool to climb onto the counter and stands high above the people sitting below. With her fiery red hair and confident stance, my sister is a burning pillar of strength commanding attention. "We are in a time of dire need. We can't go on living in the shadow of the First City. The Reckoning changed our way of life. Using the Supes for protection has taken a toll on all of you. What if you no longer needed that protection? What if we found a way to get our loved ones back?"

"Then I'd say you're crazy, Everleigh Rose." A man around our age stands at a table with two others. His blond hair runs long and straggly over his shoulders. A disheveled beard makes me believe he's long since given up on the use of a comb. "This is no longer your home. You're an occasional visitor, here for a paycheck." He raises his voice, approaching the bar. "*We* live and breathe it every damn day."

My fingers instinctively wrap around a dagger.

Evie turns on the fire in her eyes and crouches to glare at the man. "Don't for one minute think that Ferrish's death didn't affect me a million times more than it affected you, Samuel." She looks out at her captive audience, furrowing her brow. Tears well in her eyes. "My sister's and parents' deaths replay in my mind every day, but I refuse to wallow in what can't be changed. My boyfriend and sister are traveling to the Grove to collect the best battle trainers in the land. We will reconvene in Tenny Rocks to form our army." She stands again and pounds a fist into her chest. "Who will stand with us?"

"You're full of horse shit." Samuel waves a dismissive hand at her. "We'll lose more good people. No thanks." He turns back to his table.

"What if I said there's a possibility we could bring Ferrish back?" she calls out.

He whips around and glares at her. "Not even the darkest witchcraft could raise our loved ones from the dead."

"She's not dead." Evie averts her eyes and places her hands on her hips before taking a deep breath. "The First City has kidnapped our loved ones and turned them into the monsters we call Miscretes. Every time the Supes kill and bury them out in the woods, they might have murdered your mother or father or daughter or son. But we are working on a way to reverse Arazian's warped spell. To save the ones who still live."

"Is this true?" A woman sitting at the bar swirls the liquid in her glass, staring at it as it sloshes against the sides.

Evie's lips set in a straight line as she stares to the woman. "Look at me, Rina."

The woman takes her attention from her glass and rests her weary eyes on my sister.

"I would never lie to a sister in Moss Ford. Our word is truth. You know this more than anyone." Evie walks along the bar and sits cross-legged in front of Rina. "We're there for each other, no matter what."

Rina nods her head and downs the remainder of her drink. She slaps her palms on the bar. "Then I'm in."

A few voices chorus their agreement from around the room. Mostly women.

"And what about you, Samuel?" Evie doesn't move from her spot. She is holding hands with Rina in what I assume is a symbol of solidarity. "Will you and the other men of the village join us to get our loved ones back and free the village from the Supe occupation? When you no longer need their protection from the Miscretes, they can spread out around the wilderness."

I glance around. It's not like this is a Supe-free zone. Throughout Evie's pleas, I've kept an eye on a werewolf and a vamp in the dark recesses. Part of me had hoped to get the supernatural creatures of Moss Ford to join us in the fight, not paint them as the enemy.

The werewolf in human form leans over to whisper in his companion's ear.

I need to speak up if we're ever to defeat the First City. "As an outside observer, what I see is not an occupation but a mutual partnership." The Supes hate the Miscretes, but the fear the humans have of their attacks after the Reckoning gives the Supes an opportunity. "This town belongs to all of you. It's time to vanquish the enemy and live in peace."

"And you have a plan? Even if your Miscrete idea falls through?" Samuel looks from me to Evie.

"The Knox women always have a plan, Samuel Roy. You should know that by now." Evie sits and shimmies down from the bar. "We leave for Tenny Rocks in two days after we've had a chance to convince the Supes to join us." She looks at the werewolf and vampire in the corner. "Draining the same supply must take a toll on them. When we arrive at our training grounds, Commander Hale, who I'm sure you've heard is one of the two saviors, will lay out the stratagem. I have full confidence in my brother." She slaps me on the back, leaving one hell of a sting.

What would they all think if they also knew I was the Dark Prince of the First City?

"If it means we could get our loved ones back... If I could get Ferrish back, then I'm willing to risk it." Samuel scans the room as other male voices call out in agreement. "You have your work cut out for you, Commander Hale."

The hard work I put in with my soldiers in the Grove will pay off. They will have this group of humans ready to fight in a month's time.

"And where do we fit into your little plan, Bastian Hale?" The vamp from the corner creeps out of the shadows, perfection in a room full of ragged humans. "You plan to turn on us the minute we help you destroy what your father has built." His blood red eyes gleam in the lantern light. "Or do you think living in your picture-perfect world of roses and daisies will actually work?"

The heavy weight of stares from others in the room makes my skin crawl. My lineage comes with an unbearable amount of judgment. He also just called out my Valeria-status in a room full of strangers.

"Your life mission is to kill as many vampires, werewolves, and fae as you can get your hands on. Living for the past few centuries, I've seldom found a human I can trust."

I shake off the stares to speak from my heart. "Those of you who have lived here long enough know the Hales as honest, hard-working people. Jaresiah and Sarah raised me, not as the Dark Prince, but as a farmer." I scan the room, daring anyone to question my motives. "Blood means nothing to me. If anything, the access I can gain to Arazian will be an asset in this battle." Despite my distaste for the undead, I hold my hand out to the vamp. "You have my word that we'll work out a peaceful treaty for both the humans and the Supes when all of this is over."

The vampire scoffs and slinks back into his darkened corner.

Evie and I will need another day to convince the remainder of the residents of Moss Ford that joining us is to their advantage.

Samuel follows us outside, where his unkempt appearance becomes more obvious. Dark puffy circles line his lower eyelids. Grease darkens his blond hair which causes strands to stick to his forehead. The man smells like he hasn't taken a bath in three months. Evie's look of disgust tells me she notices it too.

"Samuel Roy, if you don't take a bath before the next time I see you, I might have to throw you into Miller's Pond myself." She backs away from her sister's fiancé and takes my hand.

"Do you really think she's still alive?" His bloodshot eyes glimmer in the sunlight. Hope can be a dangerous feeling.

"Some of our loved ones are alive and well, trapped in the bodies of monsters." Her brow furrows and her lips pull into a pout. Does she feel sympathy for the man? "There's no way I'll believe she's alive until I hold her in my arms. We've lived too many years grieving to do the whole damn thing all over again."

Samuel Roy follows us around like a hungry dog, scooping up scraps of the attention our presence brings. According to Evie, he used to garner the positive appraisals of both men and women in the town. In his current state, he's nothing more than a sorry has-been.

When we reach the inn where Evie secured us a room for the night, I face Samuel. "Look, I have my core seven when it comes to trainers, but I'm sure we'll need someone to fetch us supplies, you know, to head into town and scrounge up enough food to feed a hundred or so men and women. Do you think you'd be up for that?"

He squints in the sunlight and shakes his head. "I was hoping for a combat position, one more aligned to my training."

Evie elbows me and smiles. "Samuel Roy's father was in charge of the military outfit for the northern part of the wilderness until the Reckoning." She peeks at him, quirking her lip. "Until he disappeared, never to be heard from again."

I'd almost rather have my father missing than have him as the sadistic madman who provided my seed. "Sorry to hear that. What types of weapons are you qualified to instruct others in using?"

"Bow, crossbow, war hammer, mace, axe, sword, dagger, pike, and the occasional flail." He holds out both of his hands, uncurling a finger for each weapon his names.

I struggle to keep my jaw from dropping. I've never held some of those weapons, let alone used them.

"But I'm willing to learn if it means I can join the fight to avenge Ferrish." He folds his hands as he closes his eyes. "She's the only reason I go on. The woman would tie my ankles and drag me behind a horse if she'd heard I'd given up. It wasn't her nature to quit."

My attention rests on a wooden wagon full of hay on the other side of the square. Anyone with decent aim could stick a dagger in its soft planks. "Tell you what." I draw the weapon from my jacket, flipping it to lay the handle in Samuel's hand. "If you can hit that wagon, I'll let you help train."

"Where?" he says, adjusting his grip on the smooth handle.

Of all the idiotic things to say. "Hit the wagon."

He steps closer to me, and I almost gag at his stench. "I know you want me to hit the wagon, but what part of the wagon?"

Anywhere is fine, but if he's up for the challenge... "See the bolt in the upper right quadrant of the front wheel? Stick the dagger about an inch above the iron."

Samuel lifts a shoulder, sets his stance, draws back, and flings the weapon. When it hits, the handle protrudes from the upper right quadrant of the wheel like I had asked. Several villagers clap at the accurate shot.

"Impressive," I say and throw a wink at Evie.

"I told you he was good." She leans against a split rail fence, obviously done with the theatrics. "You can pair him with Rafe. The two will make quite the dynamic duo."

I hold out my hand to shake his as he gives me back the dagger he retrieved from the wagon wheel. "We can't pay you, and the job's terribly unpredictable, but if you'll take the position, you're hired, Samuel Roy."

CHAPTER TWENTY-THREE

Mari

"SEVEN HUNDRED FORTY-TWO, seven hundred forty-three, seven hundred forty-four..." Grayson walks behind me, and I've ignored him this far, but it annoys me to no end.

I whip around to face him, hands on my hips, and no longer able to control my frustration. "I give up. What in the world are you counting?"

He glances up, supplying me with his famous sheepish grin. "The number of steps I'm closer to my execution, compliments of Bastian Hale."

"This was all my idea. If he wants to kill someone, it'll be me." I step onto a flat rock crossing a stream and then hop to the next one. We're both the saviors and I have every right to make decisions in this fight. While my encounters with the werewolves were less than ideal, Grayson and I can't go back to Tenny Rocks empty-handed. If our idea with the Miscretes doesn't work, we'll need as many forces as we can muster.

Grayson jumps onto the rock behind me, holds me by the

elbows to keep me from falling in, and then passes on to the shore. "You know he's going to want to blame someone for our journey to Rumsford. It can't be you. That leaves me." He pokes his chest with his thumbs.

"Can werewolves be reasoned with in their human forms?" I think back to my time with Levi at the Ironhorse Inn. It's obvious now that he was trying to protect me from the were-wolves who live there without letting me in on his fear. While we seemed to encounter only humans, I'm not sure if I could have told the difference between a wolf and an Undesirable.

"Sure. If there's something in it for them." He follows the trail to the left around a tall stand of reeds. "You'll find that with most Supes, not just the dogs. Do you have a plan?"

This isn't my strength. I'm not charismatic like Grayson, or strong like Bastian, or someone who doesn't care what others think of her like Evie. "No. I thought we'd come up with one together. You're the wolf expert."

He laughs and snaps the top from a reed, sticking it between his teeth. "Expert, huh?"

Gruesome images of the night I first came to the wilderness fill my mind. Grayson killed a werewolf with a single silver dagger. "You sure know how to kill one."

"It doesn't mean I know how to reason with one." He shoves his fists into his pockets, slowing to let me walk beside him. "If you haven't noticed, Supes don't trust humans, especially ones from Avren."

"And how will they know we're from Avren?" I would think that in the time I've spent in the wilderness, I've covered up some of the newbie scent, and Grayson's been here for years.

"They know, Mari. We reek of sterilization and artificial perfumes." He holds his arm up to his nose and inhales. "Smells like dust and campfires to me, but most Supes can smell our blood from miles away."

"I don't want to waste time with any wolf." The lake breeze

dances over the reeds and brushes my face. Grayson said the Supes won't kill me, but I still wonder if every breath will be my last. "Only the pack leader will do. Do you know who can get me an audience with him?"

"How old-fashioned of you to assume the pack leader is male." He tromps through a patch of thick mud.

"I didn't mean to. I only assumed." Nothing in our upbringing in Avren taught us to assume that women were a weaker sex. It's only the wilderness that relays this message.

He shakes his head as if laughing at his own joke. "You're too gullible, Windsong. The lycanthropes will eat you up and spit you out. You've got to be strong. No one will believe you're the mighty savior ready to lead an army against the two cities if you're tricked so easily."

"Then teach me what I need to say." I lean against a boulder and cross my arms, refusing to let my brother humiliate me with the pack. "How do I get them to see me as someone to look up to instead of manipulate?"

He leans against the rock beside me, his hazel eyes catching the afternoon sunlight. "You've got to believe it yourself." His finger points to my chest. "Once you believe you're something special and it shows both inside and out, no one will doubt it."

I chew on his words as we follow the long path around the lake, fighting the demons holding me down. In the city, the Council told people what job they were worthy of and their marriage match. Pride was looked down upon. If the leaders on the Council didn't think you were worthy, you weren't. In the few short months I've lived in the wilderness, I've come so far in overcoming the programming I grew up with, but it still lingers in the deepest corners of my subconscious.

I'm not confident enough to convince others. I'm not strong enough to lead others into battle.

Grayson quickens our pace as the sun slips behind the Elmridden range, not wanting to arrive in Rumsford after dark.

As we walk through the town, I shudder as eyes follow me through the streets. Knowing now what I didn't last time I was here with Levi makes everything one hundred percent more sinister. The wolves sense the ending of the day, and we're what's on the dinner menu.

The wind from the lake whips the dirt up along the path, pelting my skin as Grayson pushes open the heavy door to the Ironhorse Inn. A man as large as the bartender in the First City stands behind the counter, scribbling in a ledger. His sleeves are pushed up to the elbows, and his forearms are covered in tattoos. Long reddish-blond hair, the same color as the rugged beard on his face, is tied back at the nape of his neck.

He looks up and eyes us, his nostrils flaring slightly. "Can I help you?"

"We need a place to stay for the night." Grayson places a small bag of credits on the counter. "Preferably with two beds." He glances around the room before leaning in and whispering, "Do you know where I can find the pack leader?"

The man frowns, slams a set of keys down, and slides the bag of coins into his coffer. "I don't know what the hell you're talking about. You must be from the east. Crazy as they come. Take your keys and get out of my face."

"Temperamental much?" Grayson faces me and mutters, "Typical wolf."

"I can hear you," the man growls.

"Precisely." My brother lifts his sack and climbs the stairs to our room.

Unlike the time when I was here with Levi, the werewolf has given us a room close to the stairs. Grayson unlocks it and holds the door open for me. Inside, there's a bed and a sofa covered in rose-colored fabric with tiny white flowers.

"I call the couch!" He dives for it and kicks his feet up while I shut the door. Thankfully, there are multiple locks to keep the things that go bump in the night out of our room.

I place my bag on the bed, weary from our long day. The loss of the people in the Grove weighs heavy on my heart, and I'm not sure how to deal with it. Grayson says I need to let my inner strength shine, but all I want to do is crumple into a ball and cry. It's our fault they are dead. The First City or whoever killed them would have left them alone if they hadn't felt threatened by Bastian and me.

"Do you think tall, blond, and hairy will bother us tonight?" I ask, refolding the clothes in my pack, unable to lay down and rest.

Grayson is stretched out on the sofa, his legs crossed at the ankles and his eyes closed. "He's already called up ten of his closest friends. Once the full moon hits its peak, we need to be ready."

His answer is unexpected.

"Really?" I ask, checking my boot for my silver dagger. Quinn Malum was the only one who bothered Levi and I when we were here.

His eyes flick open. "Without a doubt. The wolves claim to run a legitimate business, but they can't control their workers. They take these jobs for the benefits—free meals." He sits up and pushes the curtain to the side with his finger. "And it's a full moon tonight, baby."

"If we kill a bunch of werewolves, won't that tick the leader off?" I want the pack to join us, not to take them out with our daggers and silver-tipped arrows. It defeats the purpose.

"Of course, but the walls of the human-occupied rooms are lined with silver. We should be safe for the night." Grayson stands, picks up an oil lamp from a table, and holds it up to the wall. It's a dull gray stamped with an ornate pattern. "The owners take every precaution to make sure we feel welcomed and safe. Wolves can't stand being around the stuff, so they steer clear of these rooms."

Grayson goes into the bathroom to wash up for the night. I

dim the oil lamp and sit on the couch to gaze outside. As much as I want to convince the werewolf pack leader to join us in the fight, I'm not sure what I can say that will persuade him. "Hey, I'm the savior, so why don't you drop what you're doing and follow me." Yeah, right.

Grayson rubs a towel over his hair when he returns. "It's all yours."

"What do you know about the pack leader?" I tuck my legs beneath me on the couch, resting my head on my hand. The bartender in the First City was so easy to talk to in his human form, so I'm hoping this man will be similar.

"Nasty son-of-a-bitch." He holds up a hand. "Pun totally intended. Waylon Miggs. He needs to keep his pack in line after surviving two coup attempts. Pretty much owns this entire town."

"If he's dealing with his own internal rebellions, do you think he'll want to risk the lives of his pack?" It appears the man already has a lot going on.

Grayson tosses his towel on the arm of the couch. His hair is dark from washing it, sticking in clumps against his forehead. He runs his fingers through it to comb it back from his face. "We need to convince him that there's no better way to keep his pack occupied than giving them a singular purpose. There's power in prophecy. You are the key to opening doors we didn't have access to before we understood your purpose. Your appearance tells the people and creatures of the wilderness that the time draws near."

His words from earlier still fill me with hope. I must believe in my role for others to follow.

When the lights are out, I spread out in the bed, missing Bastian. I stare at the moon and wonder if he's missing me.

A scratching sound tears me away from my thoughts. I sit up slightly in bed to look at the door. Light from the hallway spills beneath the opening, and the shadow of something resembling claws digs into the wood floor in the hallway.

My heart hammers as I grab the silver dagger from beneath my pillow. From outside our window, the bone-chilling howls of hundreds of wolves fill the valley. I suck in a breath, hoping Grayson's right about the walls. The scratching intensifies.

Dagger in hand, I move from the bed to the couch, waking Grayson and forcing him to sit up. "They're all around us," I whisper, snuggling into my brother's open arms.

More howls rise, one sounding like it's directly below our window.

"We're safe in here." He squeezes my shoulder, reassuring me that I'm being ridiculous. "The only one not bothered enough by the walls to enter is Waylon, and I'm sure he's way too busy to deal with us."

The door bursts open and the light from the hallway spills inside. I hold the silver dagger in front of me, hand shaking. Wolves whimper behind a shadowy figure standing on the threshold. His massive shoulders and muscular chest make Bastian appear tiny. From what I can see, dark hair covers his head, face, chest, arms, and legs. He wears a pair of loose shorts. The man appears to be holding onto his humanness.

"Maribel Windsong." His deep voice rings out in a way that seems to shake the entire room. "I believe you're here to see me."

I don't want to leave the false safety of Grayson's arms. Neither of us could take on this mountain of a man on our best day. Inside, I fight the inner turmoil of wanting to show the confidence I need to accept my role as the savior and releasing the scared Avrenian girl who relies on others to run her life.

I move to the edge of the couch.

Grayson clutches my arm. "Mari, don't." He must know something I don't. This is why we're here. Why is he trying to hold me back.

I shake free from his grip and stand, taking a step closer to

Waylon. With his body blocking the light, I still can't make out the features of his face. That will make it difficult to assess his reaction to what I'm about to say. "We are not enemies, the humans and the Supes of the wilderness. Although we have differences, our true adversaries live in the First City and Avren. Have you not lost wolves to the Miscretes or Avren's soldiers?"

"Isn't it true that I've also lost pack members to both you and this man?" He points at Grayson.

I look back at him. His eyes are wider than I've ever seen them. He's fearful of the pack leader, and rightly so. If Waylon holds these killings against us, we might both die before we have a chance to lay out our case.

Lifting my chin, I search for the inner confidence I need. "Both of those killings were in self-defense. You don't expect us to sit back and let wolves rip our throat out, do you? The Avrenian soldiers murder your pack members for sport." At least, I think this is true. Flynn told me once about his older brother joining a hunting party. It confused me because I'd never thought people willingly went to the wilderness.

Waylon stands in silence. Only the low whimpers of the wolves behind him break it. "This is true. When one of our own is killed by an Avrenian's silver arrow, we exact our revenge by taking out the entire hunting party. Occasionally, one gets away."

"What if it stopped altogether?" I circle the far end of the bed to dig through my pack. "What if the two saviors of the wilderness were on your side when we storm the gates of the First City and Avren to put a stop to their tyrannical reigns?" I hold Bastian's necklace in my hand. "Bastian Hale is the savior from the First City, and I'm the savior from Avren. You must feel it like the fae."

"I'd say the fae are full of horseshit." He advances into the room, not bothered for a second by the silver walls, and sits on the couch beside Grayson. My brother scoots away from the enormous man. "Why would the heir apparent to the First City's throne give it up to take down his own kingdom? And a seamstress from Avren wielding a sword or bow? I don't care how much training you claim to have, you'll never be more than a spineless city-dweller."

"That's where you're wrong." Grayson finally has the courage to speak up. "Bastian Hale and Mari Windsong are my brother and sister. If anyone knows them, I do. Bastian wasn't raised in the First City, and he rejects his lineage. The wilderness is his home as much as it's yours. And Mari, well, can't you see for yourself?"

"See what?" Waylon grumbles.

"The square of her shoulders, the lift of her chin, the determination in her eyes? She no longer holds the zombie look of an Avrenian. She's determined to fulfill her destiny, whether you agree or not." He leans over the side of the couch and draws an arrow from my quiver, tapping the shaft against his palm. "And she shoots with deadly accuracy."

The man stares at me for an uncomfortably long time. "What if we help you? What if our side wins? What's in it for us besides doing away with the pesky Miscretes and Avrenian soldiers?"

"Freedom." The idea has come to mean so much more to me now that I've tasted it. "Freedom to live your lives the way you want. The Council of Avren has plans to exterminate Supes from the wilderness, I'm sure of it. They're working together with Arazian. It's time we stop them before it's too late."

CHAPTER TWENTY-FOUR

Bastian

THE ROOSTER'S crow before the crack of dawn has me groaning after tossing and turning on the lumpy mattress most of the night. Samuel put us up in his cottage—a glorified shack which I'm sure leaks when it rains. My mattress smells of mildew and hay.

When I finally open my eyes, I see Evie leaning against the wall, smoking stick in hand. She holds it up to her lips to draw in the tobacco and closes her eyes as she rests her head back. Being here is as tough on her as it is on me. Samuel hasn't made it any easier with his constant chatter about Ferrish.

"You got another one of those?" I ask, sitting up and rolling my neck, releasing audible cracks.

She tosses me a burlap sack. I rummage through it for her papers and tobacco.

"I don't think I could bear it if Xeno comes back empty-handed." She looks at me with a rare vulnerability. "If we need to face the Miscretes to take down the First City, I can't do this."

I roll tobacco up in the paper. "No one is asking you to, but as your commander, I have to say we're at a clear disadvantage without you in this fight. As your brother, I want you to take care of yourself first."

She purses her lips to let a ring of smoke rise into the air. Then she snuffs the end of the smoking stick on the floor. "I haven't made up my mind yet. Let's hear what Xeno has to say. I'm in on the training. The people of Moss Ford and Tenny Rocks are out of practice and need someone to whip them into shape."

"That is something you're more than capable of doing, dear sister." I strike a match I dug out of my pack and light the end of the paper. The tobacco instantly relaxes me. Not having Mari here has me on edge. I'm also not sure how our conversation will go today. Samuel promised to call an assembly, but it's not like the Supes and I have a positive relationship. I can count on two hands how many I've killed over the years—two hands on ten people.

Evie rummages through her bag and pulls out her other set of clothing then disappears into the closet. She emerges wearing her tight black fighting gear, the same clothes Mari borrowed when she first came to the cabin. Memories of seeing her for the first time in the black leather outfit make me miss her even more. As much as she drove me crazy with her Avrenian ways, she had me wrapped around her finger from the start.

"Do you think Rafe will leave Mari alone for two seconds without you there to watch over her?" Evie winks at me and then checks her reflection in a broken mirror. She runs her fingers through her hair, weaving the strands into a braid to one side.

Rafe. I place my hand on my forehead. He doesn't give up. Knowing Mari, she'll keep our relationship a secret with Susan around, so he's sure to make a move. "I'll have to give him a bit of a talking to when they show up in Tenny Rocks. He means well, I think, but doesn't know when to give up."

In the main room of the cottage, Samuel slices a loaf of bread on the counter. He looks up and smiles when we enter. Even with a night of rest, he looks no better than the day before, and it makes me wonder if he's sick.

"Good morning," He places the loaf on a table with a bowl of preserves and three mugs of coffee. "I spoke with Velm last night. He agreed to arrange the meeting of the minds for seven o'clock this evening. You'll have a captive audience to work your magic."

With all the Miscrete gravesites in the forest outside the village, I'd say the Supes are tired of dealing with their pesky neighbors. They may be easier to convince than the humans.

"Do you want to go to the secret garden today?" Samuel sits across from Evie and places a slice of bread on his plate. "They've decorated it in honor of the anniversary."

Evie glares at him. "Why in this green world would you ever think I'd want to go there?"

He shrugs then spreads a dollop of preserves on his bread with a knife before licking it off the utensil. "I don't know. Just thought you'd want to visit a place where your sister's spirit lives on."

"What's the secret garden?" I imagine an underground cave where luminescent flowers bloom despite the lack of sunlight.

"A place in the woods where few people go." Samuel rests his knife against his plate. "It's a tangled maze of wildflowers protected by mossy boulders and a stream for a moat. Rumor has it that it was planted by the nymphs of Heatherwood."

"And Ferrish spent many afternoons writing in her journal. No place in the wilderness was more precious to her." Evie pinches the bridge of her nose. "And as much as you're a bastard for bringing it up and as much as it might hurt, I long to see it again."

Samuel folds his hands on the table and a wide grin crosses his lips. "Evie's most exquisite paintings are her renderings of the Heatherwood gardens. In fact..."

I hold up my hand to stop him, staring at my sister. "Wait... you paint?" In all the years I've known her, I didn't think she had an artistic bone in her body. Weapons seem more her speed.

Knife in hand, she draws her eyebrows in, clearly not thrilled with the direction of this conversation. "Correction. I used to paint. It's not an interest of mine anymore."

Samuel pours cream into his coffee before stirring it with a small silver spoon. "You're too modest, Everleigh Rose. Her paintings used to hang all over town. Almost every resident of Moss Ford owned one. It wouldn't surprise me if they made it all the way to the First City or Avren. Her natural renditions are *that* good."

Evie taps her knife against her plate. Samuel must not know her well enough now to understand her patience threshold. There's a chance that the Everleigh Rose from before the Reckoning was a different person.

"I'm sure they are," I say before swallowing the remainder of my coffee. "Evie is someone who can do whatever she sets her mind to. But I think you'd better lay it to rest, Sam." I force out a weak smile, taking on my role as the one to defuse the situation.

"If we travel to the secret garden, no talk of painting or Ferrish. Understand?" Evie leans back in her chair, her gaze moving between us. "It might be hard to believe, but I do have feelings."

We clean up the breakfast items in silence with neither Samuel nor I bringing up Evie's hidden talent. She kicks her feet up on the table while whittling a stick. The brandished knife serves as a warning to anyone bold enough to cross the line.

"Our meeting with the Supes will be in the Needles Sanctuary, so I thought we'd return on the outer trail to save time." Samuel loads his jacket with various weapons. He reminds me more of a warrior this way, familiar with a dagger and short knife, rather than a person who spent days in the wilderness weathering a rainstorm.

Evie looks at me and purses her lips. "That passes through the Hale farm."

My desire to avoid my past outweighs any hope for efficiency of travel. If the trail back from the secret garden to this sanctuary takes longer, so be it. We'll leave earlier. "We won't take the outer trail."

Samuel watches our exchange wearily then opens the front door. "Then we'll return on the inner trail. Doesn't make a difference to me."

After locking up his cottage, Samuel leads us through the town to a trail on the north end. Thick foliage disguises the entrance, which is overrun with brambles and vines. The only clue to its existence is a break in the grass on the ground.

Samuel removes his sword to cut us a path. He doesn't have to do this for long. Once we're past the initial overgrown bushes, the trail clears out as if it's maintained.

"How do the townspeople use this trail? The entrance hasn't been accessed in years." I glance behind me, expecting to see the chopped branches lying on the ground. But the bushes fill in before my eyes, reaching thick vines over the trail like snakes. "What the hell?"

"Magic." Samuel keeps his eyes forward with his sword still drawn. "There are secrets in this forest the people and Supes of Moss Ford want to keep hidden."

"From whom?" I ask, but then it comes to me. "The Miscretes and Arazian. It's less than half a day's journey from the First City to Moss Ford. It's no wonder you keep the Supes here to protect you."

"It's not something we're proud of." He sheaths his sword, although he keeps looking around like his life depends on it. "Living a life of fear is rather like not living at all. If I'm truthful, this is my first time on this trail since the Reckoning. If we stay behind locked doors and let the Supes take care of us, we might survive to old age."

"The savior is here to change that for you. For all of Moss Ford." Evie elbows me in the ribs, not out of jest but to get me to respond.

"Yeah, um, Mari and I are both gathering forces to join the fight. If we can defeat the First City, you'll no longer need to live in fear." I hope everything I say is true. Thankfully, my lack of confidence doesn't come through in the tenor of my voice.

The canopy above us thickens as we move deeper into the heart of the forest. A bird sits on a branch and cocks its head, eyeing us with suspicion. The air is heavy with the stillness of the wooded refuge, a place hidden from the chaotic world outside. Magic keeps many from passing this way, as evidenced by the pristine nature of the beauty around us.

We no longer talk out of fear of shattering this sanctuary like a stained-glass window. The path curves down a slope into a ravine and then up again to the forest floor.

Samuel stops beside a wall of boulders. No one comes here. The people of Moss Ford saw to this by relying on the supernatural residents to protect them—the same ones who suck away their lives like parasites.

"Can I go alone?" Evie stands in the crevice between two rocks, her hand resting on the smooth surface. "I haven't been here since…" She turns away from us and appears to brush away a tear. "Just give me a minute."

I slide down the rock and rest my back against the hard surface. The amount of trauma in our little family is enough to fill fifty lifetimes. And with Levi gone, it's a wonder we get out of bed in the morning. Whatever it takes, I will get the three of them through this. They need to enjoy the fruits of our labor—freedom from the tyranny of the cities.

"Is she your girlfriend?" Samuel points his thumb toward the rocks before hooking it in his belt loop.

"Evie?" I raise my eyebrows, appalled at the idea. "No. I think of her as my sister and nothing else. She's dating my best friend. If they make it through this war alive, they'll marry and settle in a cottage in the country. I'm with my other sister."

"Sounds like an incestuous arrangement." There's no smirk on Samuel's lips as he pulls a metal flask from his hip and takes a swig. "To each his own."

"It's not what it sounds like." I roll my head to the side to look at him, disgusted with his thoughts. "We're brother and sister in name only. The Kindred Few agrees to live together because we've all been orphaned by either Avren or the First City." I yank down the neck of my shirt to show him my tattoo. "When we stand together, we're stronger than we would be going it alone."

He takes another drink, caps the flask, and sticks it in his pocket before hanging his head. "That's what I thought too. But after the Reckoning, after so many of us lost so much, Moss Ford went to hell." He slides down and sits on the opposite side of the opening from me. "Many left, no longer willing to face the dangers of the First City. The ones who stayed formed camps. I wanted to build up our capacity. To train warriors to take on the Miscretes when they returned. Others wanted to allow the rebel Supes a place of refuge in exchange for protection." Lifting a shoulder, he flashes me a smile. "You can see who won out."

I clasp my hands in my lap. This mindset isn't unlike the one many in the wilderness have, and it's something we'll have to overcome to win this war. Many would rather live in peaceful captivity than risk their lives to win freedom. "Are there more like you? People who wanted to fight?"

"A second wave of people left when we let the Supes into the village. They've settled far and wide. A small contingent went to join the Northern Duke, but I'm guessing they were sorely disappointed." He gathers a pebble into his hand and tosses it at a nearby tree. "Turns out he's connected with the Dark King."

"He definitely works under a cloud of deception." I don't want to give away too much to a stranger who hasn't proven himself to me yet. "I'd like to return to Tenny Rocks with at least a hundred people and Supes willing to join the fight. If our plan to change the Miscretes falls through, we'll need all the power we can get from the two villages."

"If you lost this sister of yours to Arazian's witchcraft, wouldn't you do everything in your power to get her back?" Samuel's words slur as his shoulders slump.

"The second they dragged her away, I'd be on their tail, ready to rip them limb from limb. I'd single-handedly tear down the walls of the First City to find her. I'd never sit around for years drinking away my sorrow."

"I imagine a strong warrior like you doesn't know what it's like to feel helpless." He lifts his sleeve and holds his wrist up to me. Jagged scars mark his wrists. "I'd rather die than live in a world where I know that I let this happen. And maybe joining this war might get me killed, but at least I'd be doing something beyond sitting around and rotting away."

This man is more respectable than I thought.

"Then I'd be honored for you to help me lead the troops into the First City. One of my goals is not to be leadership-heavy, but I can't let your talents go to waste." I stand up, ready to join Evie in the secret garden. Without Mari, I'm not ready to face my past at the Hale farm.

Samuel gets to his feet, standing a bit straighter than before. "I'd be honored, Commander."

The entrance into the garden is a tight squeeze between the boulders. I need to twist and turn my body like a contortionist to get through. The mixture of floral and moss scents hits me before I'm in the garden. It's the heady smell of perfumes I'm told women wear in the city, but the fresh air from above makes it bearable.

Evie sits on a mossy rock on the far end with a pencil and pad in her hands, not looking up when we enter. An explosion of color stands between us, a testament to the talents of the nymphs of Heatherwood. Floral vines crisscross high above, forming a roof. A trail meanders through the flowers, which reach high above us. It's as if we've been shrunk to the size of insects in this magical world.

"Ferrish and I used to come here to…" He pauses, tilting his head to the side and smiling. "Have a bit of private time. It's not like the nymphs cared. They're all into the promiscuous side of things."

"Too much information," I grumble as I scramble down the rocks to the path below. Guy talk is not my idea of a good way to bond with Samuel. Show me what you can do with your weapons, then we'll talk.

Bees zoom past me. Tiny creatures scurry along the floor of the flowerbed. Nymphs move from flower to flower, watering, preening, and singing to the plants. An entire ecosystem is teeming with life within this hidden garden. My thoughts drift to my meeting with the Supes tonight. What can I say to convince them? That I'm the savior? Heard that one before. They need to see the real benefit in it for them—for their entire race.

"Evie's changed," Samuel states behind me.

I turn to look at him and raise an eyebrow, having no idea if she can hear us from her perch above.

"She was Ferrish's carefree kid sister. Always singing and painting." The corner of his lip lifts. "Drove her parents crazy how they could never find her." His gaze shifts as he tugs on his ear. "After the Reckoning, she came back to work at her parents' tavern. She's moody all the time, obsessed with weapons, and could care less about the art she loved so much."

"People change," I mutter, knowing how much my family's deaths affected me. "She's a deep thinker who's loyal to a fault. She'd risk her life for the Kindred Few. Maybe someday, she'll find her way back to what used to bring her joy."

"I hope so." Samuel moves ahead of me to climb the wall to the ledge above the garden.

"The view from up here is constantly changing." Evie stares out over the flowers. In her sketchpad, where I expect to see a drawing, the page is blank. "It's something I'd always loved about coming here." She looks at me, her eyes glistening. "I wish now that everything could have stayed the same."

As I sit down beside her, I take her hand in mine and let her rest her head on my shoulder. Grief creeps up on us after festering inside like an invasive disease. For years, I've suppressed my own grief with my physical pursuits, both combative and in the bedroom. It took really caring about someone other than myself to allow me to dive into the black tangle of grief I've held back for so long. "I know."

"I want her back so much it hurts." Evie doesn't move her head, but I can hear her sniffle.

"And we'll get her back." I hate making empty promises, and I'm sure she sees through my bullshit. "I'll strangle it out of my father if need be. You'll get Ferrish back one way or another."

CHAPTER TWENTY-FIVE

Mari

WAYLON STANDS, still seeming unconvinced about whether to allow his pack to risk their lives in the First City. "We have our freedom. If Avren's soldiers or the Miscretes bother us, we rip their throats out. Simple as that."

"But you might not have that freedom for long." I glance at Grayson, not positive on the plan Lady Raven and Arazian have to work together. "It benefits both cities to eliminate the Supes and expand into the wilderness. They'll use the backs of the Undesirables to accomplish their plans."

Grayson remains stone-faced. Maybe he's had the same thoughts. What other reason would the two cities have for working together? Bastian's parents hate each other, so any reconciliation must benefit both parties.

The pack leader steps closer to me, filling up my personal space with his enormous presence. I keep my back straight, not wanting to show any sign of weakness as searing heat radiates from his body, making my knees weak.

He brings his hand to my face and pinches my cheek. "I like you. You're cute."

Not exactly the look I was going for.

With a small step back, he says, "I'll tell you what. If you can defeat my best warriors in the Rumsford Rumble tomorrow, we're in."

I look to Grayson. "Both of us?"

Waylon smirks. "No, just you."

Images of a wrestling match with wolves fills my mind. They'll kill me in two seconds flat. There must be a different way. My chest heaves as I suck in a musky breath of air.

"Relax, human." Waylon's enormous hands clamp down on my upper arms like a vise as he turns me toward the window. "You see the archery range over there? My best, in their human forms, will compete to be my second-in-command. My previous one was killed by twenty Avrenian soldiers. If you win, we join you."

"And if I don't?" There always seem to be consequences with the Supes. If they don't get something out of it, it's not worth doing.

"We have a hunting competition the day after. My best hunters need prey to capture in their pursuits. Both of you will do nicely." Waylon keeps his eyes on the archery range. "No risk, no reward."

"Don't agree to it," Grayson says from behind me. "Everything's a trap with Supes. He knows you can't beat his best archer."

"How?" I ask, turning back to my brother. "He's never seen me shoot an arrow. Don't you trust Bastian's training?"

"Listen to your sister, Grayson." Waylon crosses his arms, the smirk back on his face. His amusement makes me think he's playing with his food.

Grayson ignores the pack leader's remarks. "The guy has spies everywhere. Probably watched you shooting in the Grove."

"Ahh, the Grove. Such a tragedy." Waylon hangs his head in mock sympathy.

"What do you know about that?" Grayson charges across the room but takes several steps back as Waylon puffs out his chest. Their size difference is laughable.

"I know it was burnt to a crisp." The wolf man shows no emotion as he lays out what happened. "I know Avrenian guards sent flaming arrows into the huts, chased down survivors, and skewered them with their swords. The Council got wind of what was happening in that tiny dot on the map. Better watch what you're doing in Tenny Rocks. It might suffer a similar fate."

It wasn't the First City. But that doesn't mean Arazian didn't alert the Council.

"I'll do it." Without more forces, we won't stand a chance against the Dark King's army. If I need to prove myself a worthy savior by winning a competition, then that's what I'll do.

"Mari," Grayson whispers, holding his head in his hands.

Waylon's smirk changes into an evil grin. He thinks he has us caught. "Then we'll meet you on the range at noon tomorrow. And may the best wolf—I mean, person win."

After Waylon and his hench-wolves leave, Grayson drops to his knees. The pack leader's presence was too much for him. He still holds his head in his hands, shaking. "You don't know what you just did."

I drop beside him, resting a hand on his shoulder. "I'm not afraid of the wolves. Yes, they kill people. And no, I've never shot an arrow in a competition before." Energy flows from my hand into my brother's shoulder as I try to reassure him. The truth is, I've come to finally understand my role. Maybe it's not to lead the wilderness into battle but to stand as a symbol of strength. If I back down from Waylon's challenge, I might as well back down from this entire fight. "I know you're my big brother and you're only looking out for me, but I can win this tomorrow. It's not something I can explain. You must believe me."

My touch seems to strengthen him. With my hand still on his shoulder, he drops his hands to look at me. "It's difficult for me to separate the girl I escorted out of Avren and the one kneeling beside me now. Have patience with me. I want so badly to believe in you, to follow your lead, but I've seen too much in the wilderness."

The energy that first drew me to Bastian, now swirls with threads of confidence. To follow its prodding is the course I must take. The ancient fae knew something I can't begin to understand, but I need to trust it. "I know," I say, not breaking the flow between us. "I can't explain what's happening inside of me, but I won't be alone in the competition tomorrow. Waylon thinks he has us beat, and his arrogance will be his downfall."

"I hope the same isn't true for you." My brother gives me a sad smile. He gets to his feet and goes to lie down on the couch.

I settle on the bed, laying my head on the pillow. One thing is certain: I'm going to need all the rest I can get if I'm going to beat Waylon's best tomorrow.

CROWDS SURROUND the archery range before noon the next day. Massive men and women with arm muscles the size of my legs draw back arrows and send them flying into targets with deadly accuracy. The confidence I felt the night before has dissipated, so I dig deep to harness the energy.

"Are you going to warm up with the rest of them?" Grayson carries my quiver, which is filled with silver-tipped arrows in case things go south. "You haven't had a chance to practice in a while."

My hand feels awkward on the handle of my bow. The slick

of sweat on my palm reveals how I really feel about this competition. "Can we go out into the woods to practice? We have a half hour until it starts."

As we pass the range, a woman a foot and a half taller than me lets an arrow fly. It hits the target with such force that it bursts the seams. Hay flies everywhere.

"Don't break the targets before we start, Helena," growls a male competitor.

I can hear the murmurs and occasional roars of the crowd from the small meadow in the forest. Birds flutter in the branches of the trees above us, sending leaves and needles fluttering to the ground. If I don't win this competition, my brother and I will be fighting for our lives in this forest tomorrow.

Grayson sets the quiver against a tree and rubs his hands together. "Let's see what you've got." He removes an arrow and hands it to me.

Drawing in a deep breath, I place my feet, rooting them to the ground, and lift my bow, nocking the arrow as I raise it. I aim the tip toward a birch tree between two massive pines. If I can't hit a narrow target, I shouldn't be in this contest. When I'm confident in my aim, I let the arrow fly. It drifts to the left, grazing the bark of one of the pine trees.

Grayson whistles. "Do you think you can correct that in less than a half hour?"

Hands shaking as I lift the bow again, I'm not sure. The wolves shooting at the range hit the target every time. "I don't have a choice."

This time, the arrow grazes the bark of the birch. Closer.

Grayson places a hand on my shoulder as I reach for another arrow. "Last night, when you touched me, I felt your energy. It was like nothing I've ever felt before. There's something special inside of you, Mari. Tap into that. Use it to give you the strength to win."

It's not something I've tried often. Only a feeling. Using it to give me an advantage feels both awkward, like wearing new shoes, and perfectly natural at the same time. With a new arrow nocked, I raise the bow again, setting up my aim. But then I close my eyes. I visualize the arrow's movement through the air, making a perfect arch and hitting the birch tree precisely in a black knot on its bark. The bow string twangs between my fingers as I release. I keep my eyes closed the entire time it's in the air, watching it hit the imaginary knot in my mind.

"You did it!" Grayson grabs my shoulders and pulls me into a hug as I look at the results of my shot.

Sure enough, it's as perfect as my visualization. I want to do it again to make sure I can trust in the process.

"I'm going to aim for the crab apple on the tree below." I raise my bow, elated with my newfound ability. "If I hit it, I think I'm ready."

Grayson brushes the hair hanging in his face behind his ear and raises an eyebrow. "You're going to hit a piece of fruit the size of a marble?"

"Yes," I say, setting up my shot. The energy under my skin is still humming from my first attempt to use it. Like if it had a voice, it would be saying *finally*. I close my eyes and visualize the arrows journey to the crab apple, then let the arrow fly.

"Shit, Mari. I don't think Bastian could do that." Grayson races across the meadow toward the tree.

I follow and find that my arrow not only struck the apple but also drove it into the pine tree behind the crab apple tree.

"You'll have to teach me how to do that." Grayson's lips turn up into the carefree smile I love.

I twist the arrow out of the tree and walk over to the birch to retrieve my first one. "I don't think I can. It's innate with the prophecy I believe. If I thought it would work for you, I would."

"Let's go kick some werewolf ass." He slaps me on the back, almost knocking me over.

"Careful. I'm not Bastian." I narrow my gaze at him, but I

don't smile. The task at hand means too much. If I can win, we'll get the werewolves on our side. I'm confident my newly tapped energy will help.

"No, you most certainly are not." He laughs as we make our way back to the range.

The crowd parts as I enter, letting me pass to the place where the other competitors gather. Like Helena, they all tower over me. They watch me like I'm a fly they're ready to squash as I approach the man holding the list of competitors.

"Maribel Windsong," I say, my fingers aching from gripping my bow too tight.

The man scans the list and finds my name, placing a check beside it. "Here you are. Interesting that a non-lycanthrope is competing for the second-in-command position in the pack. Waylon had to approve this list."

"There's more at stake if I win than being second fiddle to a washed-out pack." They're fighting words, but I don't care. I'm sure I'll hear plenty of trash talk from the other competitors.

Low growls rise from several of the people around me.

A judge for the competition gathers us around her. "Highest score wins. There'll be no cheating, transforming, or shooting at your competition. May the best wolf win."

The other competitors lift their faces to the sky and howl, so I do the same, garnering a weary look from Grayson.

I wait my turn beside a younger wolf who appears eager to prove himself. He bounces on his feet, trying to psyche himself up. When he finally calms himself, he turns to me. "You know you're the joke of this competition, right?"

I hold my hand out to him. "I'm Mari, and you are?"

"Felix." He only stares at my hand as if it's covered in warts. "Waylon only let you in so we'd have human volunteers for round two tomorrow. Also figures it's a good way to get rid of one of the saviors."

"Then I guess I'll have to prove the overgrown hairball wrong and beat you all." I'm pushing the boundaries, but if their only plan is to use me for wolf bait, I don't care. "When I win, every one of you is bound to fight in the battle against the First City and Avren because of your overconfident pack leader."

"In your dreams, human." Felix's eyes glow yellow as his pupils reduce to slits.

When it is my turn, Felix and two other wolves line up facing targets at the far end of the range. The goal is to score high enough to stay in the competition and move on to the next round.

"Archers ready?" the judge calls out, holding up her hand. "Raise your bows."

I nock my arrow and raise my bow, setting my aim as best I can on my own.

"Shoot," the judge calls out.

Closing my eyes, I imagine the trajectory of the arrow as it impales the center yellow circle of the target, but in the middle of my visualization, Felix growls in my ear.

"Don't miss, human."

My fingers release the arrow and when I open my eyes, it's buried in an outer ring. Only the top three move on to the next round. I check the other three targets. One doesn't have an arrow in it.

"Felix, Solfang, and Maribel move on to the next round." The judge writes the official results in a notebook.

The competitors go to collect their arrows as a chorus of cheers and boos come from the crowd. I'm a hundred percent sure the boos are for me.

As I wait in line for my next shoot, Waylon strolls in my direction, accompanied by his gang of wolves. "Maribel, I'm pleasantly surprised you made it past the first round. Lucky for you, Jake had a bad day. I was wondering if you and your

Avrenian friend would join me for dinner tonight? My servants will draw basting baths for you afterward. There's nothing better for a hunt than basted human flesh."

"Leave me alone." I turn my back on him. There's no way I'll let Felix or Waylon get to me. If I win, he'll be obligated to help whether we like each other or not.

CHAPTER TWENTY-SIX

Bastian

SAMUEL TAKES the lead as we head along the inner trail through the woods to the sanctuary. The time between dusk and night-fall has always filled me with awe. Some creatures settle down for the night, burrowing beneath the leafy carpet. Others wake, ready for an evening of hunting and terrorizing the neighbor-hood. It's a transitional time. A moment to listen to the symphony of the crickets and cicadas as they play in melodic harmony.

Evie walks beside me, still a bit lost from her time in the garden. It's evident she left a piece of herself behind those glacial rock walls. As much as I want to save her sister, we all need to focus on the task ahead of us.

"I'll take the lead tonight." I'll use my strength and savior status to convince the Supes to join the fight. While Everleigh Rose is known to the residents, she's not ready to give a persua-sive speech. "You've got a lot on your mind."

She slices through a stand of tall reeds with her sword,

keeping it unsheathed as she shakes her head. "I'm sorry. Something got to me back there. It was as if Ferrish sat beside me, playing her flute and talking about boys and dances. Her ghost haunts every corner of that place." The tip of her sword drags through dirt along the trail. "When I was about eight and she was twelve, we snuck out to watch a meteor shower from the garden. Fireflies blinked among the treetops and in the bushes. The magical nature of a forbidden escape with my sister had me giddy. I had never disobeyed my parents."

"That's a bit shocking to hear," I laugh, tugging on her braid.

She doesn't respond the way I think she will to my teasing. "It's true. I've changed. I lost parts of me that I'll never get back after their deaths."

I imagine an Evie without the sarcasm, constant complaints, and snide remarks. "I wish I had known that part of you."

"You didn't miss much." She keeps her attention on her sword dragging through the dirt. "I was gullible, too trusting, and felt safe in my environment. Never again. I won't go back to where a feeling of safety allows monsters to attack the people I love."

The glow of a bonfire lights the underside of the leaves in the trees high above and casts shadows along our path. I never thought I'd work with vampires, fae, werewolves, and other creatures that call Moss Ford their home. I usually try to steer clear of them, not allowing their rhythms to dictate my behavior. Here, I'm willingly strolling into a place where the Supes could kill me.

A horde of creatures surround the fire, their faces otherworldly in the reddish-orange glow of the fire. Shadows and light dance over their visages, adding a horrific element to the scene. Most of the monsters segregate themselves, so it is easy to differentiate between them. Each is impressive in their own way. As much as I dislike the Supes, that doesn't mean I don't respect them.

The vampires are the first to sense our arrival. Pale, impossibly beautiful faces turn in our direction as we crest the hill above. If they wanted to, they could overcome us in less than a second.

Beside them stand the fae, taller than any other creature here. Dirty fae. Of all the Supes, they are the lowest on my list after what happened to Levi. But now's not the time for revenge. The fae king already got what was coming to him. They hold their noses in the air, as if standing beside the others is beneath them. Arrogance is the most likely reason, but standing beside the wolves might also offend their sensitive noses.

Most of the werewolves remain in their human forms despite the full moon above. They're much hairier and rowdier than the others, their boisterous *yips* and howls making their presence no secret. It's obvious they've been drinking all afternoon as some break into vulgar songs about women, partying, and fighting. It's strange how I relate to them more than the others.

Other Supes sprinkle themselves among the three main groups—wood sprites, dwarves, ogres, magicians, and some I don't know the names for. The word of our intention to do away with the Miscretes has gotten out to the far reaches of the wilderness.

The Supes part as we approach, letting us through to climb the stairs of a small wooden platform on the other side of the fire. My gut twists into knots recognizing the enormity of the task before us. My speech needs to deliver, or the three of us might be in for the fight of our lives. I've taken on one or two Supes before, but there must be at least a hundred gathered here.

As I look out over the crowd, a trickle of sweat rolls down my forehead as the heat from the bonfire gets to me. I close my eyes, wanting to draw on the prophecy's energy but come up empty. It's as if its left me alone to face the wolves—literally.

Standing before a group we need to succeed in this battle, I have to embrace what I've long feared: my true self.

I open my eyes, scan the crowd of Supes, and swallow back my fear. "I grew up a stone's throw from the village on a farm where the Miscretes tortured and murdered my family." Gory details might add validity to my tale. "My brother was ripped from my hands and eaten alive by a horde of the creatures. Since that day, it's been my life purpose to make those responsible pay for what their minions did on our farm. Of the six people there that night, only my brother Levi and I survived." I swallow back the tears, a replay of that night running through my mind. "To you, the Miscretes are nothing but an annoyance. To the humans of the wilderness, they are our friends and family." I look at Evie. Her eyes glisten.

A vamp steps forward, his face revealing zero emotion. "They say you're the savior, but you've killed my kind." He looks at the fae and werewolves. "You've killed all of our kind."

The giant dragon in the room. They'd expect me to address this.

"What choice do I have? I don't actively attack your kind. But if a Supe threatens me or someone I love, I won't stand back and let them take lives. The fae prophecy declares that I'm a savior. What does a savior do? He saves." I let that sink in for a moment as I contemplate my next words. "If we are to stand up against the First City and Avren, we must stand up against their ideals and embrace our own. The wilderness is a place for freedom, not oppression. Inclusion, not exclusivity. Tolerance, not hatred. We must learn to live together in harmony to show we are better."

A pale applause arises from the crowd of Supes. Not exactly what I was hoping for but better than nothing.

"If we stand by and do nothing, Arazian and the Council of

Avren will join forces and destroy us. They've worked together in secret for years despite an overt hatred of each other." I look at the vampire who stepped forward to question me. "When they take the Undesirable humans in as slaves, do you think they'll let the Supes live in peace? Not a chance. They fear you. Fear turns to hate and annihilation."

"And if we work with you, how do we know you won't turn around and do the same thing, Dark Prince?" A female werewolf steps forward, her arms crossed.

"Listen, I know you have no reason to trust me, but I stand here giving you my word. I hold no claim over my title. I'm an Undesirable as much as you are." I lick my lips, hoping my speech isn't in vain. "I hate my birth father more than anyone here. If I can kill him with my own sword, I will. But I stand here, Commander Bastian Hale, leader of the wilderness forces, to let you know that if you join us, I will do everything in my power to extend the same freedoms to the Supes as I will to the humans."

"And what about you, Everleigh Rose?" A witch steps out from behind the bonfire, her blondish-brown hair flowing over her shoulders to her bosom. She's one of the women who practices her craft in the caves deep in the woods. I avoid them like the plague. "Do you hold the same beliefs as your so-called brother? Ferrish told me you rejected her more experimental side. If you get your sister back, destroying the sisterhood might benefit your narrow mind."

"Leave my sister out of it." Evie's teeth clench as she glares at the witch.

Samuel steps forward, apparently feeling the need to defend Ferrish's honor. "Let's focus on the commander's request. All of us have a lot to lose if the cities get what they want. We plan to attack the First City in a month's time. Are you with us or not?"

I didn't realize Samuel was a *get to the point* kind of guy. Maybe I like him more than I thought.

Murmurs rise among the Supes as they huddle in their respective circles, hashing out their options. I honestly don't expect the fae to vote to join us. Although this group is estranged from Frostacre, Mari killed their king. The others come down to a coin flip.

The female werewolf who questioned me earlier calls out first. "The wolves will stand with you." She smirks and lifts her chin. "We've wanted to get our jaws around Sterling's neck for a while."

Surprisingly, there aren't any protests rising from the vamps. A male, with long blond hair only a shade lighter than his face calls out, "We agree with Portia. Sterling mars our name. His egregious acts of self-preservation make him a hazard to our community. Though he is a rebel like us, he's in bed with our enemy." The vampire's straight face is almost comical to me as it lacks any emotion. "We will also stand with you."

A member of the fae steps forward, almost floating over the ground by the fire. Glowing embers sparkle against his dark hair as he moves closer to us, an almost imperceptible crease of compassion between his eyebrows. "King Cirrus murdered your brother."

I'm not sure what to say. The admission comes as a shock because I expected the opposite. *You murdered King Cirrus.* A lump grows in my throat as I manage to respond with a weak, "Yes."

"The fae of Moss Ford understand your pain. We, too, have lost loved ones to the Unseelie Court." He reaches his hand to my forehead. His fingers are impossibly long.

I don't know why, but I let him. The mental capabilities of the fae astound me.

"You hold no ill will, but you have a complicated past." He looks past me into the woods, drawing on his supernatural energy. "The internal battle will be great, Prince Bastian. The choice will come upon you like a heavy stone."

More prophecy? There's no choice. With the help of these forces, we wipe out the First City and kill my father. End of story.

He drops his hand and meets my eyes. Sadness shields itself behind his steely fae gaze. "You love the other savior."

Did I let him delve too much? Probably. "I do."

"Don't let that stand in the way of your purpose, Prince Bastian." The fae drops to one knee and bows his head. "The ancient fae prophecies will ring true. And we, the rebels of the Unseelie Court, stand with you."

I can't wrap my head around what he said about Mari standing in my way, let alone the fact that they'll fight with us. I push aside the prophecy crap and focus on our impending battle. With my best fighters from the Grove and the Supes from Moss Ford on our side, there's only one missing piece left to the complete puzzle of how to take down the First City.

Changing the Miscretes.

"WHEN DID you plan to get around to telling me that you're the Dark Prince?" Samuel had remained quiet a majority of our walk back to the village. I didn't realize he was stewing. "It's a bit of a double-edged sword, don't you think? Part savior, part evil prince."

"Samuel Roy," Evie snaps as she turns to face him in the moonlight. "Do you trust me?"

He stutters as he blurts out, "Of course, I trust you."

"Then why are you questioning a man I call my brother?" The light from the moon is dim, but I can see her hands planted firmly on her hips. "He's known the Dark King is his father for a very short time, and he's already betrayed the man's trust.

There's not a doubt in my heart whose side he's on. I trust Bastian with my life, and so should you."

Samuel looks at me and lifts an eyebrow. "You could rule an entire city, live in a fancy house, have any woman you want, but you choose to reduce your palace to a heap of rubble? Sorry if I'm skeptical."

In the few short days I spent in Arazian's mansion, I did enjoy the food and pampering. It was so different from my time growing up on the farm where we worked hard to help our parents. But seeing the way my father treated Mari sent me spiraling into a world of murderous intentions and revenge. The look on her face when my father announced my engagement to a random woman and had her strip down naked in front of the crowd—in front of the woman I love—made me crumble inside. Never will I hurt her like this again. Title or not, there's no way in hell I want to be the Dark Prince.

"I'm the commander of the wilderness forces," I state, keeping the emotion of my thoughts out of my voice. "The Dark Prince is dead to me."

"Because of Everleigh, I'll trust you... for now." Samuel walks beside me as we continue our trek home. "The second I sense a betrayal of that trust, I'll slit your throat."

"Good to know." The dagger under my pillow will serve me well with Samuel Roy around.

CHAPTER TWENTY-SEVEN

Mari

WHEN I STEP up to the line, I'm ready. I've purposely picked the spot on the opposite end from Felix. As the arrow leaves my bow, my vision has it hitting the dead center of the target. The silence of the crowd tells me my accuracy is on point this time.

Grayson joins me in line, excitement etched across his face. "You knocked out Solfang. In the other groups, it looks like your biggest competition is Elstan, who others tell me is the clear favorite. He's hit the bullseye every time, but yours was in the exact center. You've got this."

Elstan is an enormous man, slightly shorter than Waylon but just as broad. He sports tattoos on his face, bald head, and arms like badges of honor or trophies. I watch him shoot—his stance, his posture, the way he doesn't let anything distract him. When he lets his arrow fly, there's no arc to the trajectory. It soars straight through the air with incredible speed and punctures the target just left of center, though still in the yellow bullseye.

If I beat Felix, I'll face Elstan and Helena in the finals. When I look at the young wolf beside me, I can tell there's no way he'll go down without a fight and a bit of cheating. He's red-faced. Veins protrude from his forehead and arms. I've gotten under his skin, and my heart stutters in fear that he might transform.

He bends down so his face is close to mine. His breath smells of rotting flesh and liquor. "There's no way I'm going to let Avrenian filth like you beat me. Lose this round or die, little girl."

When the two of us line up to shoot, my hands are shaking. My heart still beats rapidly with his proclamation. Will the others let him kill me in his wolf form? I'm thankful they put us on the targets at the far ends, away from each other.

I watch Felix shoot first. It's a great shot, clearly in the bulls-eye. Still worked up, he smirks in my direction. With all my focus on my shot, I'm not sure if I'll be quick enough to draw another silver-tipped arrow if he does change.

As I close my eyes, I push the wolf's demeanor out and let the energy inside me guide my shot. I hear my arrow pierce the target and then a deafening silence among the onlookers.

A roar arises from the other side of the range, so I open my eyes.

Felix is already in his wolf form, gnashing his enormous teeth in my direction. His yellow eyes narrow in on me—the predator locked in on its prey. He bounds toward me before I have a chance to think about drawing another arrow. The wolf knocks me to the ground, his teeth inches from my face.

Then Felix falls to the side, whining.

I scramble to my feet, my heart in my throat. My life just flashed before my eyes. An arrow protrudes from the wolf's side as he lies in a pool of his own blood.

"I said no cheating." The judge drops her own bow and nods to the other two competitors. "Let that be a warning."

Helena skirts around Felix, turning her nose in the air. From what I've heard about the wolf community, weakness is not tolerated. The others saw Felix as weak for not controlling his emotions.

I stand behind the white line, trying to regain my composure, and glance down at the other two archers, my arms exhausted. Bows already raised, they're ready to go.

Helena looks over at me and sneers. "You got lucky with that last shot. I'll hunt you down in no time tomorrow. You should never have made a deal with Waylon."

With my bow by my side, I swallow back my fear. As a savior, I can't let her intimidate me. "You will lose and join us on the battlefield to defeat Arazian and Sterling. No one can defeat me."

Helena throws her head back and laughs, clearly not bothered by my fighting words. "Pitiful human. I'll let you watch me rip your brother's throat out first. Your over-confidence makes you weak."

"And your face makes you ugly." I don't know why I say it, but eloquent comebacks don't come as easily for me as they do for Grayson.

"Arghhhh!" Helena lets her arrow fly before the judge's whistle, hitting the bullseye.

The judges rushes over with her hands out. "Disqualification. No one shall shoot until the whistle is blown."

The wolf woman throws down her bow, patches of hair growing from her arms. "You little piece of…"

"Go take a seat, Helena," Elstan calls out, not taking his eyes from the target. "I've got this."

She walks away muttering curse words under her breath. The threat of the judge shooting her must have kept her from transforming. With a great deal of flourish and commotion, she sits on a log beside her comrades.

Elstan looks at me and smiles. "It's you and me, human. Closest to the center wins."

I plant my feet and straighten my back before lifting the

bow. If the wolves knew about the energy, they'd probably accuse me of cheating. But when something is part of you, is it an unfair advantage?

The large wolf man lets his arrow fly directly into the bullseye, striking the target with such force that the entire structure wobbles. It's not exactly in the center, but it's closer than it was last time. I need to shoot to perfection to win.

"Where are my manners?" Elstan covers his smirk with his hand. "Ladies always shoot before gentlemen. "Guess you still have a long way to go to becoming a woman."

Ignoring him, I raise my bow, ready to show him what I'm made of. There's a lot riding on this shot and Grayson is depending on it as much as I am. The crowd chatters on as if they don't consider me serious competition for their champion. I settle my concentration on the yellow circle at the center, ready to prove my worth. I close my eyes, relying on my inner senses rather than my outer ones to get the job done.

The familiar *twang* as I release the bow string echoes in my ear. I don't look yet, waiting for the telltale sound of the arrow piercing the target. Dead center again. Never in my life have I felt truly talented in anything. Hours of practice with a needle and thread gave me a possible career in Avren, but I wasn't gifted with it. Archery is different.

In the time it takes to truly admire my shot, I've failed to notice the silence of the crowd. I've taken down their champion. They all truly believed Elstan would become Waylon's second-in-command. I've embarrassed him in front of his pack.

He stares at me, shakes his head, and walks off with his tail between his legs. I half expect him to transform like Felix, but it's obvious he's been beat.

The crowd parts and their leader steps through with a medal in his left hand. He holds his right out to me, and I take it reluctantly.

"Never in my life did I think a human could beat my best."

Waylon drops my hand before stringing the medal over my head. "And an Avrenian? Impossible."

I glance at Grayson, who stands nearby with his hand beneath his jacket at his waist. It's more than likely wrapped around a silver dagger. "I expect you to keep to your end of the bargain." The sun is high in the sky, making me squint, so I hold my up hand to shield my eyes.

"Half of my wolves will meet you at the appointed time. They will join the fight against the First City." The pack leader stuffs his hands into his pockets, looks down at his feet, and shuffles them in the dirt. Worthless piece of dog crap. He's reneging on the terms we set. He turns to walk away.

"All," I say under my breath.

"What was that?" He stops and looks back at me, daring me to question his leadership in front of the pack.

I square my shoulders, draw an arrow, and point it at Waylon. "I said, *all* the wolves will join us in the battle. That's what we agreed on."

A chorus of growls rise from the wolves around me.

He holds his hands in the air, letting out a nervous laugh. "Don't be foolish, Maribel. The instant you let that arrow fly, my pack will rip you to shreds."

"Mari, drop the bow." Grayson takes small steps in my direction as if I'm a caged animal, waiting for someone to release me.

This is about more than the impending battle. This is about the humans and Supes living in peace with each other once this is all over. People will no longer be on the bottom of the food chain. "Shut up, Gray."

"Your brother is a very smart man." Waylon takes a hesitant step backward, bumping into two pack members. "You should listen to him."

"And you will agree to send *all* of your pack to Tenny Rocks." It might be foolish, but with the energy of the prophecy coursing through my veins, I'm no longer afraid of the Supes. "If you comply, I might let you keep Rumsford as your home base after all of this is over."

"I thought the point of taking down the cities was to do away with centralized control?" Waylon shakes his head as if I duped him into believing a fairytale. "Local leaders in charge of their jurisdictions."

"That's the plan." There's a small part of me that worries about one of the Supe leaders wanting to take control after the cities are gone. That's why Cirrus and Arazian wanted the saviors. "But as one of the two leading the wilderness into battle, I want to bring everyone together to make those decisions after the smoke clears."

"Fair." The wolf man claps his hands, and the wolves disperse, leaving us alone except for Grayson. "Now, tell me how you really won that competition."

I hold up my free arm to flex my muscle. "Pure skill and strength. Not all humans are worthless."

"Elstan will go with you to Tenny Rocks. As much as I'd like to trust you, it serves my purposes to keep an eye on the operation of preparing for this battle." The pack leader glances toward the edge of town, where the bald man stands with a bag. They must be communicating telepathically. "He knows what to do if you double-cross me."

Great. I can't wait to have a hairy shadow.

"You'll make a great leader of the humans one day, Maribel Windsong. You don't put up with much." Waylon removes an axe from his belt, holding it in front of him. Intricate carvings decorate the metal blade. "A human gave this to me many moons ago when I fought alongside her in the Battle of the Gretis Expanse. I made a vow that if I ever found her equal, I'd pass along the gift. May it serve you well."

I hold the axe up and let the sun reflect off its metallic surface. Though I admire its beauty, it's a weapon I'm not familiar with. As much as this leader tried to con me, I appreciate the gesture. "Thank you."

Grayson and I leave Rumsford in silence, unsure of how to talk about the idea that we were almost werewolf prey. It wasn't a situation I wanted to put either of us in, but we escaped with the promise of a pack of wolves for the fight, a valuable weapon, and a wolf warrior in tow. I can't imagine what Bastian will say.

Although the incident in the Grove will tear him apart.

"So... what do you do for fun in Rumsford, Elstan?" Grayson turns to walk backward facing our companion. "Play a bit of billiards? Smooth talk the ladies? Hold dog food eating contests?"

Elstan stares at him, his face expressionless. It's obvious the guy would tear Grayson from limb from limb if his leader gave the word. "We play pin the tail on the jackass. Two wolves accidentally ate the last one. You up for the job?"

Grayson pulls his lips back into a fake smile, rubs his hands together, and turns around, joining me. "Yeah, I'm currently employed. Great benefits and retirement."

The afternoon sun hangs low in the sky as we skirt around the Grove and the cabin. We avoid leading Elstan to our home in case things turn south. It's still a hike to Tenny Rocks, but the moon isn't full anymore, so we're not concerned about any werewolf sightings from Elstan.

Grayson rattles off a new strategy for overtaking Arazian and Sterling without our key players from the Grove. Important parts still haven't shifted into place. Will Xeno come back with news about the Miscretes? Did Bastian and Evie convince the Supes of Moss Ford to join the fight? And what about my father?

It's almost midnight when we reach Tenny Rocks. Elstan leaves us, preferring the woods to a warm bed at an unfamiliar inn. A single oil lamp hanging from a peg nailed into a support beam halos the dark hair of a large man behind the counter as he writes in the ledger. I'm thankful it's not Katiana.

Grayson leans over and whispers, "That's Adair, Katiana's brother." He plasters on a smile and waltzes over to the counter, slapping his hands down beside the ledger. "Adair, my good man, my sister and I need a room for the night."

Katiana's brother straightens to his full height, towering above Grayson.

"Uh… that's if you have one," Grayson adds, slipping his hands from the counter and into his pockets.

"You're the weasel they call Grayson Elrod, correct?" Adair removes a set of keys from his board and swings them around his finger. He lets them go and they sail across the room into a metal bucket by the door. "Oops."

My brother walks over to the bucket and screws up his face in disgust. "You tossed the keys into the spittoon pail?"

"Three words, Elrod," Adair growls, holding up three fingers. "Revenge for my sister."

"That's four words." Grayson removes a dagger from his pocket and scrunches up his nose.

"Do you think I care?" Adair's eyes take me in for the first time. "You could stay with me for the night."

"Don't talk to her." Grayson holds the dripping key ring on the end of his dagger above the pail. "The Stevens twins are notorious players."

That's not how I saw Katiana. She seemed more like a woman looking for love and attention. My brother was clearly in the wrong playing with her heart.

Adair doesn't care about Grayson's warning. He skirts around the counter and holds his hand out to me. "Adair Stevens at your service, miss."

His hand is bigger than Bastian's.

"Maribel Windsong," I reply, perfectly fine with an innocent handshake. "We're here to recruit soldiers for our battle against the First City. We'd like you to join us."

Grayson steps in, drying the keys on his shirt. "I think with our new acquisitions, we're all set, Mari." His past with the Stevens twins has muddied our present opportunities.

"It's up to you." I smile at Adair, ignoring my brother's insulting behavior. "We'll meet in two days' time to gather the forces. "We could use another strong set of hands."

"If it pleases you, I'll be there." As Adair smiles, I see that several of his teeth are missing. The man's seen one too many bar fights in his life.

Dropping the keys into his pocket, Grayson puffs out his chest and approaches the innkeeper. "She's Bastian Hale's girl-friend. Stay away from her."

"Whatever you say, Elrod." Adair lets out a stifled laugh as we climb the stairs to our room.

Two twin beds covered in neat quilts stand against the walls. It's small but perfect for us.

As I nestle in bed, my thoughts turn to tomorrow—bringing both good and bad news to Bastian and Evie. The idea of fighting beside wolves terrifies me, but the energy inside finds a way to calm my nerves, helping me fall asleep.

CHAPTER TWENTY-EIGHT

Bastian

SUSPICIOUS WHISPERS. Deception. Betrayal.

The weight of my past feels heavy as I walk into Tenny Rocks with Samuel and Evie. Word of my ties to the First City weaves its way among the townsfolk like a venomous snake. It overshadows my role as a savior.

A group of older women watch me from their huddle, talking in hushed voices. Men place their hands on their weapons as I pass, and children are ushered inside by nervous parents.

I want to shout "I'm on your side!" but it won't make a difference. Once someone believes a lie, they are bound and determined to repeat the narrative until its insidious nature seeps into their soul. No matter what I say or do, many in Tenny Rocks will see me only as the Dark Prince.

"Ignore it." Evie walks by my side, well attuned to the stiffness of my shoulders and rigid jaw. "They're ignorant, and you're still their savior."

The townspeople only amplify the beliefs I have about myself. What if the Dark King's and Lady Raven's DNA make me predisposed to a life of evil and corruption? In my heart, based on how the Hales raised me, I want to do the right thing.

"We're back a bit early." I adjust a dagger at my hip that's digging into my thigh. "Let's get a room at the inn and grab lunch. It will give us time to organize our plan for luring the people of this town into my evil web."

I wink at Katiana as we pass the check-in counter and head into the tavern. We find a booth by the window, but I can't help but notice how many people get up to leave as I enter. It's as if they think I'm going to cast a magical spell and turn them all into rodents.

Adair, Katiana's scoundrel of a brother, approaches us. He's almost as tall as me and twice as wide. "I need to ask you to leave."

No way. I'm starving.

I slide my arm along the seat back of the booth and cross one leg over the other. "We're paying customers."

"And my sister and I own this place. We have a right to refuse service to Supes and Dark Princes." His lips curl into a snarl as he leans on the table toward me. "Your family thinks it can waltz in here and use us for your own personal doormats."

"We're sorry if Gray hurt Katiana." Evie leans against the back wall with her feet on the bench. She glances at the oaf of a man, not intimidated by his huffing and puffing. "But there are much larger things at stake here that have nothing to do with your personal vendettas."

"I'd like a beer and your special." I carry on, ignoring Adair's request. "And a double order of the rolls you bring out before the meal. They're fantastic."

Adair pounds his fist on the table, scaring away any of the remaining customers. "I'll serve you this one time, but if I see you around here again, you're going to wish you'd crossed the threshold of another inn." He stomps away, flinging open the door to the kitchen.

"Pleasant fellow." Samuel sits on the edge of the seat he shares with Evie, her legs taking up most of their side. "As I said before, I do understand their concerns."

Gathering and training forces from Tenny Rocks might prove more difficult than I thought. No one here trusts me.

A minute or so after Adair delivers our food, Gray and Mari walk down the stairs of the inn. My heart leaps at the sight of her, so I scoot out of the booth, more than ready to have her safely in my arms. Until this moment, I didn't know how much my heart ached in her absence.

She rushes into my arms as Gray heads toward the booth to see Evie. With her arms around my neck, I scoop her up, my hands beneath her thighs as she wraps her legs behind my back. Her warm breath tickles my skin with her face buried in the crook of my neck. It's as if the world around us melts away.

When I finally release her, placing her gently on her feet, Adair glares at me as if I stole his favorite doll. I look around. "Where are the others?" Knowing Susan, she's probably convinced them to stay along the perimeter in case the First City forces attack.

Mari lowers her eyes and takes my hands. They feel impossibly small inside of mine. "Gone."

"Gone? What do you mean?" I tug on her hands as a sinking feeling hits me.

Gray walks slowly up to us. "We didn't have a chance to save them, Bastian. The place was smoldering ash before we arrived."

I drop Mari's hands, brush past her, and storm out of the inn. Sterling made the first move, but I will make the last. They rush after me, their voices fading into the background of the intense pounding in my head. For months I trained my soldiers, only to lose them before the battle's begun. I'm going to make that fucking vamp pay.

"Bastian, stop!" Mari's voice cuts through my anger. Her energy wraps around me, soothing my tense muscles.

I stare at her, not able to comprehend the undeniable feeling of her warmth while she's standing twenty feet away.

She takes hesitant steps closer as if she might scare me away. "After the Grove, Gray and I traveled to Rumsford. We met with Waylon."

Another rush of fear and anger takes over. "You met with the pack leader of the werewolves?" The guy has a superiority complex that I've dealt with one too many times. "I told you to stay away from there."

"They've agreed to join the fight." She looks at Gray and gives him a half smile. "I learned to use this force within us. For years, growing up in Avren, the Council suppressed my abilities, steering me toward a life as a dressmaker. Exiling me to the wilderness was Lady Raven's biggest mistake." There's new life in her eyes that wasn't there before. "I only wish we'd made it to the Grove in time."

"None of that was your fault." I rest a palm on the side of her face, brushing away a tear with my thumb. "Arazian knows we're gathering forces to lay siege to the city. Without my key military leaders, he's weakened us."

"It wasn't your father." She bites into her lip as I drop my hand. "Avrenian soldiers burned the village to the ground. The wolves witnessed it. It's further proof that the two cities are working together to bring an end to the rebellion." She rests her hand on my arm. "But if you go rushing in there and try to kill Sterling, effective or not, we'll miss our opportunity to save the Miscretes."

My heart aches for my friends. As tumultuous as my relationship was with Susan, they had my back no matter what. But Mari's right. There will be a time to avenge them soon. As a savior and commander of this operation, I need to keep a clear head and not let emotions guide my choices. Doing so would play right into Arazian's hands.

"Do you think he'll be there?" Evie straps her weapons belt around her waist, not knowing who we could run into on the way to the dock. "From what you've said, the guy's as slippery as they come."

"He'll be there," I say, shrugging on my jacket. "I've got a hundred and fifty credits in my pocket as an insurance policy. The walls of the First City hold a lot of secrets, and his fat rat ass can probably squeeze into most of them."

"Don't trust the guy or the rodent." Gray stands by the door, sharpening blades by running their dull edges along each other. "We had a name for people like him in Avren. Called them drifters. There's something worse than not fitting in a utopia—not fitting in with the people or Supes of the wilderness."

Samuel lounges on the bed, trying to catch a few minutes of sleep.

"But he's willing to help." Mari looks amazing. She's wearing the skin-tight black fighting gear she borrowed from Evie. It hugs her in all the places that make me sweat just thinking about them. Her face is aglow at the thought of making progress tonight with the Miscretes. I'm not sure if it was the time apart or her newfound confidence, but whatever it is, I'm here for it.

"I agree with Mari." I use a tie to pull my hair away from my face, ready for news one way or another. "With or without the secret to the Miscretes, we've got to move forward with our plans."

Oil lamps sporadically line the waterfront, lighting our way on the moonless night. The dock creaks with the current of the river, setting a spooky scene. I don't fear a Miscrete attack after our last encounter, but there are other things that go bump in the night.

Gray, Evie, and Samuel stand along the perimeter of our meeting place, keeping watch. As the time passes, an attack by either of the cities' forces becomes more and more likely. Informants keep the leaders aware of most secrets.

Mari leans against the railing of the dock, staring into the swirling water below. "Am I getting my hopes up for nothing?"

I sigh, lean my back against the railing, and cross my arms. "I'm counting on him. You should see the people in Moss Ford. They've lost hope of ever recovering their loved ones. We had to snap Samuel out of the trance that occupies the rest of the village. Day in and day out, they work, drink at the tavern, and act as a food supply for the Supes who live there, promising them safety."

A howl rises from the forest on the other side of the river, so I snatch my silver dagger from my belt.

"That's Elstan, the werewolf Waylon sent along with us." Mari hasn't moved from her spot along the railing. "I don't know if that was a warning or a mating call."

Dagger in hand, I scan the edge of the woods. "Either way, I wish Xeno would hurry up and get here."

"There!" Samuel calls out from about ten feet down the riverbank.

The others draw their weapons, ready for whatever action the darkened woods bring us.

A tall man with a pale face and long brown hair exits carrying a limp man in his arms. Sterling is expressionless as he dumps the body into the river. "Sending your spies to do your dirty work, Prince Bastian?"

Xeno floats face down in the water and any hope I had of finding a reversal for the Miscretes sinks to the bottom of the river.

I reach into my jacket for my wooden dagger, ready to take

down Arazian's second-in-command right here and now. It will be one less to fight when we reach the First City. Mari has her bow strung tight with an arrow, ready to strike the vamp's chest on my command.

"Come here and fight me, Sterling." I set my stance, dagger in hand. "Or are you scared of a little wood?"

In an instant, the vampire stands five feet away from me, his eyes blood-red and deadly. Miscretes swarm out of the forest, jaws gnashing as they wait for their master's command.

"I'm not here to fight, Your Highness." He bows his head but keeps one eye on me as he lowers it. "I'm here to bring you back to where you rightfully belong."

"Never." I narrow my eyes, ready to fight him with my bare hands if needed. "You have Arazian where you want him, under your thumb. He's so drunk half the time, it's a wonder he has any say in the running of the First City at all."

He raises a well-manicured eyebrow.

"I'm not easy to control like Arazian. While I was there, I saw exactly what was going on. You control the Miscretes. You control the prisons. It wouldn't surprise me if the attack plans for Avren came from you. Why control one city when you can control two?" I adjust my grip on the dagger, ready to lunge.

Sterling claps his hands with an infuriating smirk on his face. "Bravo, Prince Bastian. You've rallied the people and supernatural beings of the wilderness to attack the First City." He puckers his pallid lips. "The sad thing is, in your absence, the king has evacuated to Avren. There's no one of substance left for you to attack."

"Except for you," I growl as I drive my weapon toward his heart.

He's too fast, easily skimming over the river and climbing a tree.

Mari takes aim and closes her eyes. Her arrow skims Sterling's ear as he moves out of its path.

"Attack!" Sterling orders from high in his tree perch.

Hundreds of Miscretes swarm toward the narrow bridge, not wanting to cross the river.

"We've got to cut them off." Gray sprints toward the entrance of the bridge, sword in hand, followed closely by Evie and Samuel.

I touch Mari's sleeve as she nocks another arrow. "You stay here."

"No," she says, not bothering to wait for me as she races along the riverbank. Drawing back, she lets an arrow fly, hitting the lead Miscrete.

I swear and run to join the others. Something in Mari changed while we were apart, which she claims has to do with the energy associated with the prophecy. Whatever it is, it's going to be the death of me. "Cut them down as they cross. Don't let them off the bridge."

Gray and Samuel take the front, slashing and muscling through the Miscretes. If one gets by, Evie is there to keep them from advancing.

The pained expression on her face as she takes down monster after monster gives me pause. "Fall back!"

My comrades move behind Mari with confused expressions on their faces.

Splattered in blood, Gray keeps his sword raised as the Miscretes keep advancing. Mari takes down another one with her arrow, but she's not fast enough to get them all.

This was not my plan.

I set down my sword, raise my hands above my head, and call out to Sterling high in the tree. "Call them off. I'll go with you."

"Bastian, no." Gray grips my shirt, pulling me away from the monsters. "We've got this."

No, we don't. Not without killing more Miscretes. Not without possibly killing Ferrish. If I go with Sterling, he won't bother my family for a little while. And it will give them a chance to train our growing army.

Sterling stands before me, one fang digging into his lower lip. He's salivating at the idea of taking the Dark Prince away to his land of indoctrination.

The vamp looks at Mari, another tempting prize to add to his trophy case. "Your father has joined Arazian in Avren, reunited with the Council that rejected them. With both saviors in the city, there will be no stopping the advancement of Avren."

"And where do you fit into all of this?" Mari holds a wooden arrow pointed at the vamp's chest. "They'll discard you as quickly as your vampire queen did." She lowers her bow slightly. "But if I were to come with you, you must promise Bastian's safety."

There's no way I'm going to allow Mari anywhere near Arazian. "Absolutely not."

"I don't believe you're her keeper." Sterling tilts his head to the side as he inspects my girlfriend. "She's developed quite the mind of her own since she left Avren."

"But I'm her commander." It's difficult to muster a convincing tone. I'm desperate to keep her safe from Sterling's fangs, my father's wandering eyes, and whatever Avren will throw at her.

"Can I speak with Bastian alone for a minute?" She looks to Sterling and then the others.

"Whatever it takes." Sterling bows away and the others warily find spots out of earshot.

"Evie, Gray, and Samuel are all capable of training the army without us." She licks her lips, probably thinking through how she'll convince me to allow something that goes against my nature. "I know Avren. If Sterling takes us there, we can gather valuable information." A hand rests on my arm as she looks up into my eyes. "Imagine having all our enemies in one city. This is a true gift for the rebellion."

"Gift or trap?" I purse my lips and glance at Sterling. "If they can find a way to use us, they will, Mari. The prophecy's clear, and they know what role we play."

She's made up her mind. I can see it written all over her face. Her eyes sparkle with the possibilities, and her lips turn slightly upward as she massages my sleeve. "I don't want to be apart from you again. Where you go, I will go, whether it's to the snowy Elmriddens or to the Outpost of the Damned. You are my life now."

I hang my head in defeat. There's no way I can change her mind. "Then I guess we're going to Avren."

As much as I know the others want to stop us, they hold back any further protests. I'm their commander and they understand that what I say goes.

"We're ready," I call out to Sterling who greedily rubs his hands together.

Ready to rip the very fabric of Avren to shreds.

ALSO BY HEATHER KINDT

They thought it was just a game.

Meg wants one thing. For her best friend to be happy. If it were up to her, Brek would leave their hometown, attend college on a scholarship, marry the woman of his dreams, and have two-point-five kids. That is until they see the flyer for the game.

Brek doesn't only want Meg's happiness. He wants her. Even if it means putting his own life at risk by playing a game with unknown dangers. And the game has built-in consequences, testing their moral compasses and friendship to its limits.

Because opening the Green Door is not only a game, but a one-way ticket to something much more deadly.

Read the entire Eternal Artifacts series now

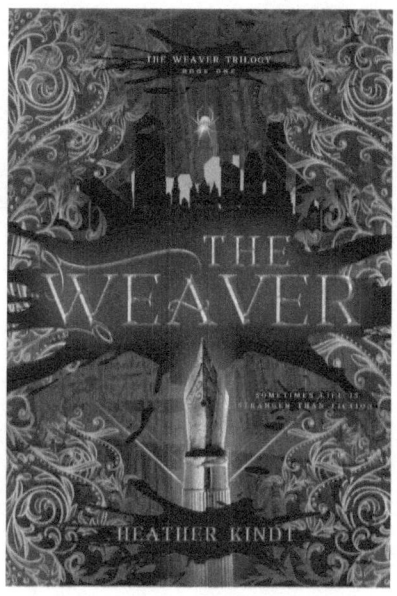

ALSO BY MIDNIGHT TIDE PUBLISHING

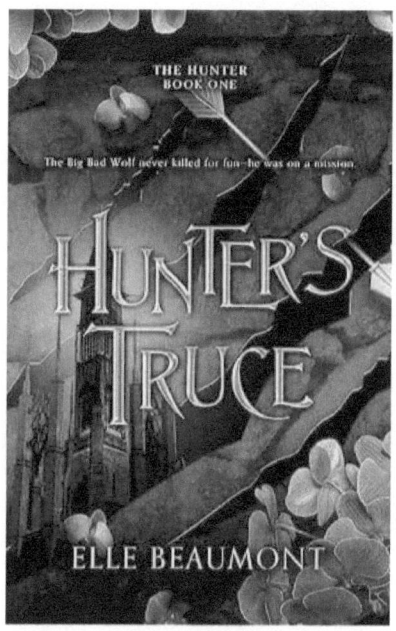

The Big Bad Wolf never killed for fun—he was on a mission.

Niklaus von Brandt is leading a double life. Some days he wields cleavers in his stepfather's butcher shop, and others, he transforms into a lethal instrument—a skilled assassin, prowling the kingdom's darkest corners.

Abendrot was founded by werewolves but is now ruled by humans who have one goal: to eradicate the werewolves. Now, to protect his family, Niklaus must embrace his moniker, the one the kingdom murmurs about—The Big Bad Wolf.

Yet within the opulent halls of the castle lies a secret, and Niklaus plans to use it to his advantage. Even if it means exploiting the eldest princess.

ABOUT THE AUTHOR

Heather Kindt grew up in Derry, New Hampshire, but now resides in the mountains of Colorado with her husband and two children. She loves writing fantasy and romance books. Her debut novel, Not Quite Dorothy, won the Dan Alatorre Word Weaver Writing Contest. To learn more about her and the great things that are coming in her writing world, visit her website at http://heatherkindt.com.